Reviewers Love the Lone Star Law Series

Letter of the Law

"Fiery clashes and lots of chemistry, you betcha!"—*The Romantic Reader Blog*

Above the Law

"[R]eaders who enjoyed the first installment will find this a worthy second act."—*Publishers Weekly*

"Ms Taite delivered and then some, all the while adding more questions, Tease! I like the mystery and intrigue in this story. It has many 'sit on the edge of your seat' scenes of excitement and dread (like watch out kind of thing) and drama…well done indeed!"—*Prism Book Alliance*

Lay Down the Law

"Recognized for the pithy realism of her characters and settings drawn from a Texas legal milieu, Taite pays homage to the prime-time soap opera *Dallas* in pairing a cartel-busting U.S. attorney, Peyton Davis, with a charity-minded oil heiress, Lily Gantry."—*Publishers Weekly*

"Suspenseful, intriguingly tense, and with a great developing love story, this book is delightfully solid on all fronts. This gets my A-1 recommendation!"—*Rainbow Book Reviews*

Praise for the Luca Bennett Mystery Series

Switchblade

"I enjoyed the book and it was a fun read—mystery, action, humor, and a bit of romance. Who could ask for more? If you've read and enjoyed Taite's legal novels, you'll like this. If you've read and enjoyed the two other books in this series, this one will definitely satisfy your Luca fix and I highly recommend picking it up. Highly recommended."
—*C-spot Reviews*

"Dallas's intrepid female bounty hunter, Luca Bennett, is back in another adventure. Fantastic! Between her many friends and lovers, her interesting family, her fly by the seat of her pants lifestyle, and a whole host of detractors there is rarely a dull moment."—*Rainbow Book Reviews*

Battle Axe

"This second book is satisfying, substantial, and slick. Plus, it has heart and love coupled with Luca's array of weapons and a badass verbal repertoire…I cannot imagine anyone not having a great time riding shotgun through all of Luca's escapades. I recommend hopping on Luca's bandwagon and having a blast."—*Rainbow Book Reviews*

"Taite breathes life into her characters with elemental finesse…A great read, told in the vein of a good old detective-type novel filled with criminal elements, thugs, and mobsters that will entertain and amuse."—*Lambda Literary*

Slingshot

"The mean streets of lesbian literature finally have the hardboiled bounty hunter they deserve. It's a slingshot of a ride, bad guys and hot women rolled into one page turning package. I'm looking forward to Luca Bennett's next adventure."—J. M. Redmann, author of the Micky Knight mystery series

Praise for Carsen Taite

A More Perfect Union

"Readers looking for a mix of intrigue and romance set against a political backdrop will want to pick up Taite's latest novel."—*Romantic Times Book Review*

"This is a fabulously written tightly woven political/military intrigue with a large helping of romance. I enjoyed every minute and was on the edge of my seat the whole time. This one is a great read! Carsen Taite never disappoints!"—*The Romantic Reader Blog*

Sidebar

"*Sidebar* is a love story with a refreshing twist. It's a mystery and a bit of a thriller, with an ethical dilemma and some subterfuge thrown in for good measure. The combination gives us a fast-paced read, which includes courtroom and personal drama, an appealing love story, and a more than satisfying ending."—*Lambda Literary*

"*Sidebar* is a sexy, fun, interesting book that's sure to delight, whether you're a longtime fan or this is your first time reading something by Carsen Taite. I definitely recommend it!"—*The Lesbian Review*

"This book has it all: two fantastic lead characters, an interesting plot, and that sizzling chemistry that great authors can make jump off the page. While all of Taite's books are fantastic, this one is on the next level. No critiques, no criticism, you only need to know one thing…this is a damn good book."—*The Romantic Reader Blog*

Without Justice

"Carsen Taite tells a great story. She is consistent in giving her readers a good if not great legal drama with characters who are insightful, well thought out and have good chemistry. You know when you pick up one of her books you are getting your money's worth time and time again. Consistency with a great legal drama is all but guaranteed." —*The Romantic Reader Blog*

"All in all a fantastic novel…Unequivocally 5 Stars…"—*Les Reveur*

"This is a great read, fast-paced, interesting and takes a slightly different tack from the normal crime/courtroom drama having a lawyer in the witness protection system whose case becomes the hidden centre of another crime."—*Lesbian Reading Room*

Reasonable Doubt

"I was drawn into the mystery plot line and quickly became enthralled with the book. It was suspenseful without being too intense but there were some great twists to keep me guessing. It's a very good book. I cannot wait to read the next in line that Ms. Taite has to offer." —*Prism Book Alliance*

Courtship

"The political drama is just top-notch. The emotional and sexual tensions are intertwined with great timing and flair. I truly adored this book from beginning to end. Fantabulous!" – *Rainbow Book Reviews*

"Carsen Taite throws the reader head-on into the murky world of the political system where there are no rights or wrongs, just players attempting to broker the best deals regardless of who gets hurt in the process. The book is extremely well written and makes compelling reading. With twist and turns throughout, the reader doesn't know how the story will end."—*Lesbian Reading Room*

"Taite keeps the stakes high as two beautiful and brilliant women fueled by professional ambitions face daunting emotional choices… As backroom politics, secrets, betrayals, and threats race to be resolved without political damage to the president, the cat-and-mouse relationship game between Addison and Julia has the reader rooting for them. Taite prolongs the fever-pitch tension to the final pages. This pleasant read with intelligent heroines, snappy dialogue, and political suspense will satisfy Taite's devoted fans and new readers alike."—*Publishers Weekly*

Rush

"A simply beautiful interplay of police procedural magic, murder, FBI presence, misguided protective cover-ups, and a superheated love affair…a Gold Star from me and major encouragement for all readers to dive right in and consume this story with gusto!"—*Rainbow Book Reviews*

Beyond Innocence

"As you would expect, sparks and legal writs fly. What I liked about this book were the shades of grey (no, not the smutty Shades of Grey)—both in the relationship as well as the cases."—*C-spot Reviews*

"Taite keeps you guessing with delicious delay until the very last minute...Taite's time in the courtroom lends *Beyond Innocence* a terrific verisimilitude someone not in the profession couldn't impart. And damned if she doesn't make practicing law interesting."
—*Out in Print*

The Best Defense

"Real life defense attorney Carsen Taite polishes her fifth work of lesbian fiction...with the realism she daily encounters in the office and in the courts. And that polish is something that makes *The Best Defense* shine as an excellent read."—*Out & About Newspaper*

Nothing but the Truth

"Author Taite is really a Dallas defense attorney herself, and it's obvious her viewpoint adds considerable realism to her story, making it especially riveting as a mystery. I give it four stars out of five."
—Bob Lind, *Echo Magazine*

"Taite has written an excellent courtroom drama with two interesting women leading the cast of characters. Taite herself is a practicing defense attorney, and her courtroom scenes are clearly based on real knowledge. This should be another winner for Taite."
—*Lambda Literary*

Do Not Disturb

"Taite's tale of sexual tension is entertaining in itself, but a number of secondary characters...add substantial color to romantic inevitability"
—Richard Labonte, *Book Marks*

It Should Be a Crime

"Law professor Morgan Bradley and her student Parker Casey are potential love interests, but throw in a high-profile murder trial, and you've got an entertaining book that can be read in one sitting. Taite also practices criminal law and she weaves her insider knowledge of the criminal justice system into the love story seamlessly and with excellent timing. I find romances lacking when the characters change completely upon falling in love, but this was not the case here. I look forward to reading more from Taite."—*Curve Magazine*

"This is just Taite's second novel...but it's as if she has bookshelves full of bestsellers under her belt."—*Gay List Daily*

By the Author

Truelesbianlove.com

It Should Be a Crime

Do Not Disturb

Nothing but the Truth

The Best Defense

Beyond Innocence

Rush

Courtship

Reasonable Doubt

Without Justice

Sidebar

A More Perfect Union

The Luca Bennett Mystery Series:

Slingshot

Battle Axe

Switchblade

Bow and Arrow (novella in *Girls with Guns*)

Lone Star Law Series:

Lay Down the Law

Above the Law

Letter of the Law

Outside the Law

Visit us at www.boldstrokesbooks.com

OUTSIDE THE LAW

by
Carsen Taite

2018

OUTSIDE THE LAW

ISBN 13: 978-1-63555-039-9

THIS TRADE PAPERBACK ORIGINAL IS PUBLISHED BY
BOLD STROKES BOOKS, INC.
P.O. BOX 249
VALLEY FALLS, NY 12185

FIRST EDITION: MAY 2018

CREDITS
EDITOR: CINDY CRESAP
PRODUCTION DESIGN: STACIA SEAMAN
COVER DESIGN BY SHERI (HINDSIGHTGRAPHICS@GMAIL.COM)

Acknowledgments

Tackling a series is a big undertaking for both the author and the reader. While the author works behind the scenes to weave several sets of plotlines and join lovers looking for mates, the reader is forced to wait upwards of a year for their questions to be answered and mysteries to be solved. A Texas-sized THANK YOU to all of my loyal readers who made the commitment to these characters and their stories. I hope you enjoy this, the finale of the Lone Star Law series.

When it comes to the finished product, a whole bunch of other folks make me look good. Thanks to:

Sheri for another amazing cover design.

Cindy Cresap for fierce edits delivered with a side of humor.

Len Barot and Sandy Lowe for making Bold Strokes Books a nurturing home where authors can thrive.

VK Powell and Ashley Bartlett for their steadfast friendship and keen editorial eyes.

Love and thanks to my wife, Lainey, who takes care of all the things while I'm holed up in my office writing or traveling to literary events around the country. None of my success would be possible without you.

And to all of my readers—your support fuels my inspiration and daily word counts. Thanks for taking this journey with me.

To Lainey. I love you—beginning, middle, and end

CHAPTER ONE

Special Agent Tanner Cohen blinked several times, but her eyes weren't the problem. Sydney Braswell, the love of her life—make that former love, former life—had just strolled into the briefing and slipped into a seat at the back of the room.

Ducking her head to keep from staring, Tanner stole a few glances at Syd, drinking in the sight of her long legs, trim figure, and the waves of auburn hair that used to fan out on the pillow next to hers. Damn, she'd aged well. Tanner shook her head to scatter the memories bubbling to the surface. She hadn't seen Syd in forever, but staring at her now, the years slipped away.

Tanner felt a sharp jab in her side and Assistant US Attorney Bianca Cruz shot her a quizzical expression. She looked from Bianca to the front of the room at AUSA Peyton Davis, who was running the briefing, and back again, slowly realizing everyone was waiting on her, but she didn't have a clue why. "I'm sorry, can you repeat that?"

Peyton looked deferentially at her boss, US Attorney Herschel Gellar, and then at Syd. "Agent Cohen, would you like to fill us in on the recovery of Queen's Ransom?"

Tanner felt like she'd missed something. She and the rest of the rogue task force had been contacted by Gellar's secretary over the weekend and told to meet at the US attorney's office first thing Monday. Tanner had reached out to Bianca, who didn't know much more than she did about the purpose for the meeting, but the consensus was that their activities the week before, although putting them within striking distance of arresting the fugitive drug lord Sergio Vargas, had also exposed that they'd been running an operation they'd been told to shut down weeks ago.

She figured they'd been called in for a dressing down, but that didn't explain what Syd was doing here and why had no one said anything when Syd, a total stranger to everyone but her, had walked into the room acting like she owned the place.

Filing away the slew of questions for later, Tanner cleared her throat and focused on a bare-bones recitation of the facts. "The horse, Queen's Ransom, was exactly where Razor, uh, Enrique Garza, said he'd be, in a stable on a piece of property about an hour west of Denton. Like the barn where Lindsey Ryan was held when she was kidnapped, the property was listed for sale and the owners haven't been there in months." She paused before offering up the piece of information she knew everyone wanted to know. "There was no sign of Sergio Vargas anywhere on the property."

Gellar pushed up from his seat and strode over to edge Peyton from the podium. "And I'm hearing you people offered Mr. Garza witness protection in exchange for Sergio Vargas's location? Looks like you screwed us over."

Tanner started to object, but Peyton beat her to it. "Giving us the location of the horse was his good faith overture. The next step is ours. We give him immunity and protection, and he delivers Sergio."

"Except the deal is off."

Tanner whipped her head around at the eerily familiar sound of Syd's voice, and watched her stand and walk toward the front of the room. All these years later, but it was like no time had passed between them. Syd was as beautiful as ever and her confidence was one of the sexiest things about her. Except it was completely out of place here, in this room. She watched in disbelief as Syd took Peyton's place next to Gellar, and she found a spot on the wall to keep from making eye contact.

Herschel Gellar practically drooled as he introduced Syd to the rest of the group. "I'd like you all to meet Sydney Braswell," he said, licking his lips. "She's here from Main Justice, appointed by the attorney general to oversee this task force." He stopped to wag his finger at the assembled group of agents and attorneys. "Everything you've done so far is being called into question because of various conflicts of interest, and don't think I don't know about them."

He turned to Syd. "Ms. Braswell, I run a tight ship, but in my focus on certain aspects of the case, this task force has run roughshod over the rules by which we conduct our investigations. I went as far as disbanding them last month, but I've recently found out they have been working on the case behind my back. I appreciate your help in getting this investigation back on track, and I assure you everyone here will give you their full cooperation."

Tanner shot a look at Peyton, who had moved to a seat next to DEA Agent Dale Nelson. She raised her eyebrows in question, but she got nothing in response from either Peyton or Dale, who remained characteristically stoic. Something wasn't right about all of this. Just a few days ago, they'd been talking about contacting the Department of Justice to investigate Gellar. Had he beaten them to the punch?

And then there was the whole Syd thing. Her last memories of Syd included Syd yelling words like "partner track," "civil litigation," and "annual bonuses," none of which had anything to do with a job at the Department of Justice. But if Syd was really assigned here by the attorney general to oversee an investigation, she had to have some significant experience with the department. Definitely not the direction Syd's fast track had been headed when they'd parted ways.

Bianca poked her in the side again, and she did her best to focus on the front of the room, while trying to look nonchalant doing it.

"As I said," Syd continued, her voice strong and confident,

"the deal with Mr. Garza is off. He hired an attorney and he's filed a motion to suppress any statements his client gave us while he was in the hospital."

"Damn." Tanner shook her head vigorously, angry Razor had turned on them. She thought she'd been very convincing when she'd spoken with him in the hospital.

"Agent Cohen, you have something you'd like to say?"

Tanner looked up and met Sydney's deep blue eyes square on. "We had a deal."

"He says you forced his confession."

"Oh, he did, did he?" Tanner scoffed, more pissed at Razor's about-face than uncomfortable about this little one-on-one with Syd in front of her group. "And how exactly did I do that?"

"He says you threatened to kill him."

❖

Syd watched Tanner stalk out of the room with the young Latina woman who'd been seated next to her following fast behind. She wanted to follow them and say or do something to make up for this stormy first meeting, which was not at all how she'd envisioned their reunion, but a room full of people was waiting for her to finish talking. Plus, she had a role to play.

After outlining the gist of the motion Razor's attorney had filed to suppress his client's confession, she instructed the group she'd be meeting with them individually to discuss their work on the case and to determine the plan going forward. Gellar, letch that he was, tried to corner her before she could leave the room. She dodged him with a promise to join him for lunch, but by the time she made it to the hallway, Tanner appeared to be long gone.

"Shit."

"What kind of language is that for a big-shot attorney from DC?"

Syd smiled at the sound of the familiar voice and turned

to see Peyton Davis smiling at her. She started to respond, but Peyton placed a finger over her lips and pointed down the hall. "My office, this way," she said.

When they were safely behind closed doors, she settled into a chair in front of Peyton's desk. "Do you think he bought it?"

Peyton laughed. "Gellar thinks he's the center of the universe, but it would never occur to him that he'd be the center of your investigation. He bought it all right."

Syd relaxed into her chair. She trusted Peyton's judgment. They'd worked together for several years at the Department of Justice, and she knew she could rely on Peyton to shoot straight with her. For a second, she considered returning the favor and telling Peyton about her history with Tanner, but it was one thing to reconnect with a former colleague and quite another to unload a bunch of personal crap. Processing her unexpected reunion with her first love would have to wait until she could grab a few hours alone.

"So, what do you recommend next?" Syd asked.

"We've been using my family's ranch as a meeting place. I think we should convene a meeting tonight and let the rest of the crew in on our plan. Things will go a lot easier on you around here if they don't think you're on a witch hunt."

"Can everyone be trusted? If Gellar gets wind of what we're up to, I'm not going to be able to offer protection."

"If they couldn't be trusted, they wouldn't be working with me."

Syd nodded, needing no further assurance than Peyton's word. "Well, if you don't need me here, then I'm going to check into my hotel before I have to endure a meal with the monster."

Peyton stood. "Need a ride?"

"I'm just down the street, thanks. Wish me luck." She strode out of the office and walked briskly out of the suite, relieved that she didn't run into anyone from the morning's meeting on the way. Once out of the building, she walked back to the Adolphus Hotel where she'd dropped off her luggage that morning.

Her room had all the modern amenities, but the refined leather and wood furnishings were in keeping with the grande dame status of the historical venue. When she'd checked in late last night, the talkative desk clerk had told her all about the hotel's recent remodel, pointing out many features she seriously doubted she'd have time to use. She'd barely listened anyway, since all she'd really cared about was getting some sleep before she had to face Tanner this morning, and now that she'd seen her, Syd was drained. Thinking she couldn't remember the last time she'd spent any time in a hotel by herself, she crawled onto the plush but firm king-sized bed and leaned back against the fluffed-up pillows, taking a moment to savor the luxury since it was the only redeeming thing about this assignment.

Sometime later, a maid's voice in the hallway woke her, and Syd crawled her way out of a cloud of sleep and wiped drool from the edge of her mouth. A glance at the clock on the nightstand told her she'd been asleep for thirty minutes. She lifted the phone, placed an order for coffee, and walked to the bathroom to freshen up.

She dreaded meeting with Herschel Gellar, but thankfully, the appointment involved lunch since she was starving. What she'd much rather be doing was finding a moment alone with Tanner to break the ice. She'd received Peyton's email with the notes about the case just before she boarded her flight and had no idea until she was midair that Tanner was living and working in Dallas, let alone assigned to the task force working the Vargas brothers case. If she had known, would she have agreed to this assignment?

She wasn't sure of the answer, and she wouldn't be sure until she faced Tanner alone. Only then could she determine if they could put their past aside and work together. If their encounter this morning were any indication, it wasn't looking good.

She freshened her makeup and looked in the mirror to check the result, knowing full well she was mostly interested in seeing what Tanner had seen. She definitely wasn't the same young, third year law student who'd pledged to spend the rest of her life with fellow student Tanner Cohen, but Syd was proud of how she'd aged. A rigorous workout schedule kept her in shape, and the tiny lines that were starting to creep up around her eyes could easily be written off as laugh lines.

Tanner, what she'd managed to see of her anyway before she stalked out of the briefing, had aged well too, and Syd couldn't help but wonder if Tanner had someone special in her life. Maybe she'd called that person after she left and bitched about her ex who'd traveled back in time to chastise her in front of her peers. Or maybe that someone was the Latina woman who'd rushed after her when she'd left the meeting.

The idea of Tanner with someone else left Syd with a dull ache, but she wasn't sure if the feeling had anything to do with Tanner or if it was a reflection of her own empty personal life. Someday Syd hoped to find someone special to share her life, someone she could call when she need to decompress.

She reached for her phone to see if Gellar had called and saw she had a new text. It wasn't Gellar. She pressed the number, deciding to call back instead of text because she needed to hear a familiar voice.

"How's my favorite legal eagle?"

Syd sighed at the sound of her friend Kate Johnson. She and Kate had started at the Department of Justice at the same time, and they formed a fast friendship. Kate knew about Tanner, the details having been divulged during a late, too much wine girls' night out where they'd swapped stories about the ones that got away. They'd woken up the next morning, both resolved to embrace the lives that allowed them to focus entirely on work. Remembering their pact caused Syd to hesitate about sharing the news that her new assignment had placed her in close proximity to Tanner, but the pause didn't last. "Tanner's here."

Silence. Syd waited for a few beats before venturing a cautious, "Did you hear me?"

"I heard you. I'm processing. She's the one, right?"

"She was. And then she wasn't."

"And when you say she's here, you don't mean standing right there next to you while we're having this surreal conversation, right?"

Syd laughed. "God no! She's here in Dallas. She's working with Peyton's task force."

"Holy shit. What are you going to do?"

Good question. Syd pondered her options. She'd traveled to Dallas, and she'd made a commitment to Peyton. If she left, she'd have to come up with some plausible explanation for her abrupt departure, and "I don't want to face my past" seemed more than a little chickenshit. So, she'd do what she always did, no matter how much focus it required. "My job. I'm going to do my job. And then I'm going to get the hell out of here."

Tanner sank into a bench in the park across from the courthouse and wished the world away. A few days ago, she'd managed to turn a major player in the Vargas organization, and the anticipated next step was taking the entire operation down. Enter Sydney Braswell, and now not only was her achievement at risk and her badge on the line for making it so, but her heart, which she'd managed to keep on serious lockdown, was pulsing with unwanted anticipation.

Whether she wanted to admit it or not, she couldn't deny Syd looked amazing. Sure she'd aged, but time had been kind, adding only the most subtle signs of maturity.

"Giving up police work to commune with nature?"

Tanner looked up at Bianca, who'd managed to sneak up on her and was staring at her with a concerned expression. "Maybe."

Bianca shoved her over and slid into the space beside her, placing a hand on her thigh. "You did what you did in that hospital room because I asked you to. If you think I'm going to let you get in trouble for it or let it keep us from nailing Jade's asshole uncles, you don't know who you're dealing with."

Tanner couldn't help but smile at the fierce tone from her petite friend as she reflected on her one-on-one with Razor in the hospital. He'd been shot after having stabbed Jade Vargas, who'd stopped him from harming Bianca's daughter. He knew where his fugitive boss, Sergio Vargas, was hiding out with Jade's prize stallion, Queen's Ransom. Bianca, distraught about her daughter's close brush with danger, confessed to Tanner that she was in love with Jade and begged Tanner to do whatever it took to retrieve Jade's horse and bring her uncles to justice. Tanner had actually enjoyed watching Razor's face as she pinched the IV drip to rob him of relief while she described telling his bosses that he'd cooperated with the FBI whether he did or not. She'd do it all over again. "It was my decision, not yours. I can take the consequences."

"We'll see. I'm going to talk to this new chick. I mean, where does she get off coming in here acting like we're a bunch of rubes?"

This was the moment. Tanner should tell Bianca about her connection to Sydney, but what exactly was she supposed to say? Being vague on details would only draw questions. If she told Bianca even a little about their past, she knew Bianca wouldn't let it go until she told her everything, and it was too complicated. Her personal life wasn't something she'd ever shared on the job— not that she had much of one—and everything about Syd was personal. Besides, she hadn't seen Syd since they'd graduated from law school. Did she really even know her anymore?

Tanner decided to hedge. "Any idea who called her in? Gellar's acting like it was him, but it seems like a weird move for him to cede territory to anyone else."

"Did you see those legs? Gellar's a pig, and when it comes to a beautiful woman, he stumbles all over himself. You should've seen him the first time he met Lindsey," Bianca said, referring to Dale Nelson's girlfriend, a renowned international journalist.

Tanner didn't want to think about Gellar drooling over Sydney, so she changed the subject. "You have any cases on the docket this afternoon or do you have some time to go over the evidence again?"

"That's what I came out to tell you. Peyton wants to see us out at the ranch tonight."

"She thinks that's wise with all of us under scrutiny?"

Bianca shrugged. "Wise or not, she called the meeting. You want to ride out there together?"

Tanner grinned. Bianca's little Miata didn't do so well on the gravel drive. "Sure, I'll pick you up." She stood. "I'm going to take a walk. Thanks for checking on me."

Bianca stared hard before she finally waved and headed back to the courthouse. Tanner knew she should follow, but she wasn't in the mood to do anything related to this case, especially not if Sydney was going to be involved. Maybe Peyton would have some insights about why she was here. Whatever the case, she'd find out tonight, but in the meantime, she needed a break. She fished her phone out of her pocket and called Dale. When Dale answered, she launched right in. "Wanna take a ride with me? I've got a few ideas."

Dale laughed. "Guess they didn't bench you after all."

"Not yet. You still at the courthouse?"

"On my way downstairs."

"Pick you up out front in five." Tanner disconnected the call and started walking to the parking lot down the street where she'd parked her car that morning. She'd planned on spending the entire day in the war room they'd created at the US attorney's office, but the idea of spending any time at all within spitting distance of Herschel Gellar was more intolerable than ever. If Sydney was teamed up with him, that only made things worse. No matter what Gellar and Sydney had planned, she'd weather Razor's allegations. All she had to do was keep a low profile and steer clear of her past, and her future would work out just fine.

CHAPTER TWO

Sydney drove down the dusty drive toward Peyton's ranch, the Circle Six, and wondered what she'd gotten herself into. She remembered Peyton fondly discussing her family's quarter horse breeding farm, but it was still hard to reconcile the career-focused woman she'd met in DC with the sprawling acreage, stables, and ranch house.

She was having similar troubles with Tanner. The last time she'd seen her was a month after they'd graduated from law school, both of them still nursing the wounds of their recent breakup. Sydney had come home from her bar review course to find Tanner packing a box with a few of her last remaining belongings.

"I'm sorry," Tanner said, keeping her head ducked low. "I didn't think you'd be home."

Sydney bit back a bunch of potential responses, most of which were guaranteed to land them back in the middle of the argument that had broken them up in the first place and settled on, "I would've packed those for you."

"I didn't want to ask," Tanner said, hurt shading her voice.

And those simple words summed up pretty much everything that had gone wrong between them. Deciding there wasn't any point rehashing it all, Sydney strode toward the closet. "There are a few things in here. I set them aside in case...in case you wanted to go through them."

Tanner stopped what she was doing and walked over to stand next to her, and Sydney pointed out the small box on the shelf, just out of her reach. She'd had to use a ladder to push the box high up on a shelf, far away from her everyday gaze. Tanner reached up and pulled it down, hugging it to her middle as she scanned the contents. It was a mishmash of memories, none particularly valuable, but each item painful for the sting of recollection it evoked, which was why Sydney had stuck them up high and out of sight. She was sorry now she pointed them out to Tanner, who sifted through them like sands of time.

"I remember these," Tanner said, holding up a pair of ticket stubs to the Beyoncé Experience. "Fred gave us these because of his fear of crowds."

Sydney managed a smile. "Right. I predict he'll make a wonderful securities lawyer, locked away from all meaningful human contact." As the words "human contact" left her lips, she was acutely conscious of how close Tanner was standing to her. No amount of emotional strife could negate the pull that had always existed between them. She wanted to slip her arms around Tanner's waist and slip back into the comfort of her arms, but it wasn't safe and it wouldn't last. The comfort wasn't real. Each day since Tanner had moved out had been easier, but seeing her here, now, the conflict came roaring back. Would they ever be able to get past the chasm between them?

A loud rap on the window jerked her from the memory. Peyton was standing outside her car window, a puzzled expression on her face. Sydney shook off her reverie and climbed out of the car.

"Are you okay?" Peyton asked.

"Sure. Fine." She brushed out the wrinkles in her suit. "Just tired. Long couple of days." *And a complete inability to speak in complete sentences, apparently.*

Peyton motioned for her to follow as she walked toward the house and grinned when her heel got wedged in the gravel. "You're not really dressed for a ranch, you know."

"About that." Syd pointed at the house. "I kind of imagined more *Dallas* and less *Rawhide*. Is this really where you live?"

"It is indeed." Peyton held out a hand. "Come on, city girl. We even have electricity."

Sydney followed her up the steps, onto the porch, and into the large, rustic house. Did Tanner live in a place like this? The Tanner she'd known had definitely been a city girl. But then again she'd only thought she'd known her. Maybe Tanner secretly loved nature and horses and the great outdoors.

When they walked inside, Sydney was struck by the homey feel. Rough-hewn beams framed the tall ceilings, and the walls were lined with family photos and other memorabilia. She caught sight of a stack of bridal magazines on the coffee table and pointed. "Are those yours? Because if they are, then ranch air changes a person for sure."

"Actually—" Peyton started to say.

"Actually, they're mine." A gorgeous dark-haired woman stepped into the room and swooped the magazines up into her arms. She turned to Sydney with a playful smile. "You must be Sydney." She stuck out a hand. "Peyton speaks highly of you."

Peyton gave the woman an affectionate smile and motioned between them. "Lily, Sydney Braswell. Sydney, Lily Gantry."

Sydney paused for a second, her hand in the air. "Gantry? Ah, yes. Cyrus Gantry's daughter."

"The one and only." Lily cast a mysterious look at Peyton, the kind only couples can interpret, and she hugged the magazines to her chest. "It's a pleasure to meet you. You'll have to come back when it's not about business and join us for dinner."

Sydney waited until Lily was out of the room before turning to Peyton. "Wow. Just wow. That's Cyrus Gantry's daughter?"

"I believe that's been established." Peyton grinned.

"Beautiful and charming. No wonder you couldn't resist." Cylinders began to click into place. "Wait a minute. All those magazines. Are you two getting married?"

Peyton nodded. "Wedding's in a month. If you don't have things wrapped up by then, you're welcome to join us."

"You're marrying the daughter of a man who's facing indictment by your office? Peyton, what the hell are you thinking?" She started to say more, but the sound of a throat being cleared behind her cut her off. She turned slowly, praying Lily hadn't returned to the room, but it was worse. Tanner was standing behind her.

"I'm pretty sure she's thinking she's in love. Of course, love isn't always about thinking," Tanner said, pointing at the door. "I let myself in."

"Guilty as charged," Peyton said, seemingly oblivious to the daggers Tanner was sending Syd's way.

Sydney nodded, but she was certain the look on her face still showed her incredulity. Tanner called her on it. "People do all kinds of crazy things for love."

What the hell was that supposed to mean? "I've heard that," Sydney said. "But I've never seen it in action."

"Neither have I."

The gall. If anyone had walked out on love, it had been Tanner, but this wasn't the time or place to point that out. Sydney broke eye contact with her former lover. "Peyton, do we have time for a quick tour before the rest of your people get here?" She prayed Tanner would stay behind. She just needed a few minutes to regain her composure. Tonight was important and she needed to keep a steady head.

A few minutes later, she was walking beside Peyton, stepping gingerly over scattered rocks and tree roots as they made their way toward the stables. Peyton was saying something about horses and racing, but she barely heard because her mind was back on Tanner's words. *People do all kinds of crazy things for love.* Yeah, right. Not in her experience. Not even close.

❖

Tanner watched Peyton and Sydney leave, wishing she could take back her harsh words, but two unexpected encounters with Sydney in one day had left her feeling jangly, and her usually reliable ability to control her emotions was severely out of whack. Sydney had always had that effect on her.

"Hey, babe, I hate to rush you, but if we don't leave in five minutes, we're not going to make it."

"Okay," Tanner *called out, hoping her voice projected confidence because she sure wasn't feeling it. She'd spent the last fifteen minutes standing in front of the closet she shared with Sydney, dressed only in a towel, wishing school was back in session. But it was June, and she and Sydney had landed coveted positions with two of DC's most prestigious law firms where they would make more money in a week than most people brought home in a month.*

She knew she should be grateful, but after a few weeks of pushing paper for the firm's partners and attending night after night of required social networking, she'd begun to seriously doubt she was cut out for big law.

Sydney's hands slipped around her waist and her whisper tickled Tanner's ear. "Wear the gray suit with the blue shirt. It's super hot on you."

Tanner turned into her arms and let the towel drop to the floor. "How about we both take a mental health day and crawl back in bed?" The moment the words left her lips, she saw Syd's eyes twitch with frustration and she rushed to make her case. "Come on, Syd. It's not like either of us are doing anything important at these gigs. They won't miss us for one day."

Syd inched away, but Tanner felt the distance between them breach into a large crevasse. "I know you're bored, but it's a rite of passage," Sydney said, all business now. "All summer associates do nothing more than carry water while the partners size us up, but the offer rate at both our firms is over ninety percent—I checked."

Of course you did, Tanner thought. Syd had done impeccable research for both of the jobs they held to make sure they fit in with the big picture plan. They'd graduate and start work as first year associates at their respective firms making piles of money that they'd earn by working ungodly hours with no vacations. The pain would last a few years until they were solidly on the partner track, and then they'd start planning more personal accomplishments like a big house, kids, and a vacation home. There was more, a lot more, but Tanner had started to tune out the rest, unable to conceive of a pot of gold worth working toward at the end of this particular passage.

She leaned down to pick up her towel, but Syd caught her halfway and tilted her face toward hers. "It'll all work out," she said. "I promise."

"I know," Tanner replied with a confidence she tried to feel. "I love you."

"I love you, too."

"Then that's all that matters. The rest is just logistics." Sydney looped her arm through Tanner's and started pushing aside hangers. "Now, about that suit."

"Where is everyone?"

Tanner turned at the sound of Bianca's voice, schooling her face into a neutral expression. "Peyton's outside with Braswell. Mary and Dale stopped to pick up some beer, but they should be here any minute. Any idea why Braswell's here?"

"Can we stop calling her Braswell? She prefers Sydney, and she's really very nice."

"*Et tu*, Bianca?"

"Seriously. I spent the afternoon filling her in on everything to do with Lily's dad and Jade's uncles, and she wasn't a jerk at all. Asked good questions. I looked her up, and she's got a pretty amazing résumé. I don't get the impression she's gunning for you."

"Well, it sure felt like it this morning." Tanner mentally

kicked herself for not employing a little Google on Syd, but she'd spent the balance of the day trying not to think about her. Big mistake. Huge. "I still don't get why she's here at the ranch. I thought we were meeting to figure out how to deal with her, not including her."

Bianca shrugged. "You got me, but if Peyton invited her, she must've had a good reason."

Tanner grunted. Bianca was a young lawyer and she had a tendency to think Peyton, her mentor, could do no wrong. For the most part she thought Bianca's assessment was correct. She'd had her doubts when she'd learned Peyton and Lily were dating, but she'd come to see Peyton could separate work and home life. "You should probably watch your back. Syd made it clear she had a problem over the fact Peyton's dating Lily Gantry. She might flip out when she discovers you're dating the niece of the two most wanted men in North Texas."

Bianca didn't look worried, but she did fix her with a laser stare.

"What?"

"Syd? That was zero to nickname in no time flat."

Shit. Tanner felt a tinge of guilt for not coming clean about her past with Syd, but she'd dug in now. "Whatever. I'm just saying you should be a little more careful before you start cozying up to her." The sound of the front door opening cut off Bianca's response, and Tanner sighed with relief to see Dale and Mary stroll into the living room, each carrying a twelve-pack of Corona. The increasing numbers gave her comfort, and she followed them into the kitchen.

Dale jerked her chin toward the front door. "Any idea why the new girl's here?"

Tanner shook her head, trying not to react to the words "new girl." "Not a clue. I was hoping you would have some intel."

"Not me." Dale stacked the beer in the fridge and then offered one to Tanner and Mary.

Tanner took hers and drank a deep draught. They'd been

meeting here at Peyton's ranch for the last month since the task force had been officially disbanded. Dale had asked her to join them when they started to suspect Gellar was working around rather than with them, and they wanted to use her position as one of the lead agents on Cyrus Gantry's case to find out what he was up to. With last week's raid and the subsequent retrieval of Queen's Ransom, the fact that the group was still operating as a task force had come to light, but now they met in secret in an attempt to keep the details of their investigation under wraps while they tried to figure out if Herschel Gellar was somehow involved in the case against Lily's father and the Vargases. All of which begged the question of what Sydney was doing here, especially if she was working with Gellar.

"You want me to ask Lindsey to do a little digging?" Dale asked, referring to her girlfriend, a nationally known investigative reporter who'd been helping them out. "Any of us start poking around, someone's going to notice."

Tanner started to scoff at the idea. She was a fucking FBI agent. She didn't need a reporter to do her job for her. But then she warmed to the idea of someone objective doing the digging, and she started to tell Dale to go ahead, but there was that guilt again, like it would be a betrayal to sic a reporter on her ex. And there was always the possibility Lindsey might discover their past relationship, and she'd feel like a fool for not telling them. She should just tell them now. Before she could pull the trigger, the subject of their discussion appeared in the doorway.

"Any chance I can get one of those?" Sydney asked.

Tanner shot Dale a warning look as she handed Sydney her beer and got a subtle nod in response. She'd talk to her later.

Peyton walked into the room and signaled for them all to have a seat. "Sydney, you met Bianca, Tanner, and Dale this morning. Mary Lovelace is our ATF connection and she's been working with us since the beginning. I'll let each of them bring you up to speed, but in the meantime, everyone meet Sydney Braswell, the newest member of our little task force."

Tanner shot a look at Dale and Bianca, who both shrugged. "I thought you were here because Gellar called you in."

"That's what he thinks," Syd responded, her voice calm and steady. "But I'm really here because of Peyton. She and I worked together at the DOJ, and she contacted me about the information you all found on Gellar. We're not opening an official investigation yet, but I'm here to check into it, and the best way to do that is if Gellar thinks I'm here for some other reason. As long as my cover stays intact, I'll have unfettered access to the office. If we develop some tangible evidence that he's involved with the Vargases, I'll convene a grand jury and we'll start looking into prosecution."

"So the stuff you said this morning about Razor was part of your cover?"

"No. You're still going to have to answer for that. Judge Casey has set a hearing on the motion to suppress for next week."

"Did you tell the weasel's lawyer that he won't get witness protection if he doesn't testify?"

"He won't need it if he doesn't. He thinks he has more to lose from the Vargases than by crossing you."

Tanner looked around, acutely conscious of the fact that everyone in the room was watching them like they were playing a high-stakes tennis match. "Well, maybe he underestimated me."

"That's entirely possible."

Tanner's ears pricked up at Sydney's words, certain she detected hidden layers of meaning.

"We'll need to meet to prepare for the hearing," Sydney continued, her face slightly flushed. "You'll have every opportunity to convince me your actions were justified."

Damn, there was definitely some undercurrent happening here, but Tanner forced herself not to react. She didn't know current day Sydney Braswell well enough to presume anything. She'd meet with her and discuss the case, but anything personal was completely off-limits because there was absolutely no way she would risk her heart again. "Fine. But now we're here to work." She looked around at the group. "Let's get started."

❖

Sydney held Tanner's gaze longer than was comfortable for either of them, and she experienced both pleasure and disappointment when Tanner looked away first. "I'm not your enemy." She directed the words to the entire group, but they were really only meant for Tanner. "I'm here to help. But we have to do this right, follow all the rules. You can't knock down a man like Gellar. You have to knock him out."

Her words were greeted with nods from around the table. "All right then. I'm thinking we should start off by going around the table and everyone can fill me in on their connection to the case. I know Peyton from DC, and she's already told me that she's engaged to be married to Lily Gantry."

"Do you have a problem with that?" Bianca asked.

"Do you?" Sydney was careful to keep her tone even. She thought the idea of Peyton in a relationship with one of the key player's daughter was ripe for friction, but she wanted to know what the rest of the team thought.

"No," Bianca said in a firm voice. "Besides, Lily isn't involved in any way with the investigation or her father's business."

"Could it be that you're a little biased considering you're dating Sergio and Arturo Vargas's niece?"

To her credit, Bianca didn't look away, instead assuming a more challenging posture, but Dale came to her defense. "You're painting with a pretty broad brush," Dale said.

"And so will the defense lawyers. They live for the appearance of conflict. And what about you? Aren't you in a relationship with one of the Vargases' victims, Lindsey Ryan?" She paused for a second to let her observations sink in and then kept going, knowing she wasn't winning any friends. "Ultimately, you all have issues when it comes to this case, but you've done some amazing work so far and I think it would be a mistake to break up the team. That said, I have some recommendations, and I need you to follow them to the letter if we're going to make this work."

She watched Tanner's face for any signs her remarks were being well received. To most people, Tanner's expression would have appeared neutral, but she could tell by the slight twitch at the corner of her mouth that she was itching to get out of there. She could totally relate.

"What if we don't?" Tanner asked.

"Then this case may come crashing down around you, and your careers with it. Haven't you sacrificed enough?" Sydney met Tanner's deep brown eyes and held her gaze. She'd promised herself she wouldn't get personal, but there was no denying she still cared. Tanner had given up everything for this career, including her, and she'd be damned if she'd let it all go to hell because her team couldn't keep their hands to themselves. Since the day Tanner told her she'd chosen to walk away from their planned future, Sydney had blamed her for the fallout as she'd picked up the rubble of their broken dreams. But somehow their paths had wound back together in a way she never would've expected, and a part of her believed there was a reason for this reconnection.

The room was quiet and Tanner's stare consumed all of Sydney's awareness. When Tanner finally spoke, it was as if nothing else existed.

"Tell us what you have in mind."

Sydney looked everywhere but directly at Tanner. It was the only way she could focus. "I've read all the reports dating back to Maria Escobar's death." She offered a slight nod in Dale's direction to acknowledge the loss of her wife, the AUSA who had led the task force initially until she'd been gunned down in front of her home. "I think that Gellar's obsession with Cyrus Gantry and the Vargases, while perhaps warranted from a law enforcement perspective, is a distraction from something bigger."

"Bigger?" Mary asked.

"Yes. There are too many pieces to this puzzle that don't fit. Like all of you, I'm not convinced that the men who kidnapped Lindsey had anything to do with the Vargases, but someone sure went to pains to make it look like they were involved. And going back further to the Gantry Oil truck with all the dead bodies inside—it appears that Gantry's company had filed a legitimate report regarding the theft of the truck. Whoever stole it wanted you to believe Gantry was responsible for those deaths, but more importantly, they wanted the public to believe it." She folded her hands on the table. "Don't get me wrong, I definitely think the Vargas brothers are bad news, but I don't think they are responsible for all of this. Someone is trying to set them and Gantry up to take the fall."

"And you think Gellar is involved somehow?" Peyton asked.

"I don't know, but apparently you all think he's up to something. The secrecy at the office, the rumor about a hidden bunker at his house, and the suspicious bank accounts—all point to someone who has something to hide. Maybe it's related to these cases, maybe it isn't, but there's only one way to find out."

"And what's that?"

"We need to set a trap."

"And how exactly do you plan to do that?"

"That's your job. And I don't have a clue, but we'll figure it out together. In the meantime, I'll distract him as best I can while the rest of you will need to gather more information about his activities." She turned to Peyton. "We can set up a regular meeting here, right?"

"Sure," Peyton said. "We'd be happy to have you join in at our regular poker game."

Sydney smiled and shot a look across the table at Tanner, whose expression was mostly unreadable, except for the slight strain behind her eyes. It was clear her presence here made Tanner uncomfortable, but there was nothing she could do about it even if she wanted to. And she wasn't sure she wanted to.

CHAPTER THREE

A gent Cohen, isn't it true you threatened my client in an attempt to gain his cooperation?"

Tanner started to say, "That's Special Agent," but she knew he was baiting her. Instead she leaned back in the uncomfortable witness chair and took a moment to size up Enrique Garza aka Razor's attorney. She'd come up against this guy in court several times before, but he obviously hadn't learned from the experience. A veteran of the courtroom would've taken his time, asking more specific questions to lead up to the conclusion he wanted to draw instead of leading with the overarching issue. His carelessness or impatience was to her benefit. She kept her tone even as she leaned forward slightly to speak into the microphone. "No, that is not true."

"But you offered him witness protection, isn't that right?"

Tanner cast a quick glance in Sydney's direction and noted her nod before answering. "I explained to him that we could explore WITSEC as a potential option to assist him with his legal troubles."

"And I imagine that you explained another, less palatable option as well."

Tanner cocked her head. "I'm sorry, was there supposed to be a question there?" She looked at the judge and hunched her shoulders. She wasn't sorry, and in front of a different judge, she might not let a hint of sarcasm invade her tone, but she and Judge Casey knew each other well and she knew exactly how far she could go before he'd admonish her to keep her remarks to herself.

"You threatened to put out the word that he'd cooperated even if he didn't, a move that would place my client's life in jeopardy. Isn't that correct?" He overemphasized each word of the last sentence to punctuate his frustration.

"I'm confused," she said, making a show of scratching her head. "If your client wasn't working for the Vargases, then why would his life be in jeopardy?" She shrugged. "In any case, the answer is no. I didn't threaten your client." She delivered the lie coolly and calmly. This entire hearing was a colossal waste of time. Razor was well known as an enforcer for the Vargases. He'd tried to kidnap Bianca's daughter, thwarted only by the quick thinking of Jade Vargas. They'd caught him in the act of a capital offense—no confession necessary. What she'd questioned him about at the hospital—the location of Jade's horse and where Sergio Vargas was holed up—was extraneous as far as Razor's fate was concerned. If he'd stuck to the deal, then he'd be able to live out the rest of his days in freedom, but he'd made the choice to go back on his word. Not her problem, and she wasn't about to confess to strong-arming him when she'd essentially been offering him a way out of his troubles.

The back-and-forth continued for a bit longer, but eventually Razor's attorney decided he wasn't getting anything else out of her. Dismissed from the witness stand, Tanner stayed in the courtroom and watched as he and Sydney made their best arguments to the judge, who told them he would take the matter under consideration. As the bailiff yelled, "All rise," Tanner slid out of her seat and ducked out of the courtroom, running smack into Bianca.

"Running from the law?" Bianca laughed. "Oh wait!"

"You're hilarious," Tanner said. "You have a hearing right now?"

"No, I was in Niven's court, but I finished up early and thought I'd check on you. How did it go?"

"Okay, I guess. I never know how these things will work out until the judge rules. We'll probably hear later this week."

"And Sydney? She do okay?"

Tanner shifted her feet and glanced back at the courtroom doors. "Sure. She was fine."

"Fine, huh? Faint praise. When are you going to warm up to her? I admit, I wasn't keen on adding a stranger to the team, but Peyton vouches for her and she seems pretty on top of things."

At that moment, Sydney burst through the doors and started walking toward them. Tanner looked everywhere but directly at her, planning an escape route, but Bianca enthusiastically waved her over. As Sydney walked toward them, Tanner let her gaze stray up Sydney's long, well-toned legs. Sydney had always been athletic. They'd spent hours in the gym and the racquetball court during law school, making a game out of quizzing each other over what they'd learned in class between sets, each of them preferring to work out with a partner instead of going solo. Clearly, Sydney still kept up some kind of exercise routine. Did she have a workout buddy back in DC? Was it a girlfriend?

"Tanner says it went fine. What say you?" Bianca asked Sydney.

"Fine, huh?" Sydney looked at Tanner, her gaze appraising. "I don't know this judge, but I'd say we have a better than even chance of winning the hearing. Never hurts to have an attorney on the stand."

Bianca's face scrunched into a frown, and Tanner shook her head, but before she could deflect, Bianca said, "Excuse me?"

Sydney looked between them, wearing a confused expression. "What?"

"Tanner's not an attorney." Bianca turned to Tanner. "Are you?"

"Kind of."

"She is." Sydney nodded.

"Which is it?" Bianca asked, looking between them.

Tanner cleared her throat. "I went to law school before I

joined the agency. I'm still licensed. Obviously, I don't practice law, but yeah, I'm a lawyer." She watched Bianca for her reaction, but Bianca was staring at Sydney.

"And you knew this? How?"

"Long story," Tanner interjected, tugging Bianca by the arm. She wanted to get her far away from Sydney before more secrets of her past leaked, but Bianca stood firm. "Wait a sec," she said. "I want to hear from her, because if she's digging around in everyone's past, then maybe I misjudged our ability to trust her."

Tanner looked at Sydney and saw sympathy reflected back, but what she couldn't tell was whether Sydney cared if Bianca knew their story.

Sydney faced Bianca head-on and it was her turn to lie, apparently. "I reviewed Tanner's file as part of my prep for the hearing so I could make sure she didn't have any prior disciplinary actions that defense counsel could use to challenge her credibility."

Bianca stared at Sydney for a moment and then broke into a smile. "Sorry about that. I have a tendency to leap ahead. I should've known it wasn't anything. Hey, do the two of you want to grab lunch?"

Tanner watched the exchange with a mixture of relief and regret. On the one hand, it would've been nice to get the fact that she and Sydney had been a couple once out in the open, but on the other hand, she kind of preferred to hang on to the hope that she'd never have to deal with it.

"Actually," Sydney said, "I need to go over some of my notes from the hearing with Tanner, and I don't want to raise any conflicts by involving any of the rest of you. Rain check?"

"Absolutely," Bianca said. "Catch you both later."

As Bianca walked away, Tanner decided to act fast. "I should go too. We can talk later, right?" She was a step into her escape when Sydney's silky but firm voice stopped her retreat.

"No, Special Agent Cohen. We need to talk and it can't wait."

❖

They were early enough to be seated right away at Stephan Pyle's popular Flora Street Cafe, located in what Tanner told her was the Arts District. Sydney took a moment to look around and size up her surroundings. They'd walked from the courthouse, and Tanner had barely spoken two words along the way. When they finally entered the doors of the restaurant, Sydney's first thought was this wasn't the kind of place she would have assumed Tanner would like, but then again it had been years since she and Tanner had shared a meal. People changed.

In some respects. Tanner was still the trim, fit, beautiful woman Sydney had fallen in love with, but her eyes were harder now, as if she'd witnessed things she'd rather not have seen, which was saying a lot since she'd done a tour in Afghanistan before they'd even met. Sydney was well acquainted with the effect atrocities could have on a person's psyche. She'd seen plenty in her time as a prosecutor, but working out in the field like Tanner did took a deeper toll, and she wished she could go back in time and do a better job of convincing Tanner to chart a different course for her life.

"This place okay?" Tanner asked as the hostess led them to a booth.

"Looks great." Sydney settled into her seat and half listened to the hostess who was giving them a preview of the specials. When she finally left, Sydney waved a hand. "Seems a little froufrou for you."

"Oh really," Tanner said, eyebrows raised. "I thought you liked froufrou. The chef's really popular with the foodie crowd."

Sydney chose not to dwell on the assumption that Tanner had picked this place especially for her, obviously remembering her love of all things food. "There are a lot of things I used to like." Sydney immediately regretted her choice of words, but rather than compound the implication, she buried her head in her menu. "What's good here?"

"The lobster and the prime rib sandwiches are both solid bets, but you're definitely going to want to start with the white asparagus soup."

"Really?"

"Are you surprised these things are good or that I know they're good?" Tanner set her menu down. "So what if I used to live on hamburgers and you used to be on the way up at one of the biggest firms in the country. Lots of things have changed for both of us."

They placed their orders and Syd fiddled with her iced tea while she worked up to what she wanted to talk about. Tanner sat perfectly still, but Syd could tell she was simultaneously casing the place and her. Unable to bear the silence, Syd asked the one thing she wanted to know the most. "Are you happy?"

Tanner inclined her head and studied her thoughtfully. "That's a tall question. Care to break it down a bit, counselor?"

"Never mind." She'd had no right to ask the question. Tanner's personal life was none of her business.

"Did you really bring me here to ask if I'm happy?"

"No. Yes." Sydney shook her head. "I mean, both. I have a million things to ask you, but it's hard to do when you seem to be trying your best to avoid me."

"I never expected to see you again."

Tanner's voice cracked slightly as she delivered the words, but her expression was impassive. Sydney fiddled with her napkin, trying to decide if she wanted to keep going. "I can't decide if you're happy or sad about that."

"I'm not sure how I feel, but I didn't have much time to prepare. But you did. Do you think maybe you could've called to let me know you were coming out here?"

Sydney took a sip of her tea. She'd seen Tanner's name in the file while she was still in DC, albeit within moments of boarding the plane to Dallas. She'd considered calling but settled on a very rational reason not to—she didn't have time to track down Tanner's number, and even if she did, the airport setting had too much ambient noise to allow them to conduct any kind of conversation. But the truth was a long-distance phone call to her ex-lover to say, "Hey, I'm on my way to your neck of the woods to help out with a secret investigation into the guy who's running your task force, and oh, by the way, looking forward to catching up," seemed insincere, not to mention crazy. She settled on a simple response. "Would you have taken my call?"

Tanner looked down at the table. "I don't know. I put everything about us so far behind me I never imagined I'd have the chance to talk to you again." She stared at her water glass as if it were an oracle. "There was a time when a call from you would've brought me running."

Sydney wanted to ask when that was. Was it before or after Tanner had cleared out all of her belongings from the apartment they'd shared? Or was it later, after she'd entered the academy at Quantico? Tanner's words, which in another context would have warmed her heart, magnified how far they'd drifted apart. The chunk of time when Tanner had loved her more than anything had passed long ago, and now they were just two women who shared a past but had no future.

"You said you wanted to talk. So, talk," Tanner said.

Sydney drew back in her seat and placed her hands in her lap. Tanner clearly didn't want to discuss anything personal, and that was for the best, but they needed to clear the air if they were going to work together and she said as much. "So, I don't care what you tell your colleagues as long as we're on the same page."

"They don't need to know specifics, but it's probably a good idea to mention we know each other from law school. I already feel a little silly that we didn't bring it up already."

"Agreed. The sooner, the better. You handle Bianca. That girl is a pistol and if she weren't in a relationship, I think she'd have a thing for you. If she knew we'd been a couple, she'd probably beat me up."

"Especially if she found out you broke up with me," Tanner said. "Don't mind her. She's super loyal, but she wouldn't hurt you too badly."

"If that were true."

"What?"

"I didn't break up with you," Sydney said, her eyes wide with surprise.

"You gave me an ultimatum, which is pretty much the same thing."

"There was no ultimatum. I asked you to put our relationship before anything else."

"You asked me to choose between a career that would make me happy and one that would crush my soul, and you made our relationship contingent on my choice. If that wasn't an ultimatum, I don't know what is."

Sydney stared at Tanner for a moment, certain that pursuing this argument would be pointless for both of them but desperate to dissect their past. When all the anger and misunderstanding was stripped away, she could think of only one thing she really wanted to know. She'd already asked it, but she tried one more time. "Are you happy?"

"Happiness is overrated."

"Said only the unhappy people."

"Are you?"

"Happy?" Sydney took a moment to reflect. "Comparatively."

"Could you be any more vague?"

"Probably." Sydney offered a smile to try to lighten the mood. "I have a job I like, a few good friends, and I'm healthy. Is there more to life than that?"

"I guess not." Tanner relaxed back in her seat. "About this job. Any chance you want to fill me in on how you went from the partnership track at Chamblee and Ives to scrubbing it with the rest of us on a government salary?"

She wanted to tell Tanner everything. How she'd spent four years working her ass off and the only thing she'd had to show for it was exhaustion and compromised ethics, but she wasn't in the mood for an "I told you so" from Tanner, who'd never hesitated to sacrifice personal gain when duty called. She distilled everything down to a simple conclusion. "That life just wasn't for me."

Tanner's slow nod was a gentle acknowledgment of the truth she'd known all along but Syd had to trip over to find. What would her life be like now if she'd taken the shorter path?

She'd never know.

Chapter Four

Sydney studied the bulletin board in the office break room while she waited for the coffee to brew. The space between the usual workplace notices about OSHA and family medical leave was dotted with random posts: free kittens to a good home, a Ford F-150 pickup for sale, a house for lease by a DEA agent on assignment out of the country for the next year. The post about the house made her think about her apartment back in Alexandria. Her neighbor had offered to water plants and take in the mail, but if she was going to be in Dallas for a significant period, she would need to make other arrangements.

The prospect of being here longer evoked mixed feelings. While she didn't necessarily relish investigating a sitting US attorney, the challenge involved in working with this task force was way more interesting than her usual gig overseeing a unit of young white-collar crime prosecutors. And then there was the surprise of working with Tanner, if she could call it that. They'd barely spoken since sharing lunch earlier in the week, and even then their conversation was a minefield with neither seeming to want to admit they'd both made mistakes that had led them down different paths. Now that they were walking in the same direction, wasn't it time to put the past behind them? And do what? Fall into each other's arms?

No. They were different people now, no longer resembling the naive law student couple who'd planned a life together. Besides, Tanner didn't seem to have any regrets about walking away from their dreams, so essentially the only thing that hadn't changed was the reason they'd broken up in the first place.

"Thinking about getting a kitten? I hear this batch is feisty."

Sydney shook her head at the sound of Peyton's voice, wondering how long she'd been standing, staring at the bulletin board. "Feisty is exactly the opposite of what I'm looking for at this point in my life."

"Is that so? Are you looking to settle down? Did you finally meet someone special?"

"Don't go projecting your happy love life on me," Sydney said, waving off the rapid-fire questions. "I'm married to the job just like you used to be. I don't need a woman or a kitten getting in the way of work."

"Yeah, yeah, that's what they all say until they meet the one."

Sydney took in the goofy smile on Peyton's face and couldn't resist asking, "The one, huh? How are you so sure?"

"Deep question, counselor, but if you're looking for a formula, I can't help you. The first time I saw Lily, she was standing across a crowd of people, all of whom were dressed to be noticed, but she was the only one who captured my attention."

"Next you're going to say that it was love at first sight."

"Actually no, but there was definite interest. She was beautiful, but it was more than that. The bright, hopeful look in her eyes, her confident stance, the way she smiled when she caught me looking back at her—I knew I wanted to get to know her, and when I did…well, then I kind of tumbled into the love part."

"You make it sound so easy."

Peyton laughed. "As if. Take two women from vastly different backgrounds and sprinkle in a criminal investigation where one of them is delving into the business dealings of the other one's father. Not to mention my well-meaning but short-sighted brother decided to put our family ranch in jeopardy by selling oil rights to Lily's father without permission from the rest of the family."

"Holy shit, Peyton. I don't see how you get past any of that."

"Very carefully, but I was pretty damn motivated." Peyton's gaze suddenly seemed very far away. "Being with Lily is worth anything, everything. It may not be easy, but our relationship is my greatest accomplishment."

Sydney nodded, but she couldn't quite relate to the concept either as it related to Peyton or in the abstract. The Peyton she'd known had been fully focused on her work, and she never would've expected to hear the words she'd just heard from her. She'd felt that way once about Tanner, but she'd been wrong, but rather than point that out to Peyton, she changed the subject. "I have an idea about the case, but I'm not sure how to accomplish it. Can we talk in private?"

If Peyton was fazed by the change in subject, she didn't show it. "Sure, my office?"

"Let's do this off-campus." She looked at her watch. "I'm supposed to meet with Gellar in a few minutes. How about lunch?"

"Sounds good. Want me to bring anyone else?"

Syd started to mention Tanner by name, but seeing her so soon after the conversation she and Peyton had just had would just be a reminder their happily ever after hadn't and would never happen. Still, they'd need a few people to pull off what she had in mind and Tanner was a key player. "Bring the whole gang."

"Okay. Let's meet at Snuffer's. It's across town, but it's less likely we'll run into anyone else from the office. I'll text you the address."

"Thanks."

"Enjoy your meeting." Peyton grinned as she left her alone in the break room. Sydney took her time fixing her cup of coffee. She was in no hurry to sit and listen to Gellar pontificate about how the office would fall apart without him, even though part of her assignment was to distract him in order to keep their investigation under wraps. When she'd first accepted the job, her goal was to get in, get out, and be on her way, but she hadn't known then that Tanner was assigned to this office. Tanner's presence shouldn't change anything because the reasons they'd broken up were all still present, but Sydney couldn't help but feel like her world had shifted. The question was whether the tilt was in her favor.

❖

Tanner stood outside Bianca's office and tapped her foot while she watched Bianca stuff her purse full of random items. "We're going to lunch, not a weeklong trip overseas."

"Sorry. I switched purses this morning, and I left half of my stuff in the bag I left at home."

"Uh-huh." Tanner didn't get why anyone needed one purse, let alone several. Bianca's rummaging reminded her of Sydney, who routinely made them rush to get to class because she was always switching bags to match her outfit.

"It's an eight a.m. class. No one will notice if your purse doesn't match your shoes."

"I notice. Besides, later today when you want something I happen to have handy—lip balm, Tylenol, a Kleenex—you'll be grateful I checked my supplies."

Tanner scoffed, but the truth was she didn't mind having the most put together girl on campus on her arm. Like her, Sydney was on track to graduate at the top of their class. To everyone else, her ascent looked easy, but Tanner knew how little sleep Syd got as she toiled late into the night to make sure she was more prepared than anyone else, and how she stressed over what to wear to project the image of success.

"I'm ready." Bianca was standing at the door, purse in one hand and the other waving in front of Tanner's face. "Whatcha thinking about?"

"Nothing."

"Bullshit. You were a million miles away. You've been doing that a lot lately."

Tanner jangled her keys. "Come on, I'm driving."

"Scared of my little sports car?"

"Key word, little." Tanner started walking out of the office toward the elevator bank, happy for the change in subject. "Too many big cars and trucks on the road. You're risking your life every time you get into that thing."

Bianca made zooming noises and mock steered. "I'm nimble and quick. I can outmaneuver anything on the road."

"Come on, Speed Racer."

Peyton and Dale were already seated at the restaurant when they arrived. Tanner counted the empty seats. "Who else is coming?"

"Sydney Braswell," Peyton said. "In fact, she called this meeting."

"Not real smart to meet in the middle of the day like this," Dale said.

Tanner silently thanked Dale for making the point she'd been about to, and she cursed her pounding heart at the idea of seeing Sydney again. "Is something going down right now?"

Peyton shrugged. "Didn't sound particularly urgent, but it seemed more convenient to meet here. The ranch is a haul for all of us. If anyone were to see us and report back to Gellar, all she has to say is she was letting us know how the audit is going to go down. I'm not too worried."

They ordered drinks from the waitress, and about fifteen minutes later, Sydney appeared. "Sorry I'm late," she said. "Judge Casey's clerk called to let me know he was sending out the judge's decision on the motion to suppress." She slid into her seat and proceeded to pick up the menu and peruse the contents.

"And?" The word shot out of Tanner's mouth before she could stop it.

Syd looked at her over the menu. "He's not granting it. Razor's confession, such as it was, comes in."

"Well, that's a win."

"Is it? He's not going to cooperate with us, and what he did tell you—where to find a horse—doesn't do anything to advance the case against the Vargases or bring Sergio in. Your tactics may not be considered illegal, but they definitely cost you in this case."

Tanner's jaw dropped at being called out again in front of her peers, and she looked around the table for a sympathetic eye. She didn't have to look far.

"It wasn't just a horse," Bianca said, slapping a hand on the table to punctuate her remark. "That horse, Queen's Ransom, is not only the lifeblood of Jade's ranch, he also happens to mean more to her than anything else in the world. Except maybe me," she added.

Sydney shook a hand at Peyton. "See what I mean? You have an AUSA and an agent who would sacrifice the chance to build a case against a notorious fugitive all for the sake of sentiment. The only one of you who isn't riddled with conflict when it comes to this case is Mary Lovelace, and she isn't here."

"Then why aren't you having lunch with her instead of us?" Tanner asked.

"Quit deflecting."

"Fine. I'll get right to the point. Why are we here?" Tanner asked.

"Because as much as I hate to admit it, I do need you."

Tanner heard the slight shift in tone but didn't want to ask out loud if "you" meant her or the entire group. "What do you need?"

Syd pointed directly at her. "Gellar likes you. He mentioned several times how you were one of the agents who took part in the raid at Gantry's office and that you may be the only one working on the case that he can trust."

Well, that answered her initial question, but Tanner wanted to know more. "Okay, but you called all of us here. Do you have a plan?"

"Not entirely. I've spent the week reviewing the task force

work since its inception and getting up to speed. I've prepared requests for Gellar's bank records and other financial information, but I have a feeling the information we really need is not going to be anywhere public. I want to figure out a way to use how he feels about you to get into his inner sanctum." Syd looked around the table. "And I need the rest of you to come up with a decent distraction."

"Maybe you should define 'inner sanctum' before we go any further," Tanner said.

Syd hesitated for a second and then blurted out, "He's not stupid, and if he's up to something, chances are good any records of it will be at his house. I'm not going to be able to get a warrant to search his house unless I have something concrete to tell a judge. And I can't get anything concrete to tell a judge…"

"Unless you search his house," Tanner finished. "You get the irony, right? First you come here and lecture us about how we run our investigation, and now you're asking us to do your dirty work."

"I'm not asking you to do anything illegal," Sydney said, shaking her head. "But if we can figure out a way for you to get a look around the house under the guise of something innocent, and you happen to see something we can use as a hook for a warrant, then it's a win-win."

"What am I supposed to do? Show up on his doorstep and ask him to give me a tour?" Tanner looked around at the rest of the group for support. Surely she wasn't the only one who thought Sydney had lost her mind. "He might think he can trust me at the office, but I'm pretty sure he'll suspect something's up if I invade his personal space." She hadn't bothered to temper the rising tone of her voice, and she could see a few diners at adjacent tables starting to look their way.

"Hey, we're all on the same team here," Peyton said, breaking the tension. "I need to make a couple of calls, but I have an idea that might work. Let's eat lunch like civilized people and I'll be in touch with a plan."

Sydney nodded and smiled her trademark winning smile and Tanner buried her head in the menu. Sydney's idea wasn't bad in theory; in fact, she wished she'd thought of it. Gellar had trusted her to review most of the discovery he had prepared for the grand jury that would hear the case against Gantry and the Vargases, which was surprising since he acted like he had to hide everything from the rest of the team. Maybe she could show up at his house under the pretense of sharing some eyes-only information with him. She started to say as much, but when she looked around the table she saw that Sydney had already captivated everyone with a story about when she and Peyton had worked together in DC. Tanner remembered well Sydney's ability to draw people in, but she wasn't about to join the fan club. She'd talk to Peyton about her idea later, when bright and shiny Sydney wasn't around to distract her and everyone else.

❖

Sydney hung back from the rest of the group as they exited the restaurant, hoping to catch Peyton as she returned from the restroom. Out of the corner of her eye, she spotted Tanner eyeing her with a curious expression, but she pretended she didn't see her. It was easier that way. It would be easier all around if she could pretend she didn't know Tanner, but ever since she'd laid eyes on her again, little bits of Tanner facts had populated her thoughts, distracting her from the work she was here to do.

"Did everyone leave you?" Peyton said as she walked toward her.

"I stayed behind on purpose." Sydney sucked in a breath. "We need to talk."

"Sounds ominous."

"Hopefully not, but I need to make a confession, and I've finally worked up the nerve to do it. Mostly."

"How about we talk over a drink?" Peyton took her arm and steered her toward the bar.

"Wait," Sydney said. "Don't you have court this afternoon?"

"No court, no meetings. Only a bunch of evidence seized in a human trafficking case to review. Gellar assigned me to that division when he broke up the task force, and I have a few lingering cases to work on while I'm back on the Vargas case. Tequila might be the only way I get through the afternoon. One glass. You game?"

Sydney nodded and followed Peyton to the bar. Peyton ordered two Sauzas, neat, and tossed some bills on the bar when the bartender asked if they'd like to keep a tab open. Sydney picked up the heavy glass and tipped it against her lips, enjoying the slow burn of the smooth amber liquid. "Thanks. I didn't know it, but that was exactly what I needed."

Peyton touched her glass to hers and said, "What's on your mind? You having second thoughts about coming out here?"

Yes, but not for the reasons you think, Sydney thought. But was that true? If she'd known she would see Tanner again before she'd agreed to make the trip, would she have turned this assignment down? Or was it just a matter of not having time to prepare? Her thoughts jumbled and she realized she was in danger of not accomplishing what she'd had in mind—coming clean. "I used to be in love with Tanner."

Peyton stopped with her glass in midair and scrunched her brow. She set the glass down and then picked it up and took a deep drink. She motioned to Sydney's glass, and Sydney did the same. When both their glasses were back on the bar, Peyton finally spoke. "Guess the tangled web extends to everyone on this case."

Peyton's even tone didn't signal any "I told you so," but Sydney felt it just the same. "I deserve that. In my defense, I had no idea she was working with you until I reviewed the file just before I got on the plane."

"It's been almost a week. Do you think you might have found time to mention it between then and now?"

"Are you mad?"

Peyton laughed "Of course not, but I am curious." She took another drink. "Well, that explains why Tanner looks like she's chewing bullets every time you two interact. I'm thinking the love thing didn't work out for either of you."

"No. It didn't. Not ultimately. Well, not between us anyway. And not for me at all. I've had a few relationships since Tanner, but nothing major. This job is my wife and I'm happy to be married to it." Sydney stopped talking, acutely conscious she'd been rambling.

"You don't have to tell me all of this."

"I know. We met in law school and spent three years studying our asses off and planning a future together that was never going to happen, but you're right and I'm sorry for oversharing. We're here to work, not for me to moan about having to work with my ex who apparently isn't any more interested in having anything to do with me than she was when she walked out the door to join the FBI."

Peyton held up both hands. "Whoa, there. That's not what I meant. If you want to talk, I'm happy to listen. I just didn't want you to feel like you have to. I trust that whatever you do with this case won't be colored by your past."

"I wish I could be so sure."

"I don't know Tanner very well."

Sydney paused to digest that tidbit. "Seems like you all are a pretty tight-knit group."

"It didn't start out that way. What I said earlier about Tanner was true. She was part of the team that led the search on Lily's father's offices. That was all Gellar's doing."

"Okay." Sydney drew out the word, not entirely sure what she was supposed to glean from this information. "So how did she wind up working with your task force?"

"Bianca brought her in." Peyton held up two fingers twisted together. "Those two have become good friends, and the fact that Gellar trusts Tanner has made her a valuable asset for the team. If it had been up to me, though…"

"You wouldn't have joined forces with her." Sydney finished the sentence.

"And I would've been wrong. I guess I'm just saying that things aren't always what they seem."

Sydney pointed at the mostly empty glass of tequila in front of her. "Are you waxing philosophical or is that the liquor talking?"

"Maybe both." Peyton took another sip. "But back to Tanner. I didn't know she was a lawyer, but I did know she was in the service. Was that before or after law school?"

"Before law school, before I met her. She didn't talk much about her time in Afghanistan, and it never occurred to me when I was plotting out our legal future that she'd want to return to government work. Not very bright on my part."

"Yet here you are, doing the same thing."

"I didn't get here by the most direct route."

"The direct route is often overrated. My brother Neil begged me to stay and work the ranch with him before I left for DC, but I wanted to go make a name for myself," Peyton said. "If my father hadn't gotten sick, I don't know that I would've come back here. I might never have met Lily and might never have met any of these women I now consider friends."

"There you go again with the sage wisdom. How is your father?"

"Some days are better than others, but the reality is he's just waiting to die."

"I'm sorry."

"Don't be. He's lived a full life and he's surrounded by people who love him. I'm just glad I came back when I did. If he'd passed away while I was in DC, I don't think I would ever have been able to forgive myself."

Sydney thought about her own parents, who'd drifted apart not just from each other but her too after their divorce, and she wondered what it must be like to have a close relationship with blood relatives. She reached over and placed a hand over Peyton's. "If you need anything, I'm here for you."

Peyton's smile was tinged with sadness. "Thanks. You being here is a big help. Once this case is wrapped up, I'd like to have a little time to focus on my family and help plan my wedding. I only plan to get married once, and I'd like to do it right."

Sydney returned the smile, but her happiness for Peyton was bittersweet since she'd stopped imagining a future with family and weddings for a while now.

"Are you okay?" Peyton asked.

"Sure," Sydney lied. "I promise we'll get things wrapped up in plenty of time for you to walk Lily down the aisle."

"To that end, I need you to do me a favor."

"Name it."

Peyton raised her glass. "Take Tanner out for a drink and break the ice. The whole team can feel the tension, and it's not conducive for us going forward. Once you two put the past behind you, it'll be much easier for all of us to focus on Gellar. Okay?"

Sydney raised her glass and touched it to Peyton's, willing to admit in theory at least that Peyton was right. The question was whether Tanner would agree.

CHAPTER FIVE

S o, why did you decide not to practice law?" Bianca asked. Tanner looked up from the files spread out on the table in front of her and didn't bother hiding a groan at the out of left field question. It had been two days since she'd confessed that part of her past to Bianca, and she'd managed to stuff it to the back of her mind. At Sydney's urging, they'd decided to re-review all of the files from the Gantry and Vargas cases to make sure they hadn't missed anything, but the task was boring since they'd been through everything so many times before. "Depends on what you mean by practice. I could argue that I practice law every day. I know the laws, I enforce them. Isn't that enough?"

"Spoken like a true lawyer. Seriously, didn't you ever consider becoming an AUSA or maybe even a defense attorney?"

"No." Tanner kept the answer short because she wanted to steer far from any conversation that dug into the decisions she'd made in the third year of law school. She and Bianca might have become friends, but reliving the memory in her head was bad enough.

"Professor Radley had a guest speaker today. It was a special agent from the FBI, a woman. She was amazing. Did you know that a large percentage of the agents are lawyers?"

"Do you know where my umbrella is?" Sydney asked, rummaging through their bedroom closet. "I've been looking

for it all day and I can't find it anywhere. It's supposed to rain tonight, and I don't need the partners seeing me in sopping wet mode."

"It's in the front closet where you always keep it," Tanner said, not bothering to hide the edge of exasperation in her voice. Tonight was the third night in the last two weeks that Sydney was headed out to attend a law firm mixer. Attendance had been mandatory while they'd worked their summer associate jobs, but now that the fall semester had started, Tanner had hoped Sydney's focus would be back on their present lives and not just the future. "Did you hear a word I said?"

"Radley, special agent, FBI, closet."

"Amazing."

"It would be if I could find it."

"No, your ability to spit out a particular set of facts and circumstances when I know you weren't really listening to a word I said."

Syd strode past on her way to the closet, pausing to kiss her lightly on the cheek. "It's called multitasking, babe."

Refusing to be distracted by the kiss, Tanner pressed on. "Radley told her I was the most promising student in her class, and she gave me her card."

"Aha!" Sydney brandished the formerly missing umbrella and then feigned an embarrassed look at Tanner's frown. "I heard you, I heard you. I'm just not sure why she felt the need to give you her card. What's up with that?"

Tanner grabbed Syd's free hand and pulled her toward the couch. "I need you to sit still for two seconds and hear me out."

"Sounds serious." Syd perched on the arm of the old sofa.

"It might be." Tanner took a deep breath. She'd been so excited after she'd spoken with Special Agent Barlow that she'd been bubbling over with ideas about how to broach the subject with Syd, but now that the time had come, her excitement had turned to apprehension. "The agency is hiring, and I've been asked to apply."

Syd's brow furrowed. "Agency? What agency? Wait, you mean the FBI?"

Tanner heard the slight rise in tone and told herself it was natural for Syd to be surprised. Working for the FBI wasn't exactly part of their big plan to take over the legal world, but she knew that once Syd had time to digest the news, she'd see how it was the perfect fit for her. Agent Barlow had already spoken with Professor Radley about her, and her military background had been a big plus. The agency was looking for more lawyers to join their ranks, and if she passed all the background checks and initial testing, she could start training right after graduation. "Yes, the FBI. It's a fantastic opportunity."

Syd reached out and stroked her arm. "Of course. And it's great that they want you, but it's not exactly what we had planned, right?"

"Sure, but—"

"I mean, you'd have to go off to training for months, and then you probably wouldn't have any control over where you're ultimately assigned. Not to mention the potential for danger. Not exactly the best environment for raising kids."

Tanner's head spun at the way Syd had just fast-forwarded their lives to a full-fledged family. "Slow down, babe. Next thing you know we'll be planning for our as yet unborn children's college education."

"You laugh now, but it'll be here before you know it." Syd stood and leaned in for a kiss. "I think it's great they want you. Who wouldn't? You're set to beat me out for the top spot in our class and you'll have your choice of big firm jobs. I, on the other hand, better go hustle. I won't be too late."

Still clutching the umbrella, she grabbed her purse and keys from the table by the door and sailed out. Tanner watched Syd go, her earlier excitement fading fast, leaving behind a sense of loss. Silly since she had everything she could ever want: stellar grades, tons of opportunity, and a beautiful, smart woman who wanted to build a future with her. She reached into her pocket and pulled out Barlow's card. She'd been flattered at the attention, and who could blame her? It was nice to be wanted, but Syd was right, that life didn't fit with their plans. She started to toss the card into the trash bin they kept by the door, but just before it left her fingers, she clamped down and hung on. When she slipped it back in her pocket, she swore it was only a souvenir.

"Have I done something to make you mad?" Bianca asked. "I mean, I know you got in trouble for helping me out with Razor, but I thought we were past that. Jade thinks you're the best person she's ever met, and we're both completely in your debt."

Tanner forced her attention out of the past. "Sorry. I don't know what's wrong with me lately," she lied. "But I promise it's not you. I'd do the same thing all over again, I swear. And I'm glad you and Jade are happy, no matter what anyone else says."

"You mean Sydney? I know she seems a little judgy, but you have to consider how all of this looks to her or how it would look to anyone coming in from the outside. Have you heard from Peyton yet about a plan to get into Gellar's house?"

Tanner laughed. She was used to Bianca's swift conversational turns, but they still left her spinning. "Not yet, but she sent me a text that she wants to meet after work, so maybe she'll have something cooked up by then."

"Keep me posted."

"Sure." Tanner opened a file and pretended to be totally engaged in hopes Bianca's probing questions would subside. She needn't have worried. What she saw would derail them both. She jabbed a finger at the papers inside. "Where did this come from?"

Bianca reached over and looked at the outside jacket and then glanced around like she'd just committed a crime. "Oh, yeah, I meant to tell you that I may have found a few additional files."

Tanner shot a look at the door. "Found?"

"Borrowed might be a better word." She lowered her voice.

"Gellar has an appointment across town and Ida says he won't be back until tomorrow. That one and," she held up another file, "this one were in his desk drawer." She hunched her shoulders. "It wasn't locked."

"Holy shit, Bianca." Tanner grabbed the other file out of Bianca's hand and flipped through the contents. Both files contained pages of handwritten notes along with 302s, official FBI witness summaries, but she didn't recognize the handwriting on either, and the signatures on the 302s were impossible to make out. She skimmed the information and her excitement grew. "Have you read these?"

"Not yet. It was kind of a grab and go operation. I figured we could look at them together."

Tanner shoved the paperwork across the table. "Brace yourself." She watched Bianca read, and it only took a few seconds before her face lit up with the realization she'd stumbled onto something very important.

"These are all about Gantry Oil's truck that was found abandoned. The one carrying all those people."

"Right. The one where all those people died and were left to rot in the middle of nowhere."

"But I didn't think there were any leads on that investigation," Bianca said. "Gantry's company had reported the truck stolen, and there were no witnesses, no forensic evidence." Bianca pointed at the fan of paperwork in front of her. "But there's a whole case here."

"So it would appear." Tanner held up one of the 302s to the light. It was definitely the official form, but she couldn't make out the signatures on a single one of them. "Have you seen Gellar's grand jury witness list?"

"No, he hasn't been in much of a sharing mood. He keeps insisting he's going to present the case solo. Why?"

Tanner pointed at the scribbled name on the 302. "Because I'm willing to bet this agent is on the list."

"Then we should talk to whoever it is. See if we can get them to tell us anything."

"Yes, we should. But first we need to figure out if this person is even real."

❖

Syd was the first one at the bar and she ordered a club soda. She didn't know what Peyton had in mind, so it was best to be prepared for anything. She'd spent the day with Gellar, traipsing around the city. First, a lunch at the Dallas Bar Association where Gellar pontificated about the work his office was doing to a captive bunch of lawyers who likely only cared about the continuing education credit they were getting by pretending to listen to him. Next, he insisted on driving her out to FBI headquarters where he made a big show about introducing her around. She'd braced all afternoon for a possible run-in with Tanner, but she hadn't been anywhere in sight. Syd couldn't help but wonder where Tanner had spent the day and who with.

Everyone on the team seemed to like Tanner despite the fact she'd joined the group later than the others and had been viewed as Gellar's pet. Syd wondered if Tanner enjoyed working on the task force more than working out of the FBI office. Whatever the case, it was apparent Tanner had settled into her job as a law enforcement agent and the profession suited her.

Their mailbox was crammed, but for once it wasn't just bills jammed into the small metal box. Syd clutched the letters in her hand and hurried into the house. She set the letters on the table, glancing at the familiar names of law firms on the top two and telling herself she'd wait until Tanner got home, like they'd agreed. Whatever their future held, they'd find out about it together, but in the meantime, she'd have to locate something to distract her attention or she'd go crazy.

The phone rang and she jumped at the sound. Hoping it was

Tanner, she answered before looking. "Tell me you're coming home soon."

"Well, I would, but then my boyfriend might be pissed since I have a date with him."

"Hey, Denise. Sorry, I thought it was Tanner."

"Uh, obviously. So, did you get the letter?"

"I think so."

"It's kind of a yes or no question."

Syd ran her fingers along the edge of the letter on top of the pile. "There's an envelope here. More than one, actually, but I haven't opened them yet."

"Oh my God, you're waiting for Tanner, aren't you?"

"You say that like it's a bad thing."

Denise sighed. "Your lovey-dovey thing just makes the rest of us look bad. When does she get home?"

"In a little while. I can wait." Syd hoped she sounded believable.

"Sure, whatever. Well, I'm headed out to celebrate. Got my offer from Burles and Preston, and I already emailed to accept."

"Good for you."

"Any chance you can at least tell me who you got letters from?"

Syd pulled the stack of mail a bit closer. "I suppose just looking at the outside of the envelopes wouldn't be such a bad thing. I mean, it's the responsible thing to do to make sure this mail is all for us."

"Sure. Now dish before Lance gets here to pick me up."

Syd started flipping through the mail in earnest now. There were letters from each of the law firms where she and Tanner had done their summer associate positions, and she read off the names to Denise. Next came a few bills and the obligatory coupon pack and a large postcard from a local car dealership. "That's it."

"Three out of three is pretty good odds."

"I'll say, but I'm going to wait to count the odds until I see *what's inside." Syd gathered the pile and stacked it neatly, but when she did she realized one thin envelope was stuck to the back of the postcard. "Hang on a minute."*

"What is it?"

Syd stared at the envelope. It wasn't the heavy linen stock of the others, but it looked just as official since it was addressed to Miss Tanner Cohen. But in the upper left-hand corner instead of the name of a top tier law firm, the initials FBI blazed over a Washington, DC, address. She turned the envelope over and over as if a clue might reveal itself. There was nothing overt to signal what was inside, but the mystery filled her with a growing sense of dread.

"Syd, are you still there?"

"Sorry. Hey, Denise, I need to go." She didn't wait for a response before she disconnected the call. In a trance, she arranged the mail into stacks. Bills, junk, and offer letters. She stood in front of the neat piles and tapped the FBI letter against the counter several times before finally tossing it on top of the letters from law firms, unable to deny her instincts.

When the door opened behind her, she turned slowly, trying her level best to hide any worry from her expression. Tanner stood framed in the doorway in her favorite jeans, T-shirt, and boots, looking more like a park ranger than a sought-after candidate for a high-powered law job. "Hey, babe, have you been home long?" Tanner asked as she tucked her backpack away.

"Not long."

"Good. Sorry to keep you waiting. Radley asked me to stick around and talk about my research project. She had some great ideas."

Sydney sank into one of the bar stools at the counter. "You're really going to stick with Radley as your advisor for the project?"

"Sure. We get along great and she's brilliant. Not to mention well connected. I don't get why you have a problem with her."

Syd didn't need to hear any more to put the pieces together. "Maybe I think it would be better for your future if you picked a project that might be useful to your future career. But you know, maybe I'm wrong. Maybe you already did that." She pointed at the stacks of mail. "Looks like some offer letters came today. We did get one piece of mail I wasn't sure what to do with. Wanna check it out and let me know?"

Tanner followed her pointing finger to the letter from the FBI. "Syd, I can explain."

"Explain what? Are you telling me I'm right? That there's an offer inside that envelope?"

"I don't know for sure, but I think so."

"When were you going to tell me you applied?"

Tanner's face reddened. "I've tried. Several times, but every time I bring up the possibility, you change the subject or shut me down entirely. I had to know if I even had a chance."

Syd grabbed the envelope and shoved it toward her. "Well, by all means, let's find out." She shook it in the air. "Go ahead, open it."

"Come on, Syd, don't be like that."

"Don't be like what? Someone who plans for a future with someone who says it's what she wants when it isn't true? Is that what you mean, because that's pretty much what's happening here." She shook the envelope in the air. "This isn't what we had planned."

"Key word 'we,'" Tanner barked back. "There's no we when it comes to our future. There's you and everything you have planned, and I'm just a piece of the puzzle you're busy constructing. You decide where I fit in the picture, and as long as I make enough money and have enough prestige, then I fit into your grand scheme."

Sydney sank against the counter. "Is that what you really think?"

"What am I supposed to think? You micromanage my schedule, my clothes, my study groups. It's a wonder I was able to manage the application process without you finding out."

Sydney paced for a moment and then tugged Tanner's arm

and led them toward the couch. This wasn't at all how she'd expected this evening would go when she'd opened the mailbox to find missives about their future. She'd expected they would bust into the bottle of decent champagne they had tucked away and toast their success while deciding which of their options would be the gateway to their bright future. She'd handled everything about this encounter wrong and needed to make it right or she'd lose the woman she loved and all their plans would be for nothing.

"I'm sorry," she said. "A, I shouldn't have gone through your mail, and b, you should be able to talk to me about anything that's going on in your life without fear of judgment. I love you, Tanner."

"I love you too, Syd." Tanner's voice was quiet. "And I'm not mad at you for going through my mail. If I'd really wanted to keep it a secret, I wouldn't have had them send the letter here. I want to share this news with you, and it's been killing me not to."

Syd forced a smile and said, "Tell me now. Tell me everything."

"You remember I told you about the agent that Professor Radley had speak to the class last spring, right before the end of the semester? Well, it turns out she was here specifically to meet me. They need more lawyers in the ranks, and they did a preliminary search nationwide of 2Ls—grades, special skills, that kind of thing. They picked me, Syd. Me."

Syd slid a hand down Tanner's arm. "That doesn't surprise me at all, babe. Lots of people pick you, present company included. You're brilliant and talented. You're going to be an amazing lawyer." She placed a special emphasis on the word "lawyer."

"I hear you. You think working for the FBI as an agent isn't practicing real law."

"Well, it's not, but that's not really the point." Syd took a deep breath to gather her thoughts. She was wading into dangerous waters here. "There's absolutely nothing wrong with

becoming an FBI agent, but not for you." She ticked off her points. "It could be dangerous. Your talents will be wasted, not to mention the fact they could send you anywhere, and then what am I supposed to do?"

"I don't know, Syd. What would happen if I got a job offer from a firm with offices in New York or LA? Suppose it was an amazing offer, a huge salary with bonuses and lots of fringe benefits? Would we be having this same conversation in reverse or would it be a foregone conclusion that we'd be going where the money is?"

"Wow, you really think I'm that shallow?"

Tanner hung her head. "No, no. I know it's about security to you, but security isn't everything. Do you really want me to work at a job that might suck the life out of me rather than do something that makes me happy?"

"I'm not asking you to work for a big firm for the rest of your life. You're oversimplifying this as usual."

"Maybe I'm using my incredible legal talent to distill the facts down to what's important and what isn't."

"Quit acting like security isn't important," Syd said, no longer trying to hide the exasperation she felt. "You of all people should know how much it means to me to be secure." Syd rushed on, wishing she hadn't bared her vulnerability so boldly. "And what about kids? You think I'm going to have children with someone who spends her days chasing bad guys and might not come home at night? Dammit, Tanner, we had plans."

Tanner pulled her into her arms and held her close against her beating chest. Syd felt her eyes water and she tried to will back the tears, but they fell despite her efforts, leaving traces of moisture on Tanner's shirt. She rarely cried. It was a weakness she wouldn't indulge because she'd learned a long time ago tears didn't accomplish anything but lay open her vulnerabilities. Tanner leaned back and wiped the tears from her face. "Don't cry, Syd. We'll figure this out."

"Will we?" Sydney sobbed the words.

"Of course we will. It's you and me, babe, for the rest of our lives." Tanner cracked a smile. "Hell, I haven't even seen the letter. All of this could be for nothing."

Sydney reached over to where she'd set the letter on the coffee table and handed it to Tanner. She'd always said you need to know all the facts, good and bad, before you could formulate a strategy. Once that letter was open and she knew for sure what she was facing, she could take care of it. One way or another, she'd find a way to make it work because a future without Tanner was inconceivable.

CHAPTER SIX

Peyton slid into the seat next to Sydney and ordered a beer. "You ready for another?" she asked, pointing at Sydney's glass.

Sydney was tempted to indulge. Anything to stem the flow of memories bubbling up, catching her unawares, but she had enough distractions complicating her focus. "I'm good."

"Tanner should be here any minute. Traffic is a bitch today."

"I thought we were here to talk about work, but now it looks like you're arranging some kind of clever kumbaya."

Peyton raised her hands. "Who, me?" She grinned. "Seriously, though, if you two can figure out a way to put the past behind you, that would be great, but I really asked you here because I have a plan."

"Really? Dish."

"As soon as our partner in crime shows up. She factors majorly into what I have planned." Peyton lifted her glass. "And here she is."

Syd turned slowly and watched as Tanner strode toward them looking sharp and confident in a trim black suit with a pale gray shirt. Sydney pictured Tanner on the witness stand, testifying for the prosecution. The jurors would've been captivated by the cool confidence of her demeanor, like she was now. Before Tanner reached them, Syd turned back to Peyton. "On second thought, I'll take a glass of wine."

"Tanner, drink?" Peyton asked.

"Sure. I'll have a Blanton, neat."

Once they all had drinks, Peyton led them to a small table in the corner of the bar where they could talk in relative privacy. They were barely seated when Peyton tossed a brochure onto the table.

Sydney picked it up and began perusing the contents, grateful for the prop to distract her from studying every inch of Tanner. "What's this?"

"It's the key to getting into Gellar's house." Peyton pointed at the front of the brochure. "Every year, the Junior League holds a holiday tour of homes. All the homes are decorated for the holidays and open to the public, or at least the portion of the public who had the funds to purchase the high-dollar entry fee. The proceeds go to charity, and it's a big deal to be included on the list. The annual tour is scheduled for this weekend."

"Let me guess, Gellar's house is on the tour?"

"It isn't, but it's about to be. I called an old acquaintance who's on the planning committee and got her to pull some strings. She's meeting with Gellar right now to beg him for his help. Something about filling in because of a plumbing emergency at one of the other houses on the tour."

"And there's no real plumbing emergency?" Syd said.

"I have no direct knowledge either way. The point is, once Gellar's house is on the tour, we can get in. And by we, I mean Tanner."

Tanner took a sip of her bourbon. "I think I missed a step. I heard the words high-dollar entry fee. No way is Gellar going to believe I suddenly took an interest in expensive, well-decorated housing."

"I've got that part handled," Peyton said. "Trust me. Syd will be there too. Gellar's definitely going to want the chance to show off his house to you. It actually is pretty nice for a guy on a government salary, but his wife comes from money, so it's never raised any questions."

"Okay, what's the plan?" Sydney asked. "We need to make sure there's no way Tanner gets caught poking around. Gellar's not stupid enough to leave anything incriminating in plain sight."

"True, but he'll be off guard for the night, glad-handing a bunch of socialites. We'll wire you both so you can communicate. If Sydney notices Gellar getting suspicious, you can get word to Tanner to stand down. It's not the perfect situation, but it's as close as we can get without a warrant." Peyton drained the last of her beer and stood. "I've got to head out. Tanner, I'll text you the details. Dale and Mary will get you both set up before you go, but you'll need to show up separately so as not to raise any suspicion."

As Peyton walked away from the table, Sydney started looking around the bar wondering how long she should stay before making her own excuse about having to be somewhere.

"Wait here," Tanner said as she sprang from her seat. "I'll be right back."

Tanner jogged through the bar, caught up with Peyton, and tapped her on the shoulder. Peyton turned and raised her eyebrows in question and Tanner started talking, waving her hands for emphasis, same as she used to do when she and Syd engaged in heated debates while they were in law school. A few minutes later, Tanner was back at her side. "Are you hungry?" Tanner asked, pointing at the menu propped against the salt and pepper shakers.

It was an ostensibly easy question, but Sydney found it difficult to respond. Peyton's idea about how to gain entry to Gellar's house had been a little bit of a bombshell. Basically, she and Tanner would be working this weekend as a team, and she'd be responsible for making sure Tanner didn't get caught. If things went wrong, Tanner could lose her job and they'd both be in trouble. But hey, sure, let's grab a bite to eat like it's nothing.

She looked at the hopeful look on Tanner's face. Maybe sharing a meal was the perfect solution to bridge the gap between them. If they were going to work together, they needed to be in tune instead of constantly engaging in the push and pull they'd had going all week. And she was hungry. Hungry for food, but also hungry for information about Tanner and how she'd wound up here in Dallas and whether she loved the life she had more than the one she'd given up. Syd wasn't sure how she would digest the answers, but it was time to start swallowing some truths, no matter how hard and unappetizing they might be.

❖

Tanner led them out of the bar and asked the hostess for a booth, her mind half on the information about the ghost agent listed on the 302s and half on the reality that she was about to have to be social with her ex.

She'd given Peyton a quick preview of what she'd found, and maybe she should have included Sydney in the information she and Bianca had discovered at the office. But her guard was still up, and she wanted to keep the information tight until she was certain she could trust that Sydney was on their side. Guilt about excluding Syd had motivated the impromptu dinner invitation, and she was having serious second thoughts about whether that had been a good idea, but now that Sydney had said yes, she was fully committed. Besides, a casual dinner might be the perfect way to clear the air between them—a necessary step if they were going to work together. They settled into the booth and studied the menu.

"The steaks here are really good," Tanner said.

"You know how I love a good steak."

"I wasn't sure if you still did." She watched the slight blush creep up Sydney's neck and she tossed her menu down. "I think we should start over."

"We haven't even ordered yet," Syd replied.

"You know what I mean. You and me. Us. It's time to put the past behind us."

"Is that so? And how do you propose we do that?"

"Well, we can't start completely over. That's a little impossible, but over like this week over. Like if we'd met again after however many years and not under circumstances where you were accusing me of breaking the law."

"Ten years." Syd fixed her with a stare. "It's been ten years. How can you not know that?"

Tanner shifted in her chair. "I do know." She set her menu down. "I know a lot of things, but what I really want to know is why you fought so hard for a life you're not even living. Where's the big firm gig and the family and nice house, and the rest of the trappings? The last place I expected to see you working was a government job."

"Things change. I'm not the same person you knew."

"Clearly."

"Just because your life worked out exactly the way you expected doesn't mean mine did. Everyone's not Tanner Cohen, born to be a hero to the downtrodden and a champion of justice. Some of us have to make some mistakes before we find our way."

Tanner flinched at the edge in Syd's voice, but what really struck her was the undercurrent of pain she heard. "Is that how you see me?"

"It's kind of hard not to." Syd's expression was sad. "You knew exactly what you wanted and you went for it."

Not everything, Tanner thought. "So did you."

"I was wrong."

Tanner shook her head. "Don't beat yourself up. You went for the brass ring. What everyone thinks is the brass ring, anyway."

"That's for sure."

"Do you want to tell me what happened?" The words were out before Tanner had time to think them through. After all this time she shouldn't care why Sydney's dream life hadn't turned out the way she'd thought it would. Why should she? The lure of the perfect life had been the thing that had torn them apart. Finding out it wasn't so perfect after all wasn't a big surprise, but if Syd needed to tell her story, needed to make peace with what she'd done to break them up, Tanner was willing to give her the space to do so.

"I'm fairly certain my story is not unique, and I probably should've seen it coming. If I thought it was competitive to get into one of the top tier firms, it was nothing at all like the competition once I arrived. It started on the first day when we were told how many hours we'd need to bonus aka enter the partnership track. There was barely time to eat lunch, let alone go to the bathroom, and there was absolutely no time for a social life. All that crap during the summer months—the happy hours, the courtside tickets to the games, and the front row seats at the theater—over. Completely over. Those bennies were reserved for firm clients, people we'd barely ever get to see."

"Are you really bitching because you had to do a bunch of grunt work?" Tanner said, not bothering to hide her frustration. "I saw your starting salary offer. Hell, for that amount of money, I'm surprised they didn't also have you shining their shoes and washing their cars."

Syd shook her head. "You know me better than that. I might not have always pursued the kind of work you valued, but I have always worked five times harder than most people. I'm not scared of work, even menial work far beneath my qualifications. But I was scared of losing my license so rich attorneys could get even richer." She took a drink of her wine.

Tanner nodded. It was true. Sydney was one of the hardest working people she'd ever known, and even if Tanner didn't always appreciate who she worked for, she had to admit that. "So, this firm liked to play fast and loose with the rules?"

"That's being generous. They liked to pitch to their clients that they were real sharks, unafraid to engage in whatever tactics were necessary to get the win, in or out of court. They kept a whole stable of private investigators on staff to do opposition research on opposing counsel and their clients, and they had reporters at all the local rags on speed-dial. But unfortunately, that was fairly status quo for this level of litigation."

"You're saying it was more than that?"

Syd met her eyes with a deep stare as if gauging how much she could trust her with the next bit of information. "Yes. They were helping some of their clients with less than savory connections cook their books by setting up shell corporations in places like Curaçao."

"Holy shit. I can't believe they let you in on that your first year."

"Oh, they didn't. They waited until I was completely invested in the partnership track, and even then, they didn't tell me about it. I did some digging on my own when I noticed some things weren't adding up. When they found out about it, they called me in and explained the importance of loyalty as a quality they were seeking in their prospective partners."

"What did you do?"

"Besides thinking about Tom Cruise in *The Firm*?" Syd's smile was humorless. "I told them I was well acquainted with the concept of loyalty, but not at the expense of my license and my freedom."

"I'm sure they rewarded you for your honesty."

"It's funny how even lawyers forget the rules when they're in the middle of breaking them. They did exactly what I would have cautioned them against if I'd been their lawyer. They asked for my resignation, and when I refused, they fired me on the spot. I took my four-terabyte flash drive directly to the US attorney's office and spent the next year helping them build a case against the firm."

Tanner blew a low whistle. "Wow, that's rough. Is that how you wound up working for the DOJ?"

"Yep. By the time the case was over, I was broke and pretty much unemployable in the private sector. The bounty I got as a whistle-blower was barely enough to cover my outstanding debts. I considered chunking it all and taking a job as a barista."

"As I recall, you would've been really good at that." Tanner smiled.

"Thanks. Anyway, the white-collar division chief offered me a job. He's the same guy who recruited Peyton out there. I figured it was time for me to give back to the agency who helped me through it all. It wasn't the direct route you took toward government service, but here I am."

Instinct drove Tanner to reach her hand across the table and cover Syd's. "No one's judging you. I'm sorry you had to go through all that."

"Thanks, Tanner. And that's nice of you to say, but people do judge. I know based on all the doors that got slammed in my face when I tried to find new work. It was like I was the dishonest one. I was definitely the one who couldn't be trusted to keep firm secrets."

"You didn't do anything wrong."

"I guess."

Tanner fished around for the right words to ask the question she really wanted to know. "And all your other plans, the house, the family? Did any of that work out for you?"

"Let's see. The woman I was dating at the time was another attorney at the firm, not on the same partnership track as I was, but still way more concerned about being tainted with my misfortune than standing by me when the shit hit the fan."

"Ouch." The pain in Syd's voice pierced Tanner and she squeezed Syd's hand, wishing she knew what to say to make it better.

After a few moments, Syd drew her hand back. "So, no family, no house with a picket fence. None of that fit into my life before, and now...Well, let's just say I've come to realize my limitations. You?"

"Me?" Tanner suddenly felt uncomfortable having the attention refocused on her. "No, nothing like that. This life isn't really conducive to having someone to share it with. No one outside really understands the demands, and if they're on the job, then—"

"The demands are all you talk about, right?"

"Right." Tanner studied Syd for a moment before blurting out, "Is it bad for me to say I'm surprised you get that?"

"Hardly. You don't have any reason to expect anything from me after how I acted when you told me you were serious about joining the FBI."

"It wasn't just you. I went behind your back. You had every reason not to trust that I'd be there for the long haul."

"We both know it wasn't that simple." Syd reached her hand back and twisted their fingers together. "I'm glad we did this," she waved her free hand between them, "clearing the air. Maybe we can be friends again."

Friends. Tanner rolled the word around in her mind. She had plenty of friends, but it never hurt to have another, especially not one that she'd known for years and who knew her better than most. If she and Syd were going to work together, this detente would be best for both of them. She squeezed Syd's hand in hers, doing her best to ignore the heat that coursed between them. "Friends for sure."

❖

Syd strode through the lobby of the Adolphus, pausing briefly before the bar. It was late and she should go to her room and call it a day, but dinner with Tanner had stirred up feelings long laid to rest. If she was going to get any sleep at all, she'd need a nightcap.

The bar was sparsely populated, mostly solo businessmen nursing their martinis and whiskey neats. She scouted out a corner table far enough away from the bar to keep from having to engage in conversation and ordered a Baileys from the bored cocktail waitress. As she savored the first sip, she remembered how Tanner used to tease her about her penchant for sweet liquors.

"I don't see how you can drink that sweet stuff."

"It's not like I'm eating a box of donuts. Be glad you don't have a sweet tooth."

Tanner pulled her close and dropped kisses along her neck. "Oh, but I do."

"Baileys?"

Syd looked up into the curious eyes of the waitress, and then reached for her drink and handed over a more than generous tip to account for her zoning out. These little memory nuggets were interfering with her ability to focus, but she supposed she should've seen them coming. Their relationship had ended with too many frayed edges, and working with Tanner now was pulling at all of the little strings that had been hanging loose for so long. Maybe this reconnection was a good thing. If she and Tanner could actually become friends, she'd finally have some closure, and she could move on with her life.

The realization hit home. She'd never allowed herself to consider the possibility that the reason none of her other relationships had panned out was because the one relationship she'd always considered the big one had blown up in her face, and when it did she'd erected walls to keep anyone else from having that kind of power. How long was she going to let the fears of her past keep her from happiness? Making friends with her ex was exactly the closure she needed to tuck her ideas of what could have been neatly away and move on. All this time she'd been stagnant, and maybe it was as simple as letting go.

But if letting go of the past was the answer, then why couldn't she stop thinking about Tanner in the here and now?

CHAPTER SEVEN

Tanner walked up the steps to Peyton's house and raised her hand to knock on the door, but it swung open before her knuckles connected with the wood. "Hey, I know I'm early, but..." Her words trailed off at the sight of Syd standing in the doorway, looking amazing in a midnight blue cocktail dress. Tanner glanced down at her plain black suit and pale green shirt and felt decidedly underdressed.

"But I'm earlier," Syd finished her sentence. She swept her hand toward the inside of the house. "Come on in. The gang's all here."

Tanner walked through, lightly brushing Syd's arm. She cursed inwardly at the more than friendly way the contact shuddered through her, and she hid her reaction by talking over it. "You seem a little more excited about this plan than you did the other day."

"I've had time to warm up to the idea," Syd said. "Besides, it's a holiday tour of homes. I'm imagining bright lights, the smell of fresh cut pine trees, and mulled spices. It might be glorious."

Tanner smiled. She'd forgotten Syd's love of all things holiday. Even their bare-bones apartment in law school had always been decorated for the season. "I'm doubting we'll find any hand-strung strings of popcorn and cranberries decorating the trees at these houses. This neighborhood goes all out for the holiday, and there are businesses whose sole purpose is making these houses look like something out of a Dickens novel." She watched as Syd's expression turned dreamy.

"Do you remember that time we took the Jeep out in the woods to cut down our tree and got trapped in a mud hole?"

Tanner felt a surge of warmth at the memory of the two of them huddled together in the car, way off the beaten path for AAA but content to take their time sipping hot chocolate while they figured out a plan to get out of the mess. "I do. Thank goodness you insisted on packing all that food. That was the last time I ever pitched a fit over your intense preparations."

She started to say more, but the words "last time" rang in her head, calling her attention to memories. There were so many last times where Syd was concerned. She'd put them all behind her, certain the very last time had been the final one. Maybe this newfound friendship meant they would have a second chance to be in each other's lives, even if they'd never be lovers again.

Why couldn't they be? The idea slammed her in the chest and she fought for breath. Where had that come from? She hadn't even considered the idea, but now that it was facing her square on, she took a minute to roll it around in her head before rejecting it outright. Nothing had changed. They'd both made choices that had sent their lives in completely different directions. Syd might have eventually come around to realizing there was more value to public service than racking up big wages in the private sector, but she sure hadn't made the choice for the sake of their relationship. In fact, it was desperation, not desire, that resulted in her crossing over to her job with the government. Sentimentality aside, nothing had changed between them. Syd made decisions based on self-preservation, and Tanner wasn't a necessary part of her survival, then or now.

"I miss those times," Syd whispered, barely loud enough for Tanner to hear. Every part of her wanted to respond in kind, but her own instincts for self-preservation held her back. It was like those trust exercises where you fall back into the arms of your coworkers, trusting them to catch you. There was a time in her life when Tanner would not have hesitated to fall back into Syd's arms, confident in the knowledge she'd always be there, strong and sure enough to break the fall. But that was then. Now they had a job to do and that was all. "We should get started." She didn't wait for an answer and started walking toward the kitchen, trying not to care that Syd's smile had faded at the sound of her words.

❖

Syd took the seat farthest from Tanner at the table. The push and pull between them was getting to be a bit much, and she needed some distance to regroup before they had to spend the evening together on the job. From the moment Tanner had walked through the door, looking incredibly handsome in her well-tailored, sharp suit, Syd had lost her focus. It wasn't her imagination—she was certain there had been a flicker of affection from Tanner while they reminisced over Christmases past. She'd started to tell Tanner she still had the ornaments from their very first tree, packed away in a box she'd never managed to open but had not been able to discard either. But the sudden distance between them was palpable, and she didn't need to put herself right back in the position of being rejected again when it was clear Tanner wanted nothing more than a surface level relationship under the guise of being friends.

That was fine. She could be professional. In fact, it was easier this way, not having to navigate the minefield of personal involvements. She'd work this case and head back to DC. Maybe when she got back home, she'd work on that vow she'd made years ago to settle down, trust in someone else to be the one. In the meantime, she needed to put her sole focus on this job, so she tuned in to Peyton asking Tanner a question.

"And you can't figure out who the agent is?"

"I'm telling you, there's something completely off. I looked at the handwriting and it's not familiar. We have a big office, though, and without checking in with everyone who works there, it's impossible to know for sure."

"But you have a theory," Bianca chimed in.

"I do, but it's a little crazy," Tanner said.

"Spill."

Tanner looked around the table, and Syd noticed her quickly glance away when their eyes met. "What if Gellar wrote the 302s himself to support his own conclusions?"

"That is crazy," Syd snapped. "You're saying you think a sitting US attorney would violate a federal law to get a conviction?"

"I'm not saying anything for certain. I just posed the question. And it wouldn't be the first time."

Syd started to say *you would know*, but she bit back the words. She and Tanner might not be close, but she didn't need to pick a fight to prove it. "You have anything to support this theory?"

Tanner shook her head. "Like I said, it's just a theory. And I get that it's crazy. Maybe we'll find something tonight to support it. Maybe not."

Syd looked around the table but couldn't quite get a read on whether anyone else bought into Tanner's theory, which was totally out there. It was way more likely Gellar had found some green agent and promised him or her access to a big case in exchange for slanting the reports the way he wanted them. She'd have to find a way to do some digging herself, but she doubted tonight's expedition was going to help. Gellar wouldn't be stupid enough to leave a bunch of evidence lying around, especially not when his house was open to the public. She never should've pitched her plan to get into his house. If she'd known it would have her spending the night with Tanner when her feelings were raw and just below the surface, she would've kept her mouth shut.

But she hadn't, so it was time to either make this work or abandon the plan, and since everyone else seemed to be geared up to go, she was going all in. "What do you need me to do?" She directed the question to Peyton, not Tanner.

"Your main goal is to distract Gellar so Tanner can get a look around. Knowing him, he'll leave his wife to play hostess so he can muck it up with all the elite folks he wishes he were a part of, but even an attention hog like him gets bored now and then. That's when you'll need to be watching to make sure he doesn't start paying more attention to the action behind the scenes." Peyton pointed at Dale. "You want to tell her about the wire?"

Dale fished a small packet from her pocket, opened it, and shook a few tiny pieces of plastic in various shapes onto the table: "These are state-of-the-art Bluetooth transmitters and earpieces. You'll each wear one of these in your ear and somewhere else," she said, looking Sydney up and down, "which means we can all hear each other during the night."

Syd flicked her eyes in Tanner's direction. "So, I'm part of the 'we' in this situation?"

Dale nodded. "You and Tanner will be able to talk and convey your movements to each other throughout the night, and Mary and I will be set up nearby recording everything just in case some random conversation winds up being important later."

Syd nodded, making a mental note to watch her words carefully during the evening, lest some stray muttering wound up being recorded for everyone to hear. "Sounds good. Can you hook me up first? I should probably get going. Gellar told me he has some people he'd like me to meet and suggested I come over a bit early."

Dale had just placed the earpiece and was looking for a place to fit the transmitter when the doorbell rang. Syd inclined her head. "Busy place here tonight."

Peyton stood. "Hang on a minute, Syd. I think this is the last addition to our team for the evening."

While Peyton went to answer the door, the rest of the group started talking amongst themselves. Syd watched Tanner smile and nod at something Dale whispered in her ear, and for a flicker of an instant, she wished she'd been the one to put the smile there. Before she could give the thought any more time, Bianca asked, "Have you done this before?"

"Pardon?"

"Gone undercover? Seems a little scary if you ask me, but I guess Tanner knows what she's doing, so you'll be okay. And it's not like you're headed into a drug lord's house. I mean Gellar's an ass, but if he catches you looking around, he's not going to lop your head off or anything."

Syd stared at the younger attorney, unsure whether to be amused or mortified. "Has anyone ever told you you're a little dramatic?"

Bianca grinned. "All the time. And the rambling—it's an unfortunate by-product."

Syd smiled. "It's fine. Really. Everyone has something they do to compensate for nerves."

"What's yours?"

"What?"

"What do you do to compensate for nerves?"

Syd opened her mouth to answer, but before the words could tumble out, Peyton reappeared in the doorway, flanked by a tall, gorgeous stranger. Bianca's question faded to the back of her mind, behind thoughts of who this delicious woman was and how she fit into the work they were about to do.

Peyton rapped her knuckles on the doorframe. "Hey, everyone, I'd like you to meet Virginia Taylor. She's on the committee for the tour of homes, and she's the one we have to thank for adding Gellar's house to the tour."

Syd took in every aspect of Virginia Taylor while Peyton introduced her around the table. When the intro got to her, she smiled but otherwise kept her expression guarded so as not to give away her curiosity, but she couldn't help but notice the way Virginia kept sneaking glances at Peyton like she was a tasty snack. But when Peyton introduced Virginia to Tanner, everything changed and Virginia seemed to forget Peyton was even in the room.

"Agent Tanner Cohen, my date for the evening." Virginia sashayed over to Tanner and held out her hand. "The pleasure is going to be all mine." She surveyed the rest of the group like she was holding court. "Normally, these things are dull, dreary affairs, but I can tell tonight's going to break with tradition."

Syd looked back at Peyton, who shot her an "I'm sorry" expression. When Syd managed to gather her courage, she looked at Tanner square on, but Tanner was staring into Virginia's eyes, completely mesmerized. *Great.* A simple stakeout had just turned into a long night of listening to her ex being flirted with by Miss America. Suddenly, the unobtrusive listening device in her ear felt like an albatross. This evening was going to be way more work than she'd ever imagined.

CHAPTER EIGHT

Tanner glanced around as they walked up to the door of the Gellars' house. The two-story Tudor home dressed in red and white lights with a lawn display of happy snowmen was nice, at least from the outside, but it was nowhere near as impressive as the large-scale homes they'd just visited with front yard displays rivaling something you'd find at Disney World.

"Stay close," Virginia whispered.

Tanner did as she was told, because after touring four other houses, she'd determined there was no use resisting Virginia's will. The woman was a force, and Tanner had to admit she was the perfect cover because everyone in her path seemed to bend to her will. She was no exception. From the moment they'd driven away from Peyton's ranch in Virginia's Aston Martin roadster, which she'd insisted Tanner drive, she'd allowed her date for the evening to steer her around as if she owned her.

But this house was different. Somewhere past those doors, Syd was waiting inside, her only job to keep an eye on this operation. To keep an eye on her. And suddenly, Tanner was very uncomfortable at the prospect of Syd seeing Virginia tucked up against her.

They were ambushed the moment they walked through the door, but not by Syd.

"Hello, Virginia, I see you managed to keep your hands on this one."

Tanner appraised the speaker, a sixtyish woman wearing

expensive clothes, but with too much Botox and not quite enough hair coloring to hide her advancing years. She resisted the impulse to snap back some comment about how she wasn't something to be held on to, but Virginia's light squeeze on her arm cautioned her against it.

"Aunt Ginny," Virginia said, turning to Tanner and winking. "She hates when I call her that, but it's the only way to tell us apart." She drew Tanner into a tight embrace. "I don't need to hold on tight to get them to stick around, but why wouldn't I when they are as delicious as Tanner?"

Tanner winced inwardly, but forced a big smile. "That's right, sugar. You just hang on and enjoy the ride." No sooner had the words left her lips than she wished she could reel them back in, but the best she could do was hope the rest of the team had been zoned out for her lapse into Texas twang. She didn't have much time to think about it before Virginia steered them away, smiling and nodding to various people they passed who waved and called their names as they strolled by.

"See what I mean," she said. "Everyone here is already used to seeing you. If Gellar asks around, he'll find out you've been by my side all evening, and it won't look strange that you're here with me now."

"That's kind of brilliant," Tanner said.

"You act surprised. I might appear to be nothing more than a flighty socialite, but I actually graduated in the top five percent of my class at Richards."

Tanner held up her hands, truly sorry for the implication. "I didn't mean to assume anything. This is not my scene, in case you hadn't guessed."

"Oh, I guessed, but you're adapting quite well." Virginia leaned in and kissed her cheek. "You look great, and these people may be curious about you, but I promise none of them think you don't belong." She paused and deepened her smile. "Maybe we can get to know each other better when this whole mess is over."

Tanner swore she heard an exasperated sigh through her

earpiece, but she resisted the urge to assure Syd nothing was going on between her and Virginia. Besides, why should she? She was a free, single woman, and Sydney wasn't her keeper. Why should she care what Sydney thought about who she dated or was attracted to?

But she did. The brush of heat they'd shared earlier at Peyton's had been undeniable, and a large part of her had wanted to follow through on their connection and see where it would lead. She closed her eyes and imagined Syd's voice, soft and silky in her ear. *I miss those times.*

She missed them too. As chaotic and stressful as law school had been, she'd loved every minute of sharing the experience with someone she loved. Both of them had witnessed the breakups their colleagues endured when it became clear to them and their loved ones that law school required absolute devotion. Even the ones who'd left the busy corporate world to enter school were surprised to find the classroom was all-consuming. She and Syd had offered condolences in public, but in private they took comfort in the knowledge they were immune from the ravages of study since they were enduring its rigors as a team. Which is likely why when they reached their breaking point, it was so unexpected. Tanner didn't miss anything about how their relationship had ended.

"There's Herschel," Virginia said, subtly inclining her head toward the left side of the room. "What's the plan?"

Tanner snapped back to the present. She had a job to do and it was time to switch her focus from what might have been to what was going on now. "As much as I'd like to avoid him altogether, it's probably best to go ahead and get the pleasantries over with."

"Good plan," Dale chimed in through her ear. "And you're coming in loud and clear. Syd, can you say something so we can check the sound?"

Tanner stopped moving and waited. One, two, three beats passed and finally Syd said, "Why yes, I think I will have another glass of champagne. Thank you for asking."

Tanner looked around at the passing waiters, hoping to catch a glimpse of Syd reaching for a tall flute of bubbly. Tanner had never liked the stuff, but Syd lived for it.

The first thing Tanner spotted when she walked in the door was the bottle of champagne Syd had been saving for a special occasion, precariously balanced on a bed of ice in their big melamine salad bowl.

She caught Syd's eye and pointed at the bowl. "Nice improvisation on the ice bucket."

"Thanks. It was all I could come up with on the spur of the moment."

"Are we celebrating something?"

"I'm not sure yet." Syd pointed to the table where a pile of envelopes leaned against the bowl.

"Ah, judgment day."

"That sounds so ominous."

"Well, I suppose it's up to you how ominous it is."

Tanner followed Syd's gaze and spotted the familiar FBI seal on the envelope at the top of the heap. Damn. She'd been meaning all week to talk to Syd about the possibility of an offer, but when they'd managed to snag a moment here and there, it was never the right time. She knew deep in her gut it would never be the right time, and she'd been gambling that the letter would arrive on one of the days when she got home first. But it was too late now. She looked at the champagne and then back up into Syd's questioning eyes, wishing she had the answers her lover wanted to hear.

"Are you ready?" Virginia asked.

Tanner nodded and followed her through the growing crowd of festival partygoers, nodding at the familiar faces she'd seen earlier in the evening. When Virginia reached back and grabbed her hand, it felt almost natural, like they were on a second or third date instead of strangers on a mission to spy on the host, and she relaxed into her role. Gellar's house was impeccably decorated on the inside; keeping with the red and white theme, red bows and white snowflakes were everywhere. For a last-minute addition to the tour, Gellar and his wife had gone all out to display their holiday spirit.

She spotted Gellar standing with a group of men she didn't recognize. He was animated, waving his arms to punctuate whatever story he was telling, but then his eyes widened as he spotted someone in the crowd to his left and waved for whoever it was to join them. Tanner watched as the crowd parted for the favored guest, and Syd walked over to join Gellar's throng. They shared a laugh and Tanner emitted a low growl when Gellar placed his arm around Syd and squeezed as he introduced her to the men in his circle.

"Watch it, tiger," Virginia said. "Your envy is showing."

Tanner took a deep breath. "It's not envy. He's just such a sleaze."

"Right." Virginia pursed her lips and shook her head. "Shall we join them?"

"It's a bit crowded, don't you think? Maybe this would be a good opportunity to take a look around after all." Tanner swiveled her head to take in the rest of the room, and when she turned back, she caught Gellar staring at her with an expression that was mostly curious but slightly annoyed. "Uh-oh," she said under her breath. "Looks like I've been spotted." She took Virginia's arm. "Let's get this over with."

Every step toward Gellar was a step toward Syd, and Tanner wished she could shed her jacket to cool the rising heat inside her. Syd was easily the most beautiful woman in the room, and in a sea of well-coiffed socialites, that was saying a lot. But it was more than her natural beauty, it was the ease and grace with which she carried herself. She always made everything look so easy, but Tanner knew Syd worked hard to project the confidence she exuded but didn't always feel. Tanner couldn't help but feel a sense of pride at the woman Syd had become even as a blaze of trepidation burned through her.

"Agent Cohen," Gellar bellowed, casting a quick glance at the dark-haired man directly to his left. "I didn't take you for a holiday home tour kind of person."

Before Tanner could respond, Virginia jumped in. "Oh, she's not, but she's a dear and agreed to accompany me." She tugged Tanner close. "Next week, we're doing her favorite thing and going on a hayride out in the country." Virginia leaned her head back and stared into Tanner's eyes with a dreamy look. "Compromise is the secret to a long-lasting relationship." She shifted her gaze back to Gellar. "Wouldn't you agree?"

Tanner watched him squint for a second as if trying to figure out if her question was serious, and then he broke out into a lazy smile and laughed. "Of course it is. Dearest Virginia, let me introduce you to my friends." He waved at the men and Syd and said, "Friends, this is Virginia Taylor, the sweet siren who talked me into hosting this soiree. If she tries to get you alone, run, or next thing you know, you'll be the headline sponsor of the next big benefit she has on her radar."

The men laughed, and Syd smiled a tight smile that Tanner was certain was hiding a grimace. "Sounds like you all need a short course in resistance," Syd said with a laugh. "And on that note, I think I'll get another drink. Would anyone else like one?" She nodded to Gellar and the other men and edged away from the crowd. Tanner resisted the impulse to reach out to her, but only barely.

"I'd give up my entire trust fund to have a woman look at me the way you look at her."

Tanner felt the hot whisper of Virginia's breath on her neck, but it did nothing for her. She started to deny her assumption, but the words would be a lie, so she settled for a simple "I need to get to work."

She tore her gaze from Syd and back to Virginia, who

introduced her to the rest of the group around Gellar. She needed to focus on something other than her growing desire for Syd if she was going to get through this night.

❖

Syd stalked off to the bar, offering pleasant but fake smiles to the other partygoers she passed along the way. On a purely intellectual level, she knew Virginia's flirting was all part of the act they'd planned, but her remark about Tanner and a hayride hit a little close to home since that was exactly the kind of thing Tanner would rather be doing right now.

When it was her turn at the bar, she ordered a martini and silently promised to nurse it for the rest of the night. What she really wanted to do was slug it back and let the heat of the alcohol burn away her frustration, but a buzz wouldn't bridge the uneasy distance between her and Tanner. She'd been silly to imagine they could be friends again. Friends didn't feel jealousy. Not like this.

Despite her promise, she took a healthy drink from her glass and settled into a space between a couple of bookcases where she could catch a glimpse of Tanner and Virginia talking to Gellar and his pals. The feed in her ear told her Gellar was doing most of the talking, which didn't surprise her. Most of the men were sycophants, laughing a little too hard in all the right places, bowing and scraping to one of the most powerful men in Texas, who with his ability to put people in jail topped them no matter how much money they had. But Syd noticed the man just to Gellar's right didn't seem to be playing along. He was tall and slender, very cosmopolitan. Dark hair and dark eyes, but not obviously Hispanic. She listened carefully to the conversation, but the stranger didn't say a word. She raised her glass to her lips to cover and said, "The guy next to Gellar is being awfully quiet."

She heard Dale's voice in her ear. "Tanner?"

Syd watched Tanner lean toward Virginia and whisper something in her ear. The conversation continued a bit longer, and then Virginia reached a hand across to the man and introduced herself.

"I'm always looking to meet new donors for our holiday drive," Virginia said in her smooth silky voice. "I don't believe we've met."

The man leaned forward and took her hand, drawing it toward him as he bent and kissed her knuckles. "We haven't. I would have remembered meeting such a beautiful woman." Before he let go, he looked up at Tanner and smirked. Tanner met his gaze, her expression steely. If Syd didn't know better, she'd believe Tanner was actually jealous of the stranger. She took another drink of her martini to wash away her distaste and strode back to the group. As she approached the fringe, Gellar waved at her.

"Sydney, join us. I didn't have an opportunity to introduce you to one of my most important guests." He pulled her closer and motioned to the stranger. "Sydney Braswell, meet Carlos Aguilar. Carlos is visiting Dallas for the week to scope out some new locations for Paladar, his successful chain of restaurants. Sydney is visiting as well."

She looked down at their joined hands and braced for the kiss, but Carlos didn't bend forward, instead fixing her with a steamy stare. "Ms. Braswell, I'm very pleased to make your acquaintance. Mr. Gellar didn't tell me there would be so many beautiful women attending this event."

"You flatter me, sir," Syd said with her best imitation of a flirty girl, taking some pleasure in the frown Tanner wore as she watched the exchange. "How opportune that you were able to be here for this splendid event."

"And you. Where do you call home?"

"Sydney's from DC," Gellar interjected. "She's here to help me on a case I'm working." Gellar winked. "A very important case."

Sydney nodded but quickly added. "It may be important, but it doesn't sound as interesting as the restaurant business." She held up her glass. "I could use a refill. Would you like to accompany me and tell me all about it?" She caught Carlos's eyes and held them, hoping he would rise to the bait while Dale's voice whispered in her ear. "Careful, Sydney. You're going to need to be near Gellar when Tanner takes off to have a look around."

Carlos flicked a glance at her glass, which was still half full. "The lady is here to have a good time. Who am I to deny her what she desires?"

Sydney ignored the voice in her ear and the stinging looks Tanner was shooting her way. "I'll lead the way, Carlos. Come with me."

In line at the bar, Carlos rambled on about the weather, and Syd focused on concentrating, which was hard because Tanner was rambling in her ear, echoing Dale's words.

"You're only here to distract Gellar and keep a lookout. How do you expect to do that when you're off courting some random guy?"

Syd smiled through the tirade, unable to acknowledge Tanner's admonitions while Carlos was so entirely focused on flirting with her. Part of her experienced a twinge of satisfaction that Tanner had to witness her being the object of someone else's desire the way she'd had to witness Virginia pouring it on. Petty, but true.

Out of the corner of her eye, she saw Tanner peel away from the group and wander off. Gellar didn't seem to notice, and Virginia stuck around to keep him and his cronies occupied. Syd's first instinct was to follow Tanner, but that wasn't the plan. The best thing she could do was talk to Carlos to cover up the fact she was keeping an eye on Gellar to make sure he didn't wander off.

Once she and Carlos had their drinks, she steered him to a couple of chairs across the room. After a few moments of pleasantries about the holiday decorations and the unseasonably warm weather in Dallas, Syd dove in. "Tell me about this business of yours."

"Right," he said. "I haven't yet opened any of my restaurants in DC. Paladar is a chain offering homemade Mexican food, but in a fast casual setting. Nothing special."

"Well, that's not true," Syd replied, hoping she sounded sincere. "I've seen a couple since I've been here and everyone says it's the hottest new concept in town. Paladar means palate, yes?" At his nod, she said, "Clever. I admire someone who can build an empire from the ground up. For someone like me who has nothing concrete to show for her work, it's an amazing accomplishment."

"A man can do anything when he works hard enough and is focused on his goals."

There it was, the steely eyes again. Syd resisted the urge to shift in her chair. A quick glance across the room told her Gellar was still in place. She started to formulate another question, but Carlos beat her to it.

"What is this case you are working on with Herschel?"

She took note of the fact Carlos had used Gellar's first name for the first time since they'd met and filed it away, while she sifted through various potential responses to his question. She shrugged and settled on what she hoped would be the perfect bait. "Some agents seem to have gotten off track. I'm here to make sure things get back to running smoothly again."

Carlos raised his eyebrows. "You're here to help Herschel."

"Absolutely. That's my only purpose."

He tilted his glass toward her. "That's excellent news. Any friend of Herschel Gellar is a friend of mine. Fortune always favors my friends."

Syd toasted the remark and took a drink. She knew she'd just crossed a line, but she wasn't sure whose side she'd wound up on. While she sipped her martini, she subtly glanced over at Gellar, who was standing all by himself, with his head swiveling around like he was looking for someone. Tanner and Virginia were nowhere in sight. Shit.

She smiled at Carlos and handed her drink toward him. "Do you mind holding on to this for me? I need to make a trip to the ladies' room." At his nod, she added, "I'll be right back."

She didn't have a clue where she was headed, but she took a chance that the bathroom was near the kitchen and headed that way just long enough to get out of sight. She'd been so focused on listening to Carlos, if Tanner had announced where she was off to, she'd missed it. "Tanner, where are you?"

Instead of Tanner's voice, she heard Dale, "I've been trying to roust her for a bit now, but she's not responding."

Syd looked around, but there was still no sign of Tanner or her date in the teeming crowd. She saw a lot of new faces, likely fresh visitors from the tour. Surely if Virginia and Tanner had decided to move on to the next house, they would have found a way to let her or Dale and Mary know. And what would have been the point of that since Tanner hadn't had a chance to look around here, which was the sole purpose of this crazy outing? "I don't see her, but I'm on my own for a few, so I'll have a look around."

In case anyone was watching, Syd made a show of asking one of the waitstaff where she could find the restroom and walked in the direction the waiter said he thought was the right one. The corridor was long and surprisingly empty considering the crowd in the front of the house. Syd walked slowly, taking time to note the number of doors and any other details that might prove to be important if they ever had grounds to search the property. Legally.

A flash of guilt stopped her. She could hear the echo of Tanner's voice, telling her things weren't always black and white. Funny since those weren't words she'd ever expected to hear Tanner say since everything to her had always seemed to fall on one side or the other without room in the middle for doubt. Guess they'd both changed quite a bit in the years since they'd naively planned happily ever after together.

With a quick glance over her shoulder to make sure no one was watching, Syd pushed on one of the partly opened doors. The interior of the room was pitch-black, and she took that as a sign no one would be inside to catch her doing a mild Nancy Drew bit of snooping around. She stepped in and pushed the door back into its original position. Using the light of her phone as a guide, she surveyed her surroundings. Desk, chair, bookshelves, and filing cabinets. Score. This had to be Gellar's home office, but she was surprised it hadn't been locked down for the party. Of course Gellar would have to be an idiot to leave anything important lying around.

She laughed. She'd been a prosecutor long enough to know that intelligence wasn't a prerequisite to misdeeds. If it was, she would have spent the last six years twiddling her thumbs instead of sending criminals to prison. She looked longingly at the rows of file cabinets, wondering if they were locked.

Sydney shook her head. The key to sending people to prison was making sure all the right procedures were followed to keep them from getting off on a technicality. Tonight's adventure was already approaching the bounds of the Constitution, but looking—only looking—around in a house they'd been invited to wasn't against the law. If she opened a drawer without some urgent reason to do so, she'd be crossing the line, but anything in plain sight was fair game. Plain sight. She repeated the mantra and walked the room, hoping something, anything, would be right there, waiting to be discovered.

"Can I help you find something, Ms. Braswell?"

Shit. Syd whirled around at the pinched tone in Herschel Gellar's voice, hoping her attempts to hide the surprise on her face was successful. "I'm sorry. It looks like I took a wrong turn on the way to the bathroom."

Gellar flipped the switch by the door, bathing them both in bright light. "So it appears. I'd be happy to show you the way. I'm looking for Agent Tanner. Perhaps you can help me find her."

Syd nodded and followed him out the door while Dale

whispered a warning to Tanner that Gellar was looking for her. Tanner didn't reply and Syd crossed the threshold behind Gellar, thanking her lucky stars that she hadn't gotten caught rummaging through his drawers and praying they wouldn't catch Tanner doing the same.

CHAPTER NINE

Wine Cellar. Tanner read the decorative sign over the door and reached out to test the door handle. Locked. Could it be Gellar was worried his holiday guests would take the opportunity of free rein to pinch a bottle from his prized collection? Come to think of it, Gellar didn't seem like the wine connoisseur type. She started at the door, certain there was a more nefarious reason it was locked.

"Are you looking for the restroom?"

Tanner turned to see Gellar's wife standing behind her. She was a beautiful woman. Tall, slender, with just the slightest hint of Botox in the immovable smooth skin on her forehead. How had Gellar managed to land a wife who clearly outclassed him? "You're Amanda Gellar."

"Yes, I am. And you're one of Herschel's work colleagues."

Tanner reached out a hand. "I guess you could say that. We have worked on quite a few cases together. Tanner Cohen, nice to meet you."

"Let me guess. Law enforcement? DEA?"

"FBI."

Amanda circled her, appraising her closely. "I noticed you earlier. You came with Virginia Taylor."

"Yes, ma'am."

"Ma'am?" Amanda threw back her head and laughed. "Please don't ma'am me. It makes me feel old." She poked a finger in the middle of Tanner's chest while letting her eyes rove over the rest of Tanner's body. "Be careful with Virginia. She doesn't waste time taking what she wants."

Tanner, certain Amanda was flirting with her, made a swift choice about the right way to play the situation. "No one can take something I'm not willing to give."

"Is that right?" Amanda rocked back on her heels. "I can tell we don't run in the same circles." She held up a hand as Tanner started to protest. "I don't mean it as an insult. I merely meant that the women you'll meet here tonight are used to being able to buy or steal anything they want, no matter who it belongs to or who wants it more. Someone like you..." She paused and ran her finger down the length of Tanner's arm. "You represent a distinct challenge."

"And why is that?"

"Because you will resist being bought. But everyone has their price."

Tanner figured that might be true for these women, but she wasn't interested in getting into a discussion of the ways people could be bought and sold. Desperate to change the subject, she pointed at the sign above the door. "Who's the collector, you or him?"

"I don't collect things. I use what I want and move on. For all I know there's nothing down there but a man cave stocked with beer and pornography. He keeps it locked and only uses the outside door." She leaned close and whispered. "If I wanted to go in, nothing would stop me."

Tanner forced herself to remain still, thinking any sudden movement would send Mrs. Gellar off to seek her next conquest. She pondered the words "outside door," and wondered if the other entrance was in the front of the house or the back and if any of the lock picks she'd brought with her might pry it open. She needed to extricate herself from Amanda Gellar so she could make a plan. "I doubt anything stops you when you want something bad enough." She glanced back in the direction she'd come. "But I should get back to my date. Thanks for the conversation." She edged away, hoping she'd struck the perfect balance of flattery and regret but not lingering to find out.

Tanner avoided the crowd in the front of the house and swiftly located a patio door. A quick look around the backyard and she found a small set of stairs leading down to what she was certain was Gellar's wine cellar. She took a minute to reach around rocks and planters but didn't turn up a key, so she reached in her inside suit pocket and pulled out a set of lock picks her mentor had given her years ago. "Only use these if you have to," he'd said. "Most of the time you should be able to talk your way into places." She probably could've talked Amanda Gellar into giving her access, but the price would've been higher than she was willing to pay. Conscious that Dale and company might be listening to her about to commit a felony, she dug out her earpiece, turned it off, and shoved it into her pocket.

Five grueling minutes later, the lock fell open. She leaned an ear against the door and, satisfied at the silence she heard on the other side, pushed it gently open, bracing for whatever she might find.

The room was totally dark and her footfalls echoed against the walls. Tanner switched on the flashlight for her phone and shined it back and forth, surprised to find a cavernous empty space, lined with tall, industrial strength shelves, also empty. She shined the light up high, looking for spy cams, but didn't spot any. She walked the space and measured it out to be about ten by ten. *Wine cellar, my ass.* There wasn't a wine bottle, barrel, cooler, or anything else remotely related to wine in the place.

She found a stairway at the far side of the room and followed it upward to a door locked from the other side. She could hear the sounds of the party going on outside and wondered where Sydney was at that moment. Was she still tailing Gellar around or had Carlos the slick businessman managed to corner her in a room somewhere? The idea of him thinking Sydney was available to him caused her to shudder.

Finally satisfied there was nothing to find in Gellar's secret cellar, Tanner turned the flash on her phone and shot a few pictures to document her little adventure. She pressed her ear against the door she'd entered, and when she didn't hear anyone on the other side, she pushed it open and eased her way outside. As she rounded the front of the house, she spotted the valets running back and forth, fetching cars as guests arrived and left for the next house on the tour. If she'd driven her own car, she would leave now, but as it was, she was trapped for the night since Virginia had to make the rounds, stopping at every house on the tour. She wished she'd paid attention to how many more houses that entailed. The best she could hope for now was to slip into Gellar's house unnoticed and endure whatever was left of this evening.

She waited near the corner until she spotted a group of women dressed to the nines make their way up the front walk. She strode over and did her best to blend in, but when the door swung wide the first face she saw was Gellar's.

"Agent Cohen, we've been looking for you." He glanced pointedly at the women surrounding her. "Did you decide to abandon Ms. Taylor?"

Damn. Tanner started to reply when she caught sight of Syd standing behind and to the left of Gellar, motioning wildly. She had no idea what message Syd was trying to convey, but she took her gesticulating to mean she should tread carefully. "No, sir. Just needed a breath of fresh air." She leaned closer. "I think your house is the most popular one on the entire tour. Good work."

He hesitated a second before responding like he was trying to decide if she was serious, but then he offered a guarded smile. "Thanks. Since you're still here, I wonder if I might have a word with you. Alone." He didn't wait for a response before ushering her off to a room down a back hallway. Syd shook her head at Tanner as they passed.

She followed Gellar through a doorway and he flicked on the lights revealing an office even nicer than the one he had downtown.

"Have a seat, Agent."

She slid into the seat feigning nonchalance, but her increasing blood pressure told her she should have spent more time in the pseudo wine cellar looking for hidden cameras since she couldn't think of any other reason he would have pulled her aside at his own party.

"I assume you know why I wanted to see you."

"I actually don't have any idea, sir. Has something come up?"

"How well do you know Sydney Braswell?"

The question threw her, but she struggled to maintain a disinterested facade. What did he know and how much could she get away with fudging? Certain he knew something, she settled on a simple summary. "Not very well. We went to law school together, but that was a long time ago."

He crossed his arms and fixed her with a stare. "I never knew you were a lawyer, but it explains a lot."

"Sir?"

"You're very thorough. And you think like a lawyer, always a few steps ahead, unlike some other agents who can't be bothered to look at the big picture. That's why you're so valuable to me."

Tanner noted the "to me" but didn't bother clarifying if he meant him as an individual or in his position as US attorney since she was pretty sure she knew. Instead, she merely nodded and braced for what he was about to say.

"I would like you to keep an eye on Ms. Braswell."

Whoa. No amount of bracing prepared Tanner for Gellar's request. She assumed what she hoped was a contemplative expression while she cast around for a response designed to get him to reveal more. "I thought she was here to help with the investigation into Cyrus Gantry and the Vargas brothers."

"Yes, that's what I was told as well, but I didn't get to where I am without being naturally suspicious. I'm sure she's fine, but she's not one of us."

Tanner tapped her fingers against her thigh and waited for him to continue. She was dying to ask who the hell his source was, but years of experience had taught her that silence was the best way to get someone to keep talking. She didn't have to wait long.

"Use your prior relationship to get close to her, to make sure she's really on our side." He dropped his voice to a whisper. "Men like the Vargases and Cyrus Gantry have a wide reach, and they will stop at nothing when their livelihoods are threatened, even if it means bribing or blackmailing a government official." He wagged a finger. "No one is above suspicion. Understood?"

She nodded, even though understanding what he meant was so completely out of reach. All she could think about was where Sydney was now and how she could get to her.

❖

Sydney edged past Virginia to beat her to Tanner's side, too flustered to care about keeping up pretenses. "Where have you been?"

Tanner shook her head and whispered, "Not right now," before turning to Virginia and lightly kissing her on the cheek. "I'd love to accompany you to the next house, but duty calls."

"I completely understand."

Sydney watched Virginia squeeze Tanner's hand and lean in for another kiss. She averted her eyes, but not in time. She knew the display of affection was for the benefit of anyone watching, but it still made her want to claw Virginia's eyes out.

"Syd?"

She looked up to see Tanner's expectant expression. "What?"

"I asked if I could catch a ride with you."

Not what she'd expected, and she wasn't entirely sure she wanted to be alone with Tanner, but she answered before she could give it any more thought, "Sure."

The valet took his sweet time getting her car, and Syd was

pretty sure it was because the Corolla she'd rented wasn't nearly as exciting to drive as the parade of Porsches, Bentleys, and Jaguars arriving and departing the party. Sydney attempted small talk during the wait, but Tanner's responses were clipped and short, signaling her mind was elsewhere, and Syd gave up until they were finally settled into the car.

"Do you want to give me the turn by turn or just put the address into my phone?"

"What?" Tanner asked.

"I don't know where you live."

"Oh, sorry." She pointed at the stop sign ahead. "Turn right there and take the next left."

Syd put the car in drive. "Any particular reason you decided to bail on your date?"

"Date? Oh, you mean Virginia?" Tanner laughed. "I didn't see much point in continuing the charade. Apparently, there are three more houses on the tour. Who in their right mind wants to go to that many parties in one night?"

Syd didn't respond, but she remembered a time when she would have been the last one to leave a party if it meant the possibility of seeing and being seen. She'd always given Tanner a hard time about not wanting to stick around until the end, but nowadays she got it. The socializing took a toll, and the payoff was never worth the energy it sucked from more important pursuits. "You seemed to be having a good time." She hoped her voice didn't sound as whiny as she felt.

"Are you still wearing your earpiece and transmitter?"

Syd instinctively touched her ear. "Yes. You?"

Tanner raised her voice. "Dale, Mary, we're going offline now. Tell Peyton we'll report in later." Tanner reached out a hand. "Time to shut it down."

Sydney pointed at the steering wheel. "Busy here. I'll take it off when we stop." Before she knew it, Tanner was pressed up close against her, her fingers exploring. "What are you doing?" Despite her protest, Syd's breath hitched and she summoned all her focus for the drive while she tried to ignore the swift wave of arousal at Tanner's touch.

"Got it." Tanner leaned back into her seat and held up the tiny listening device with a triumphant smile. Syd grimaced. "How do you turn it off?"

"Little bitty button." She turned the device over and over in her hands. "Done."

"And what about yours?"

"I took care of that a while ago."

Syd thought back to Dale and Mary trying to get Tanner's attention to tell her Gellar was looking for her and realized Tanner had been out of range on purpose. She didn't bother censoring her response. "That was careless. Not at all what I'd expect from the Tanner I used to know."

"It was necessary," Tanner replied matter-of-factly, ignoring Syd's other observation. Syd wanted to press the point, but sensed it would start an argument that might keep her from finding out exactly why Tanner was acting so mysterious. "So what did you want to say to me that you didn't want anyone else to hear?" she asked instead.

Tanner pointed at the intersection ahead. "Turn right there. It's the parking lot over there, on the left."

Syd followed Tanner's directions into the gated parking lot of a double row of 1960s style apartments with a flat roof, clean lines, and geometric metal accents. She wasn't sure what she'd expected, but the funky, vintage style residence wasn't it. "Cool place. Apartment or condo?"

"Condo." Tanner pointed again. "There's an extra parking space over there."

Tanner's condo was on the second floor, and it was every bit as cool inside as out. Syd handed her coat to Tanner and walked around the living room, taking in the well put together ensemble of mid-century modern furnishings.

"Do you like it?"

"I love it. It's not what I expected."

Tanner grinned. "I eventually had to figure out how to decorate for myself or continue to live with whatever garage sale castoffs I could cobble together. Do you remember that air hockey table that Ian helped me drag home?"

Sydney laughed at the memory of Tanner and their mutual friend Ian, moaning and groaning as they dragged the table they'd found on the side of the road into the house only to find out it didn't work when they plugged it in. She'd made them drag it right back out again despite Tanner's insistence it would be a great conversation piece that could double as their dining table. "Your tastes have definitely improved."

Tanner's expression morphed from amused to reflective. "People change."

"Yes. Yes, they do." Sydney traced her finger along the edge of the teak sideboard. A month ago, if anyone had asked her if she thought she'd ever have feelings for Tanner again, she would've said no and meant it. Tanner was a piece of her past she'd stored away neatly behind a door marked *Done*. Even after all of the reasons they'd broken up had fallen away years ago, she'd never even let herself consider reopening the door. Tanner had made the choice to walk away. If they'd been meant to be together, nothing could have come between them. The feelings she had now were the product of residual affection, natural responses to seeing an old lover, but they didn't signal anything about her future other than it wasn't going to find root in her past.

"Are you hungry?" Tanner asked.

Syd looked into her eyes, for a split second seeing more than a simple question about sustenance, but just as quickly the desire disappeared and Tanner's expression became neutral, guarded even. Good. She didn't need any complications right now. All she needed was to work this case to its natural conclusion and then she'd be free to go home and resume the life she'd built. The one without Tanner. No matter how dull and monotonous that life had become, it was easy and painless and all she needed for now. She'd share a meal with Tanner, talk about the case, and go back to her hotel.

It sounded so simple, but like most things, it wasn't nearly as easy as it appeared.

❖

Tanner dug through her drawer of delivery menus—that much hadn't changed since college—partly to avoid making eye contact with Syd. She'd half gambled on Syd saying no to her impromptu dinner invitation, and now that Syd had accepted, she was out of sorts. She wasn't used to being out of sorts.

"What are you digging for? The Tanner I know would have the best pizza joint in the city on speed dial."

"Yeah, well, the Sydney I know would want something a little fancier than pizza."

"Not true." Syd placed a hand over her heart. "Pizza will always be my first love."

Tanner laughed. "I knew it wasn't me." As the words fell from her lips, she wanted to bite them back. "Sorry, that was lame."

"It wasn't lame." Syd slid her hand along Tanner's arm. "But I'm glad we have that truth out of the way. Now, about that pizza."

They both broke into laughter. It felt good, a much-needed release, breaking the tension between them. Tanner pulled out her phone and started dialing. "Hamburger and green olives?"

Syd nodded, her smile signaling pleasure that Tanner remembered her favorite order. Tanner placed the order and pocketed her phone, ushering them to the couch. "So, you want to tell me what you and Carlos Aguilar were so deep in conversation about tonight?"

"Sure, if you'll share where you wandered off to."

"You first." Tanner settled into a chair across from the couch, telling herself it was so she could see Sydney's face while she talked, but really she didn't trust the sparks between them not to ignite into something dangerous. Gellar's words echoed in her head. She didn't believe for a minute that Sydney was a threat to anyone but Gellar, but tiny seeds of doubt had been planted and they were already doing damage. What if Peyton didn't know Sydney as well as she thought? Maybe Peyton's plea to Main Justice to send someone to look into Gellar had backfired and they'd sent someone to look into the task force instead.

"He was sickeningly charming, but that's it. I didn't get any kind of read off him other than he might've wanted to get in my pants if I'd given any indication that was a possibility."

Tanner held back a growl. "You didn't talk about anything else?"

"He did ask why I was in town."

"What did you tell him?"

"Just that I was here to help Gellar out with an investigation. No specifics. He said something like any friend of Gellar's is a friend of his. Very clichéd."

"Any other vibes about this guy?"

"Why the intense interest? Do you have some reason to believe this guy is involved in something illegal?"

"Come on, Syd. Just answer me." Tanner watched as Syd scrunched her brow and thought hard.

"I just recall feeling he was a little too intense for my taste, but I wrote it off to my aversion to him hitting on me. Now, tell me what you're thinking."

Tanner considered her options. She didn't have anything concrete to go on, but something about Aguilar had set her on high alert, and she'd learned to trust her instincts. She wanted to talk it out with Dale or Mary or Peyton, but none of them were here right now. Only Syd, who years ago had been the one person she'd talked about everything with. Until she'd held back on the one thing that had driven a wedge between them. Oh, what the hell. "I don't have anything to base this on, but I don't trust Aguilar, and I don't think he just happened to be at Gellar's house."

"Okay," Syd drew out the word. "Let's go through how you got there."

Thankful Syd hadn't dismissed her theory out of hand, Tanner ticked off the reasons. "Carlos is known in West Texas as a very successful businessman. If he is really looking to expand here in North Texas, he's not going to cozy up to someone like Gellar. He's going to make friends in the business community."

"Good point, but maybe showing up at Gellar's would be a good opportunity for him to make those contacts."

"Except he wasn't at any other house on the tour."

Syd started to say something, but the doorbell rang. "Hold that thought," Tanner said. She paid for the pizza and motioned for Syd to join her in the kitchen. She opened the box and watched Syd swoon.

"Oh my God, that smells amazing."

"Tastes even better. I'll get some plates."

"Who needs plates?"

She turned back from the cabinet at the sound of Syd's muffled voice and found her midway through a slice. "I'm guessing you didn't get your fill of finger food at the party."

Syd reached for the napkin Tanner handed her and swiped hastily at her mouth before taking another bite. "Those high society bitches ate all the jumbo shrimp before I got to them."

Tanner laughed. "You should've been with Virginia. She would've made sure you got your share of shrimp." She watched Syd chow down on the slice of pizza like it was her last meal and an observation tumbled out. "You know, once upon a time you wanted to be one of those high society bitches."

"Maybe, but not the kind who hogs the shrimp." Syd turned her focus from the skimpy piece of crust left in her hand to face Tanner. "I wanted a lot of things. When you're young, you don't really know what you want. Sometimes you miss out on really important things because of it."

Tanner caught her gaze and held it, trying her best not to read anything into Syd's words. But how could she not? They had been young, and Sydney especially so. Tanner had already served two tours in the Army before she entered law school while Sydney had gone straight through. Now that they'd both been out in the world, their outlooks were probably more closely aligned, but too much time, too much hurt, and too much life had passed for it to matter.

Tanner wanted to ask Sydney if, looking back now, she would've made the decision to walk away from their relationship, but what would be the point? The answer would be full of either satisfaction or regret, but it wouldn't change anything. Friendship was the most she could hope for, and in the spirit of friendship, she decided it was time to lighten the mood. "I know you well enough to know you would never be a shrimp-hogging, high society bitch." She grabbed the pizza box. "Let's take this back to the couch and eat the entire thing."

An hour later, they were sprawled on the living room furniture with the box of pizza bones lying open on the coffee table. They'd shared a couple of beers and more than a couple of memories of law school.

"Do you remember Colin Danvers?" Sydney said, enunciating their former classmate's name with a nasal voice.

"You mean Colin 'may I ask one more question to clarify your point, Professor' Danvers?"

Syd punched her playfully in the side. "That's the one. He'd press on with his question no matter how loud we all groaned."

"How could I forget?"

"He's a freaking judge now. State court. Pretty sure his rich daddy got him elected."

"No way."

"Way."

Tanner shook her head. "Just goes to show who you know is more important than what you know."

"Sometimes." Syd sat up. "Hey, that reminds me. You were

talking about Carlos Aguilar, and why you think he's up to no good."

Tanner shifted to an upright position to match Syd's and felt the intimacy between them whoosh out of the room. Probably best, but definitely not welcome. She pressed on. "I don't have any hard evidence. It's more instinct."

"And your instincts—are they usually spot-on?"

Tanner stared at Syd's eyes as her husky-voiced question penetrated her consciousness. The question was loaded, and a trickle of sweat down her back told Tanner to tread carefully. Normally, she trusted her instincts completely, but right here in this moment every one of them urged her to lean forward and kiss Sydney, to charge back into the memory of the past like years hadn't passed between them. Syd leaned closer, her darkening eyes a signal she was ready and willing to join her in this throwback moment. Inches. They were only inches from touch, and Tanner's heart thumped wildly when Syd reached out to touch her face.

"Pizza sauce," Syd said, gently stroking her thumb along Tanner's lip.

"What?" The word was thick in Tanner's mouth and it was all she could manage.

Syd thrust her hand in Tanner's sightline. "Dregs of dinner."

The words fell like ice picks, slicing neatly through the growing heat, but they didn't cool her desire, only her determination to act on it. She struggled to remember what they'd been talking about. "You were saying? You know, before the pizza sauce incident."

"I believe I was asking about your instincts."

Syd's pupils had returned to normal size and her voice was even and matter-of-fact. For a second, Tanner wondered if she'd imagined the crazy attraction, the almost kiss, and decided it was possible the entire episode was one-sided. Just to be sure, she inched away from Syd. "Usually."

"Tell me more."

There was that husky innuendo again. Stick to the case. Just the facts. Tanner cleared her throat. "Observations. He acted like he'd been to Gellar's house before. He knew his way around. He was very friendly with Gellar's wife."

"What else?"

"Like I said, he's a successful businessman, but he didn't mingle other than to hit on women. I'm guessing he made a move on you." Syd looked downward and Tanner knew she was right.

"Okay, so what are you going to do about it?"

"I haven't thought that far," Tanner said. It was true. She hadn't had time to give much thought to Aguilar since she'd been consumed with thinking about Sydney since they'd walked through the door of her place. She shook away the personal thoughts and cast about for something else work related to talk about. She should tell Syd about the fake wine cellar, but she wasn't ready to confess she'd picked the lock, and she heard Gellar's words in her head, cautioning her about Syd.

She should tell Sydney that Gellar had suspicions about her, but she held back. Instinct told her to do some checking of her own. She didn't seriously suspect Sydney wasn't everything she said she was. Hell, Peyton had vouched for her. But what if they'd all been fooled? As much as she touted her well-honed instincts, they'd never been one hundred percent, and she'd never worked a case with a former lover. She was too close to this. What she should do was tell the rest of the team she needed backup, but doing so meant confessing she had doubts about Sydney, and she wasn't ready to go there.

No, she'd look into Sydney on her own while ostensibly working the case with her. If something turned up to tell her Sydney might actually be working against them, she'd tell Peyton and bow out. In the meantime, she'd get as close as she could. Gellar would be happy, thinking she was doing his bidding. And bonus—she'd get to spend more time with Sydney.

CHAPTER TEN

Syd stared at the files spread out on the table in front of her. It was Monday afternoon, and Peyton and Bianca were in court, and she'd set up in Peyton's office to review the case files. She'd been at the office for three hours and had nothing to show for it because every time she started looking at paperwork, her mind glazed over with thoughts of the kiss she and Tanner had almost shared Saturday night.

She'd spent yesterday writing up a report of her impressions of everyone Gellar interacted with at the party. She knew Tanner was meeting in person with Dale and Mary, and she'd half hoped they'd include her as well, but apparently it was an agent-only gathering. She didn't care so much about the debriefing, but the sooner she saw Tanner, the sooner she could figure out if the desire to kiss her lingered into the light of day.

Maybe she should have just gone for it when she'd had the chance. If she had, then she wouldn't be left with this hollow feeling, the kind you have when you go to bed hungry. Bad analogy. Bed and Tanner were two things that were never going to happen simultaneously.

Why not?

The question popped up out of nowhere, and she wondered why she hadn't asked it before. They were both adults, working together on the same side of a case, so no conflict there. And if the waves of heat coming from Tanner were any indication, it was clear she felt the attraction too. Syd was only going to be in town temporarily. They could have a fling—work on the case by day and let off steam at night, and when the case was over, Syd could go back to her boring, normal life in DC, and Tanner could do whatever Tanner did when she wasn't around.

What did Tanner do when she wasn't working? She'd said she wasn't dating anyone, but that didn't mean she was celibate. Did she go out to clubs, pick women up at bars? Did she have a steady, friendly fuck?

Why the hell am I obsessing about this? This is exactly the reason you can't have sex with her.

Syd shook her head. If she slept with Tanner, no matter what she told herself, she wouldn't be able to contain whatever feelings might surface, and she was certain some would. Since she'd been here in Dallas, close to Tanner, all kinds of emotions she'd thought were long buried had managed to tunnel their way to the surface. No, it was better to let things settle back into a friendly, but not too friendly, professional relationship. Nothing more.

"Hey you," Bianca said as she walked into the room. She pointed at the files. "There's nothing more boring than reading about a case you haven't actually worked, am I right?"

"You are indeed right." Syd stretched her arms over her head and yawned. "And I think someone switched the coffee to decaf when I wasn't looking."

"It's weak. I don't know why anyone bothers drinking it. You should taste the stuff my mother makes—it will grow hair on your chest."

"Not a big selling point."

Bianca laughed. "I hear you. Are you ready for a break? Peyton thought it might be a good idea for you to meet Jade, but there's no way she's coming to the office, so we'll need to go to her."

"Jade is your girlfriend?"

"Yes." Bianca punctuated the word with a sharp nod. "But before you say anything, I just want you to know—"

Syd cut her off with a smile. She wasn't in the mood to get into an argument over who was sleeping with whom, especially not considering the thoughts she'd been having. "Save it, counselor. Let's go meet her."

Bianca's tiny Miata raced through the streets of downtown toward the east, and the wind whipping against Syd's face was exactly what she needed to wake up. "Where's the meeting?"

"My place."

"Okay."

"We're not living together, me and Jade. Well, we may as well be, but as much as my daughter loves Jade, having another adult in the house would be a big adjustment. I'm the only parent she's ever known, and we haven't had a chance to sort out how it would work with both of us parenting. Besides, Jade's mother needs her at the ranch."

Syd couldn't help but laugh. "Are you always such a fast talker, or did I do something to make you feel like you have to explain everything before I even manage to get a question out?"

Bianca's face flushed. "It's me. My mouth is my Achilles' heel." She ducked her head. "Don't worry, I know how to keep it shut when it's really important, but I figured I could trust you to listen to my ramblings."

"Is that right?"

"Peyton says you're good people, and I trust her, so by default I trust you."

"Thanks. I appreciate the vote of confidence." Sydney meant the words. This team was obviously close-knit, and she figured it was hard for them to welcome a stranger into their midst. "Tell me about Jade."

"I'll warn you right now that you're probably going to swoon when you first see her. The first time I met her, she was riding toward me on a beautiful horse. Central casting for dream cowgirls. That was it for me."

"Love at first sight?"

"Hmm, maybe. I'm not sure I believe in love at first sight,

but I do believe the first impression kind of plants the seed for love to grow. Is that too corny?"

"Not at all." Sydney remembered the first time she'd seen Tanner. They were sitting in a large lecture hall, about as far apart as two people could get from each other. Professor Dautry had singled Tanner out for one of his sadistic Socratic examinations on the finer points of criminal procedure, and Syd had watched with rapt attention at the smooth, steady way Tanner fielded all of his questions, never once displaying the nerves that took most students down. Syd had typed one simple sentence into her outline during the exchange. *I'm going to marry that girl.*

She'd come close.

"I definitely think first impressions are important, but unfortunately, they don't always tell the whole story." She looked over at Bianca, who was frowning. "I'm not talking about you and Jade, of course."

"It's okay. Everyone's different."

Sydney wished she'd kept her mouth shut. She had no business judging these people and their relationships, and she could use some friends instead of scaring them away. She reached over and touched Bianca's shoulder. "Everyone is different. I can't wait to meet her."

Bianca talked the rest of the drive about how Jade had overcome her sketchy lineage to graduate from Wharton and run a successful quarter horse breeding ranch. She'd managed to avoid the lure of the quick money drug trade run by her uncles and run a legitimate business. Bianca ended with the story of how Jade had saved her daughter Emma's life just as they pulled up to a modest bungalow-style home.

"This is it," Bianca said as she parked in the driveway.

"Nice. Will your daughter be home?"

"She's at my mother's, a block over. I figured it would be better for us to talk alone."

Sydney had a bunch of other questions about whether it was hard for Bianca to raise a child alone when she worked a job that commanded so much of her attention. Syd had taken for granted the idea of having children, but she'd never met anyone after Tanner that she'd wanted to raise children with, and the prospect of motherhood on her own had always seemed too daunting. Or maybe she just hadn't wanted to live a dream that hadn't turned out the way she'd planned. Her need to plan had definitely robbed her of opportunities, but it had kept her safe as well, so there was that.

Jade met them at the door and she was everything Bianca had said. Tall, dark, breathtakingly beautiful. Even sans horse, she was the type of woman who could have anyone and anything she wanted.

Bianca made the introductions. "Jade, this is Sydney. She's here from DC to help us on the case. She and Peyton worked together when Peyton was living back East."

Syd reached out a hand before settling onto the couch. "It's nice to meet you."

"And you. Bianca says you want to talk about my uncles."

"I do, but it would be helpful first if I knew a little more about you for context." Syd hesitated a moment and then ripped off the Band-Aid. "You're Lily Gantry's sister, right? So when she and Peyton get married, you'll be Peyton's sister-in-law?"

Jade cast a cautious glance at Bianca. "That's true, but I'm not sure why any of that matters."

"I'm sure you do, actually. If any of the pending cases go to trial, opposing counsel is going to have a heyday with the entanglement of relationships in this case and the possible conflicts they imply. I may be able to work around them, but I have to know what I'm dealing with before I can make that assessment."

She looked over at Bianca, who nodded and placed a hand on her lover's knee. "Honey, she's just doing her job."

"I know. I just hate the loss of privacy my uncles have cost me. Us."

Jade twisted her fingers through Bianca's, and Syd felt

like a heel for challenging them when it was clear they were in love. Who was she to judge two people's decision to let their passion trump practicality? She softened her voice. "I am just doing my job, and I promise I'm not judging you. I can deal with complicated as long as I have all the facts. Why don't you tell me everything you can about your uncles, and I promise you won't hear another word from me about bad romantic timing?"

Jade looked first at Bianca who nodded as if to say Syd could be trusted. "I'll tell you whatever you want to know. Bianca has heard everything already. Does she need to stay for this?"

"I want to," Bianca said.

Jade looked like she wanted to protest, but Bianca inclined her head, her jaw set, and Syd watched the power balance shift. "Okay," Jade said. "Where would you like to start?"

Syd started with some softball background questions to get some idea of the progression of Jade's relationship with her uncles. Jade's answers were detailed and thoughtful, and Syd had no reason to believe she was holding anything back. During Jade's youth, Arturo and Sergio Vargas were kind and generous uncles who everyone in the family respected and revered, but Jade had overheard snippets of conversations, and her increasingly curious mind led her to look into why her uncles, who were so vague about what they did for a living, always seemed to have tons of money and were consistently feared by those outside the family.

"When did you first know for sure they were drug dealers?"

"I was in college when my mother told me the truth. She and I had an argument—common for us—about what I would do with my life when I graduated. She wanted me to work with her on the ranch, and like all young people who rebel against their parents, I thought that was the worst idea in the world. I told her I wanted to be like Arturo and Sergio." Jade closed her eyes for a second. "She spat the words out in a fit of anger. Did I really want to waste my Wharton degree running a business that could put me in a prison cell for the rest of my life? I didn't believe her at first, but the more I thought about it, I knew she was right. It was more than the money they had; it was the fear they engendered from everyone they met. What I'd naively thought was adoration was more like terror. Everyone was afraid they might someday cross my uncles and wind up the victim of a gruesome murder meant to send a message."

"It's kind of a miracle that Lindsey Ryan wasn't harmed," Bianca chimed in.

"But wasn't the whole point of kidnapping her so Gellar would release Arturo from prison? They wouldn't have harmed Lindsey as long as she was valuable to them, right?" Syd asked.

"About that," Jade said. "I know you already have reason to doubt that my uncles were involved in kidnapping Lindsey." She cast a guilty look in Bianca's direction as if to apologize for sharing what Bianca must have told her about the ongoing investigation. "I think those doubts are well founded. Sergio and Arturo don't ask nicely for what they want. They take it. If they want to bust Arturo from prison, they will make it happen, but it won't be by threatening someone's life. They would be more likely to just slit the throats of every prison guard at Seagoville. Asking is a weakness they would never indulge, even when it comes to family."

Syd paused to digest the horror of finding out someone you loved was a monster. "It must have been really hard on you to find out what they really were."

"It was. When they threatened me if I didn't work with them, I thought things had hit the bottom, but I was wrong. The worst thing they could do was threaten someone I loved." Jade reached over and took one of Bianca's hands in her own. "I will never let anyone hurt the people I love."

Syd watched Jade and Bianca share an intimate moment, knowing she should look away to give them privacy, but she was unable to tear her gaze from their exchange. The fierceness of Jade's declaration was admirable, but more than that, it was concrete, measurable evidence of her love. Syd had no doubt Jade would do anything for Bianca, no matter what tried to separate them. Had she ever felt that way about Tanner? If so, what had happened to diminish her resolve in their relationship? Clearly, something had happened, because when it was time for her to choose Tanner over anything else, she'd let Tanner walk away.

CHAPTER ELEVEN

Tanner led Dale and Mary back to one of the conference rooms at the FBI field office and shut the door behind them. "Thanks for coming out here to do this."

Mary slid into a seat. "Happy to accommodate, but would you care to let us in on the secret? What is the *this* that we're here to do?"

Tanner motioned for Dale to join them at the table. "You remember what I said last week about the 302s that Bianca found in Gellar's office? I've been doing some digging to find out the name of the agent who wrote them up."

"Isn't the name of the agent supposed to be typed on the form?"

"It should be, but whoever filled these out signed them instead." She fished some papers out of a folder she'd carried into the room and set them on the table between Dale and Mary. "See here." She pointed. "Can you make that out?"

"Looks like my doctor signed it," Dale said. "How are you supposed to figure out who it is? And what happened to your theory that Gellar wrote the forms himself?"

"I've abandoned that idea for now. He's got to have someone lined up to testify if the case goes to court, and I'm going to find that person using good old-fashioned detective work. I started scouring case records to see if there were any other 302s in the office with handwritten signatures instead of typed ones."

"And?" Mary asked.

"No luck. Then I looked for handwritten case notes, but no luck. That doesn't necessarily mean anything since we're supposed to memorialize everything with a typed 302 to stay consistent, but I thought maybe whoever did this had a penchant for his or her own handwriting."

"The suspense is killing me," Dale said dryly. "Get to the point, Cohen."

"I didn't find any case notes, but I did some snooping and came across three agents whose handwriting might be close to the one on the form. They're coming in, one by one, to talk to us today. We'll find a way to figure out which one of them wrote up the 302."

"And then what?" Dale asked. "We accuse them of working with the US attorney to prosecute a case? Newsflash—that's the way the job works."

"Ease off. Give her a chance to tell us what she's got planned," Mary said. "You do have a plan, don't you Tanner?"

"Sure," Tanner lied. "Mostly. I plan to ask each one point-blank if they authored the report, and when we find the one that did, tell him/her that we're following up on some leads generated by their investigation and we wanted to know if there were any impressions not included in the report that they could share with us. Also, I plan to gently remind them to type their name legibly on the report for official reference."

"If the report is fabricated, you really think the agent who wrote it is going to admit they wrote it?"

"No, but I do think three well-trained federal agents should be able to tell when someone is lying and convince them it's in their best interest to tell the truth."

"It's not a great plan, but we're here, so let's do this," Dale said. "Bring in the first victim."

Tanner shot a look at the door to make sure she'd remembered to shut it. "Before we get to that, there's something I've been meaning to tell you both."

"Let me guess," Mary said, narrowing her eyes. "You're

working as a double agent, spying on Gellar's behalf, and you're ready to come clean."

"You're kidding, right?" Tanner said.

Mary laughed. "Of course I'm kidding. I'm not crazy."

"I don't know," Dale said. "She has been acting kind of twitchy since Sydney Braswell showed up. Scared she's going to root you out?"

Tanner felt her face redden at the mention of Syd. Now was as good a time as any to say what she'd planned. "Actually, it's about her, Syd. I've been meaning to mention that we know each other. We went to law school together, back in the day."

"Okay," Dale said, drawing out the word. "What? Did you feel like you were holding out on some big secret by not telling us that?"

"It's more than that, isn't it?" Mary asked. "How well did you know her? Can she be trusted?"

Tanner shook her head at the complex set of questions. Whether Syd could be trusted professionally was a whole different issue than whether she could ever trust her on a personal level, but she knew what Mary was asking. "I don't think we have any reason to think she's here for any purpose other than what she's said. Now, as for how well I know her, let's just say that once upon a time we thought we knew each other well enough to have a white picket fence, raise a family, and grow old together."

Dale let out a low whistle. "Wow."

"I know." Tanner took a deep breath. "But that's all in the past. Until last week, I hadn't seen her since about a month after law school graduation when we went our separate ways. It's felt weird pretending to you guys that we didn't know each other, and we don't need weird getting in the way of this investigation."

"Like we don't have enough weird already," Mary said. "We're about to interrogate a few FBI agents in hopes of figuring out which one might be working with the US attorney on some kind of twilight zone parallel universe to our investigation. Your twenty-something love life doesn't even begin to compete."

Tanner wished she felt the same. "So, we're good?" she asked.

"All good," Dale said. She pointed to the door. "Let's do this."

Tanner held up a hand. "One more thing. It's about Syd. As we were leaving the party at his house, Gellar pulled me aside. It was strange." At Mary's eye roll, she added, "Stranger than usual. He made a point of letting me know that he knew Syd and I had some kind of past and he acted a little suspicious about her, like he wasn't entirely sure her reason for being here was to help him bust the task force into shape."

"Do you think he's on to us?"

"Not sure, but it felt more like he was trying to dig for information. I get the impression he trusts me, although I don't have a clue why, but maybe he was hoping I'd let him know if I had any suspicions." She shrugged. "Just thought you should know."

"Why didn't we pick this up on the mic?"

"Uh, I might have turned it off earlier, and then didn't have a chance to turn it back on when Gellar pulled me aside."

"Dumb move. Any chance you want to tell us why?" Dale asked.

"Not right now," Tanner said. There was no chance someone could overhear their conversation, but she didn't think it was a good idea to admit she'd picked the locks at Gellar's place while sitting in the conference room at FBI headquarters. "Let's just say I may as well have left the damn thing on."

Mary gave her a look like she knew better, but seemed to let it go. "Have you told Sydney about your conversation with Gellar?"

"No." Tanner thought back to the evening she'd spent with Syd at her apartment. She'd meant to tell her, but part of her thought it would be better if Sydney didn't know about Gellar's suspicions since it might affect how she acted around him.

"You should," Dale said. "She has a right to know if Gellar suspects something's up."

Tanner knew Dale was right, but she'd kinda missed the window. "I'll tell her. I promise." Eager to turn the conversation away from Sydney, Tanner said, "Let's get started on these interviews."

The first guy was a tall, skinny agent who'd been with the bureau for five years and worked in securities fraud. Tanner didn't offer any explanation to lead off; instead she thrust one of the 302s at him and asked if he had prepared it.

"We don't get a lot of dead bodies in securities," he said, his face deadpan. Tanner couldn't tell if he was joking or if he was always that serious, but she was pretty sure he wasn't lying. One look at Dale and Mary told her they thought the same.

The next agent was a woman. Woman was a generous term since she barely looked old enough to be a college graduate. Tanner motioned for her to take a seat. "Agent Rachel Kelly, thanks for coming in to talk to us." She introduced Dale and Mary. "You're currently assigned to the cyber crimes division, correct?"

"Yes, ma'am."

Tanner tried not to wince at the ma'am, and slid one of the 302 forms across the table. "Is this your report?"

Kelly barely glanced at the paper. "Yes, ma'am."

Tanner resisted the urge to pump her fist in the air. "We're following up on some leads generated in a parallel piece of this investigation. Do you have any observations or impressions not included on these 302s that you'd like to share with us?" She finished her statement with a hard stare designed to bend the young agent to her will. Agent Kelly shifted in her chair, picked up the paper, and set it back down again, looking everywhere but back at Tanner.

"Agent?"

Finally, Kelly focused on her. "I'm not entirely sure I'm at liberty to talk to you about this."

Tanner walked over so she was standing right next to Kelly's chair. Without her saying a word, Dale and Mary scooted their chairs closer so they effectively formed a huddle. Tanner bent slightly at the waist, but her towering height was still enough to intimidate. "How long have you been working for the bureau?"

"This is my first year."

"I remember what it was like when I was first starting out too. Someone higher up gives you a big assignment right out of the gate and you think you owe them your career. I get it. I really do. But if you aren't careful, the someone you tied your hopes and dreams to might wind up being the one that sinks your career." She sat back down in the chair next to Kelly and assumed a less imposing stance. "Now, I'm going to give you the benefit of the doubt. I believe you were only doing what you were told, but we need to know everything," she stabbed at the stack of 302s on the table, "not just what you wrote down. Who were your sources? What were your impressions? Every single detail about your investigation."

Kelly turned pale, but she didn't speak. Tanner wasn't sure if she'd poured it on too thick or if Kelly needed a little bit more of a push. Deciding on the latter, Tanner pulled her phone from her pocket and dialed. When Syd answered, she didn't give her a chance to say anything, and she prayed Syd would play along. "Thanks for taking my call. I've got Agent Rachel Kelly here. She's the agent who turned in those 302s you were asking about, but she doesn't appear interested in providing us with any background information about her investigation." She didn't wait for Syd to respond before chugging on. "I know, I know. I just thought maybe if she spoke to someone from Main Justice, she might understand how important it is that she cooperate if she wants to save her career. Do you mind talking to her?"

Tanner made a show of holding out the phone toward Kelly, who looked at it like it was a coiled snake. "You can talk to a DOJ attorney or you can talk to us. Your choice."

Kelly waved the phone away. "I'll tell you whatever you want to know."

Tanner pulled the phone back to her ear and said, "We got this." She clicked off the line as Syd was asking her what the hell she was doing and wished she had a moment alone with Syd to explain. She turned her attention back to Kelly. "Let's hear it. Start by telling us who assigned you to this case."

Kelly looked sick again, but she managed to blurt out a name. "Herschel Gellar."

"US Attorney Gellar came to you personally and asked you to work a case?" Tanner asked, injecting incredulity into her voice.

"I know it sounds crazy, but it's true. He was here in the building for a meeting, and he apparently asked the special agent in charge for a highly motivated young agent to work on a project." Kelly blushed, probably from embarrassment at the way the assessment sounded once she'd said it out loud. "Like I was going to turn down an opportunity to work directly with the US attorney."

"Of course you weren't. No one would. So your boss recommended you, and what happened next?"

"I met with him and he told me about a case he felt hadn't been fully investigated. He wanted someone to take a second look."

"The bodies found in the truck owned by Gantry Oil."

"Yes."

"Where did your meeting with Mr. Gellar take place?"

"We met at a restaurant in Denton. The Mellow Mushroom."

"And you didn't think it was strange not to meet at the office?" Dale asked.

"I thought everything about this was strange, but I also figured a sitting US attorney wouldn't have asked me to look into a case without a good reason. What was I supposed to say? Hey, this isn't the way I heard it worked when I graduated from the academy about ten minutes ago?"

Tanner smiled. Considering most people were intimidated by Dale's gruff demeanor, Kelly had a lot of spunk. "Okay, so you met at a restaurant. Tell us exactly what he told you about the assignment."

"He gave me the local police report and photos of the scene. He also gave me a list of potential witnesses. There were only a few names, but he wanted me to talk to them all, write up 302s, and report back."

Tanner flipped through the 302s and showed them to Kelly. "Are there any more besides these?"

"No, that's it."

Tanner considered her next question carefully, not wanting to spook Kelly into clamming up. "These aren't part of the file here at the office. Any particular reason why?"

Agent Kelly's face reddened again. "Mr. Gellar told me to give the reports directly to him. He had me sign a log sheet, but I didn't keep copies for our office. He implied there were some issues with the task force working on the case. That maybe the investigation they'd been conducting hadn't been as thorough as it could be."

"Like hell!" Dale was on her feet before Tanner could stop her, but Mary caught her arm before she could reach Kelly.

Kelly's head started swiveling like she was looking for the best escape route. Tanner put a hand on her shoulder to get her to stay put and motioned to Mary to try to calm Dale down. Dale grumbled but took her seat. "Do you have a copy of that log sheet?" Tanner asked.

Kelly pulled out her phone and started swiping through photos. "I took a picture of it before I gave it to Mr. Gellar."

"Good. Text it to me." Tanner gave her the number. "I don't suppose you kept a copy of the list of witnesses Gellar wanted you to interview?"

Kelly swiped some more. "Here it is. I just sent it to you."

Tanner's phone pinged twice with the sounds of incoming texts and she handed her phone over to Mary, who glanced over the witness list. "I don't recognize any of these names other than from the 302s Agent Kelly wrote up," Mary said.

Tanner took a moment to review the list and pointed one of the names out to Kelly. "This one here. Lab tech Roy Washburn, where did you meet with him?"

"At a Starbucks near his office." Kelly looked severely uncomfortable, like she realized how silly that sounded now. "Are you trying to say this person isn't who he's supposed to be?"

"Depends on how you look at it, I guess. Agent, have a seat outside. We'll be with you in a minute."

Mary followed Agent Kelly out of the room and stayed with her while Tanner picked up the desk phone, put it on speaker, and dialed the Southwest Lab that the FBI and other local law enforcement used for all their reports. When the call connected she introduced herself and asked to speak with Roy Washburn. The woman on the other end rustled some papers and then informed her no one by that name worked there.

"Now or ever?"

"I'm looking at a personnel directory that was updated at the beginning of the year, and I don't see anyone by that name on it."

"Do you have any contract employees who might not be included in the directory?"

"I'd still have their information. I just ran a search of our database and that name doesn't come up at all. Sorry, Agent. Wish I could help you out."

Tanner disconnected the call and looked at Dale. "We've got a problem."

"You're damn right we do," Dale said. "We need to run down every name on that list and find out what's going on. In the meantime, what are we going to do about her?" she asked, pointing at the door.

"Tell me what your gut says. Is that kid up to no good or was she just overly impressed by Gellar's position, so much so that she didn't feel like she could challenge him?"

"She does seem really wet behind the ears."

Tanner braced for resistance, but she was ready to convince Dale her proposal was a good idea. "I think we should up the stakes and make Agent Kelly the newest member of our task force."

CHAPTER TWELVE

Syd reached for her ringing phone as it slipped from her grasp, wishing she'd upgraded her rental to one with Bluetooth features. At the next stoplight, she leaned way over and patted the far side of the passenger's seat until she located the slippery device. The missed call was Tanner. Hoping she was calling to explain her odd, abrupt phone call earlier, Syd didn't bother waiting to see if a voice message showed up and pressed the button to call Tanner back.

"Hey, where are you?"

"In the car. Somewhere in East Dallas."

"That's pretty vague."

"In the driver's seat—how's that for more specific."

"You're hilarious."

"So I've been told. I was with Bianca, but now I'm navigating on my own and I'm pretty sure I've taken more than one wrong turn."

"Where were you?"

"Her house. Peyton thought I should meet with Jade, and since it's likely her ranch is being watched, Bianca set up the meeting at her house."

"How did it go?"

Conscious that this was probably the longest conversation they'd had about anything other than their past since she'd arrived in town, Syd chose her words carefully. She truly believed Jade was not involved in anything to do with her uncle's business, but she wasn't quite sure what to make of Jade's proclamation that the Vargas brothers must not have had anything to do with Lindsey Ryan's kidnapping. Her assessment was either spot-on or a blind spot that rendered her opinion too subjective to count on. "She wasn't what I expected."

"I felt the same way the first time I met her. Business degree from a fancy school…"

"Tall, gorgeous—doesn't look like she spends much time mucking around in stables."

"Like you'd know anything about what's entailed in mucking around in stables."

Syd laughed at Tanner's teasing tone. "True." They'd had an ongoing tug-of-war over things like camping versus wine tasting during their relationship. She'd won most of those skirmishes, giving in only once to Tanner's request that they spend time in the great outdoors. Tanner had been a good sport and made sure she'd had a French press for coffee and other creature comforts for what could only be considered glamping.

What Tanner had no way of knowing was that a few years ago, she'd given in to a request from her friend Kate and joined a group of attorneys from the office to go camping in the Shenandoah National Park. The trip hadn't been as basic as the ones Tanner would have preferred, but it hadn't been glamping either. Syd had actually enjoyed the peaceful quiet of the great outdoors and wished she'd taken more time during their stressful law school term to enjoy the experience with Tanner. She started to tell her now, but stopped. What would be the point? It wasn't like Tanner was suddenly going to whisk her away to go camping. She had changed, but Tanner didn't know that. And there was really no point in telling her now when as soon as they had this case wrapped up, she'd be heading back to DC, leaving Tanner to the life she'd chosen over the future they'd planned.

"Are you still there or did we get disconnected?"

"I'm here. Got distracted by some traffic," Syd lied. "What's the plan now?"

"We should talk." Long pause. "So I can bring you up to speed. I have an idea and I want to make sure you're on board with it."

"I'm guessing you don't want to have this conversation at the office."

"You'd be right. I don't want to have this conversation where anyone can hear it."

"How about your place? If you can direct me to the nearest big street, I bet I can find my way back there."

"Oh, yeah, sure. That works."

Syd thought she heard hesitation on the other end of the line. "If you'd rather meet somewhere else, that's fine."

"No. My place is fine."

"What's the matter? Can't remember if you left last night's takeout lying around?"

Tanner laughed. "Maybe."

Syd smiled to herself. Tanner might not have changed that much after all. "Give me the directions, and I promise I'll try to catch some red lights on the way to give you time to pick up after yourself."

Syd followed Tanner's directions to the nearest big intersection and then counted out the left and right turns until she arrived back at Tanner's condo. Despite her best efforts to delay, she arrived in less than thirty minutes. She'd heard Dallas traffic was bad, but it had nothing on DC. She spotted Tanner's car and parked in the adjoining space. As she climbed the stairs, her mind flashed to the almost kiss from last Saturday night, and she vowed to keep her distance to prevent another close encounter. She lifted her hand to knock on the door, but it swung open before her knuckles could connect. "I tried to be slower," she said, "but the traffic gods—" She stopped cold when she saw the frown on Tanner's face. "What's wrong?"

Tanner shook her head. Syd looked over her shoulder as if the reason for Tanner's swift change in mood might be standing behind her, but she was all alone on the balcony. "Guess it's me," she muttered, and walked into the apartment.

"You mind telling me why you're Miss Friendly on the phone, but now that I'm here, you don't look happy to see me?" Syd asked Tanner, who was standing in front of the open refrigerator.

"You can't keep giving everyone a hard time over things you don't understand."

"You're going to have to explain that one to me because I have no idea what you're talking about."

"I talked to Bianca on the way over."

"So?"

"She told me about your conversation with Jade."

"Again, I have no idea what that has to do with us."

"She and Bianca are in love. It might not be an ideal situation for Bianca's job and it might seem unlikely to anyone on the outside looking in, but what they have is real and neither one of them should have to apologize for choosing each other when the rest of the world thinks it doesn't make sense."

"Did Bianca say she was upset, because she sure didn't seem upset when I spoke with her."

Tanner hung her head. "No, but I can only imagine how she must've felt."

Syd heard the frustration in Tanner's voice. "You're right."

"Really?"

"Don't look so surprised. Yes, you're right. They shouldn't have to apologize, and only the two of them can know what's best for them, both as a couple and individually."

Tanner sank into a chair. "Okay, so we agree."

"We didn't used to, but we do now," Syd said, praying Tanner would read the deeper meaning behind her words.

"I'm sorry for scolding you."

"You don't have to be. Apparently, neither one of us has truly healed from the hurt we inflicted on each other." She glanced at the door. "Would you like me to leave?"

"Leave? No, that's the last thing I want you to do."

Tanner spoke the words with a sigh that sounded like relief and nothing more, and Syd tried her best not to read in any deeper meaning. "Good. I don't want to either. But, Tanner?"

"Yes?"

"If we're going to work together, really work together, we've got to be able to trust each other."

"I know you're right." Tanner hung her head. "It's hard."

"Everything worth having is." Before she could dwell on that, Syd rushed to ask, "Why don't you start by telling me more about what happened at Gellar's house. Where did you sneak off to, what did you find, and what did he want to talk to you about?"

"You're not going to like it, and it's probably best I don't share."

"There are a lot of things I don't like, but I get through them. Share, Tanner, or I'm out of here." She assumed her fiercest expression as she delivered the declaration, hoping Tanner didn't see through her facade. She didn't want to be anywhere else but here tonight, no matter what Tanner was about to say.

❖

Tanner stood up and walked to the kitchen. She was going to need that beer she'd been looking for earlier if she was going to confess what she'd done at Gellar's party, especially to Syd. "You want a drink?"

"Sure, I'll take whatever you're having."

"I'm having a beer."

"Then that's what I'm having."

Tanner arched an eyebrow but complied by opening two bottles and thrusting one at Syd's outstretched hand.

"Sometimes a girl wants a beer."

Tanner tipped her bottle at Syd. "Sometimes she does." They clinked bottles, and then they both took simultaneous deep draughts like they were washing away the discomfort of a few minutes earlier. "Truce?"

"Truce," Syd answered. "Now that that's out of the way, tell me everything."

"I broke into a locked room at Gellar's house." Tanner spat out the words and then took another drink from her beer while she waited for Syd's reaction. It wasn't what she expected.

"I figured you were up to something. I assume you didn't find anything incriminating or you'd be asking me to get a warrant."

"While I find it extremely weird that he has a locked room labeled Wine Cellar that he accesses from the outside of the house that has absolutely no evidence of anything to do with wine, I have to admit that's not incriminating. All I found was a plain room with a concrete floor and a bunch of empty industrial-sized shelves." She crossed her arms and prepared for the fallout. "Aren't you going to lecture me about the perils of skirting the law?"

"Nope. I mean, if you had found something incriminating, it would definitely be problematic. We'd have to come up with some other way of corroborating the evidence to get a warrant, but I can be as creative as the next person."

Tanner squinted and cocked her head. "Who are you and what have you done with Sydney Braswell aka Miss Law and Order?"

Syd playfully punched her arm. "Seriously, Tanner. I want to get to the bottom of this case as much as you do. I don't condone what you did, but during the party I wandered into Gellar's office, and I have to say that I was sorely tempted to dig through his files." She took a drink from her beer. "I know I gave you a hard time about the way you handled Razor, but I'm not as uptight and controlled as you make me out to be." She looked down at her lap. "Not anymore."

Tanner reached over and slid her hand into Syd's. "I'm sorry."

"For what?"

The apology was pure instinct and she wasn't prepared to distill one reason from the many. Sorry she'd skirted the rules. Sorry she hadn't been honest about it. No, her regrets weren't about the job, not where Syd was concerned. When it came to Syd, her regrets were rooted in the past. Sorry she'd kept her decision to join the FBI secret. Sorry she'd rebelled against Sydney's careful and specific plans for their future.

But was she really sorry for those things? For the better part of their last year in school, she'd dropped hints to Syd that they didn't share the same vision of what the future should hold, but Syd had brushed aside her comments because they didn't fit with her view. Not telling Syd when she'd finally made her choice was necessary to keep her own dreams alive. Her only miscalculation had been that Syd would eventually come around once she knew it was a done deal. She spent the last ten years not wanting to assign blame out loud, but beneath the surface, she knew she'd always blamed Syd for their separation. If she had only been willing to compromise, then they could have had a life together, but even as she had the thought she had no idea what that compromise would have looked like.

"I'm sorry things between us ended the way they did," she said. It was a poor summary, but the best she could manage right now.

"Me too." Syd squeezed her hand and sighed. "I remember graduation. You looked so handsome in that light gray suit. All year I'd been looking forward to celebrating being first and second in our class and moving on to the next phase of our lives. I spent that night by myself because I couldn't handle everyone talking about all their plans when ours had fallen apart."

Tanner thought back to graduation night. Unable to stand being around her classmates for exactly the reason Syd said, she'd gone out with a few of her Army pals and they'd toasted her future as an FBI agent. She'd spent the rest of the summer studying for the bar and getting in shape for the grueling rigors of the academy while resisting the urge to call Syd to patch things up between them. The last time she'd seen Syd had been the day she'd gone back to the small house they'd shared to retrieve a few things Syd had found when she was in the process of moving out.

"I guess that's everything," Tanner said, pointing to the small box on the floor. She fished in her pocket and pulled out a piece of paper. "Here's my new address. If you want to give this to the landlord, in case there's anything..." She let her voice trail off. There really wasn't anything else to say or do. The box on the floor represented the final connection she had to Syd, and the minute she picked it up and walked out the door of this house, all the memories, all the possibilities would evaporate.

She leaned over to lift the box, but Syd's hand on her back stopped. "Yes?"

"I wish things had worked out differently. Between us."

Tanner wanted to say something about choices and consequences, but she'd said enough of that. They both had hashed through the end of their relationship with shouts and tears, and she didn't have the energy for either. Not anymore. So all she said was, "Me too," before she picked up the box and walked out the door and away from the life Syd had chosen for them.

"Okay, now you've told me what you did at Gellar's house, but I still don't know what he said to you when he dragged you off to his office."

Tanner shook off the haze of the past and focused on now. "I wasn't sure what to make of it at the time. I'm still not, and it's probably nothing."

"Quit stalling and spit it out."

"Gellar is a little suspicious of why you're here. It didn't sound like he had anything to base it on, but he asked me to keep an eye on you and report back if you did anything strange."

"And you didn't think that you should tell me that right away?"

"He's suspicious of everyone, and I figured you're already on notice not to alert him in any way. But Dale and Mary thought I should tell you."

"When are you going to stop keeping things from me?"

"Syd, it's nothing. He's as paranoid as Nixon. Pretty sure Peyton's already filled you in on that. Nothing new here."

"That's not for you to decide," Syd said, her voice rising. "It's so like you to think you're the only one who needs to know what's going on. When are you going to realize you don't get to go through life alone? You have to learn to share information with other people, especially when it affects them?"

Tanner drew back and studied Syd's pained expression, certain they were no longer talking about Gellar. Syd was right. She'd always kept her thoughts close, but she'd always thought she was justified. She pulled Syd close. "Hey, I'm sorry. You're right. I should've said something sooner. I didn't want you to worry and I didn't want you to change your behavior because you thought he was watching you extra close because, trust me, he would've noticed that for sure."

Syd relaxed against her side. "That's it?"

"I promise."

"Okay, but don't do that anymore." Syd looked up into her eyes. "From here on out, the information highway goes in both directions. Got it?"

Tanner nodded. "Got it." She mentally combed through the other details about the case to see if there was anything else she was holding back. "There's one more thing, but it's not something I've been holding back. I just found out this afternoon."

"Spill."

"I found out the name of the agent who prepared the reports Gellar plans to use for the grand jury. Dale and Mary and I interviewed her at the division office this afternoon." She told Syd about how Gellar had approached Agent Kelly on his own and enlisted her aid in looking into the task force work behind their backs.

"I don't get it. How was she able to get access to information the rest of the task force didn't have?"

"She didn't. Gellar gave her a list of witnesses, but they're all made up. We spent this afternoon trying to track down the people on the list, but they don't appear to exist."

"What does that mean? Did he pay these people to say what he wanted to make a case against Cyrus Gantry?"

"Paid or threatened, your guess is as good as mine. All I know for sure is that I don't trust a word in those reports, but I still don't get what he has to gain by toppling Gantry. If we could figure that out, then I think we'd have the key to solving this case."

"Something Jade said really stuck with me today," Syd said. "She has no lingering love for her uncles, but she's adamant that they weren't behind Lindsey's kidnapping."

"Well, the kidnappers were Barrio Azteca, sworn enemies of the Vargases, but they were asking for Arturo Vargas's release in exchange for Lindsey. It's possible they were former Barrio Azteca and had switched over to the Mexican Mafia."

"Or," Syd said, "maybe they were trying to make it look like the Vargases were behind the kidnapping. Maybe it was a setup, like the bodies in Gantry's company truck."

"That still doesn't explain Gellar's angle."

"No, but it narrows the focus." Syd shot up straight in her seat. "We need to examine every case that's been prosecuted involving a Barrio Azteca member in the last two years."

"You think Gellar's in bed with the BA?"

"I have no idea, but do you have any better ideas?"

"I guess it's possible."

"And you said this Agent Kelly is willing to help us out?"

Tanner grinned. "Willing might be a strong word. I might

have suggested to her that an attorney from Main Justice would have her ass if she kept doing Gellar's bidding."

"Way to use your resources," Sydney replied. "Hey, I've got a better idea. Why don't you tell her to keep doing Gellar's bidding, but report back to us on everything he tells her. No sense cutting off the source before we drain it."

"You're so smart. That's what I always liked about you." Tanner's mind drifted back to law school. She'd been plenty smart in her own right, but it was Sydney's constant pushing that had landed her at the top of the class. Ironic since her grades were one of the things that sealed her position at the FBI. It struck her that she'd never told Syd how much she appreciated her for the motivation she'd provided, and she blurted out, "I'm a better person for having known you. You know that, right?"

Syd looked stunned and Tanner wondered if the compliment was a little too double-edged and a little too late to be of any meaning. "I'm sorry. That was pretty insensitive."

Syd leaned into her and slid her arm down her thigh. "I get it. I do. You know, when I was at the firm and all that shit was going down around me, I looked around at everyone else and they were all acting like nothing was wrong. I get that they had families to support and loans to repay, and so did I, but all I could think was what would Tanner do?"

Tanner's heart ached as she pictured Syd, finally in her dream job, on the road to her perfect future with her present crashing in around her. "You did the right thing because you're a good person, Syd. You've always been a good person."

"Not as good as you. Never as good as you."

Tanner hugged her close. "It's not a contest, babe." The endearment slid off her lips and she didn't even try to stop it. She looked down at Syd in her arms, close and comfortable, a perfect fit. If she could will away the years between them, would she? Would Syd?

"I should go."

The three words tugged at Tanner's heart and filled her with sadness, but she had the answer to her question. No matter what feelings Syd's reappearance had stirred up for her, Syd wasn't interested in revisiting what they'd once shared. And that was for the best. In a few weeks, maybe even days, Syd would be on a plane, back to DC and the life she made there, a life where Tanner didn't exist except as a distant memory. Syd had managed to separate the past from the present, and she'd do well to do the same.

CHAPTER THIRTEEN

Syd stared at her phone wishing it was anyone but Herschel Gellar calling. She'd spent the morning at the office, enjoying the fact he'd been out on appointments, leaving her free to comb through the files in peace. Tanner's warning about his suspicions echoed, and she braced for whatever crazy new idea he might have on his mind. "Braswell."

"Sydney, it's Herschel. Herschel Gellar."

She rolled her eyes at his whisper. *Like I know a ton of guys named Herschel.* "Good afternoon, Mr. Gellar," she said, refusing to adhere to his insistence that she call him by his first name. "What can I do for you?"

"I'd like you to come by the house so we can catch up in a more casual atmosphere. How about four o'clock?"

It was three now, which didn't give her much time to stall her answer. She would've preferred more time so she could reach out to Tanner or Peyton for advice. His invitation seemed innocuous on the surface, but set in the context of everything Tanner had told her last night, it was likely replete with pitfalls. She could beg off—there were plenty of potential excuses she could offer—but she wanted to go. Whatever Gellar was up to, he was smart enough not to be conducting it from the office, making it likely his house was home base for operation trouble. She might not have a chance to look around, but if she was in the house again, without all the partygoers and associated paraphernalia, she might get a vibe.

When she was in the car on the way, she picked up her phone and started to call Tanner, but changed her mind. Last night, at Tanner's, she'd slipped into a zone of comfort. They'd sat close, touched often, and Tanner had called her babe like no years had passed between them. She could close her eyes and pretend they were back in school, still in love where their only worries were passing the bar exam and choosing which big firm would get to hire them. It had taken all the resistance she had not to curl up into Tanner's arms and time travel back to when things had been right between them.

But time travel was a fantasy, and so were any thoughts that she could ever unwind the effects of time and distance. And so she'd left before she could act on her impulses, but she'd spent the rest of the night alone in her hotel room trying to convince herself that she'd done the right thing.

Today was a new day and she'd regained her focus. She'd find out what Gellar wanted, make some notes, and later she had plans to have dinner at the ranch with Peyton and Lily. No talking to or seeing Tanner today. Distance would help her stay on track.

All the holiday trimmings were still up at Gellar's house, but it was too early for the lights, and without the valet and constant stream of partygoers, the house no longer seemed festive. She rang the bell and heard the sharp sound of heels on the marble entry clicking toward her. When the door opened, she was surprised to see Amanda Gellar on the other side.

"Sydney, how nice of you to drop by."

Syd started at the mischaracterization of her visit. This wasn't a social call; she'd been summoned, but there was really no point in saying so. "Is Mr. Gellar in?"

"He is, but he's on the phone. May I get you something to drink? Coffee, water, martini?"

Syd remembered the stiff drink she'd downed at the party while Virginia hung on Tanner's arm, and a sour taste formed in her mouth. "Water would be great."

"Perfect. Follow me. We can chat while Herschel finishes up."

Amanda didn't wait for an answer and headed toward the kitchen. Syd followed, running through a mental checklist of what she knew about the woman. Amanda Gellar, formerly Amanda Kingston, came from money. Her parents had made it big in the trucking industry and she had a trust fund that would last three luxurious lifetimes, especially since she'd chosen to live beneath her means since her husband was in a very public position and it just wouldn't do to show off their wealth. Rumor had it Herschel had signed a strict prenup. Amanda didn't have a job outside the home other than serving on the boards of several high-profile charities, none of which apparently required her attention at this particular moment. Syd hadn't had a lot of time to interact with Amanda at the party, and she wondered what Herschel had told his wife about her.

"You have a lovely home."

"Thank you. It's sufficient for our needs." Amanda pulled a couple of crystal glasses from the cabinet. "You live in DC, right?"

"Nearby in Alexandria. It's a short commute."

Amanda poured them each a glass of water from a chilled pitcher in the fridge. "How are you enjoying Dallas?"

"I can't complain about the weather. Right about now I'd be digging out boots and long coats. I don't think I've even worn a sweater the whole time I've been here."

"Enjoy it, it could change at any moment, but you're probably safe from snowstorms and the like, at least until after the first of the year." Amanda looked down the rim of her glass. "Do you think you'll be here that long?"

Syd raised her shoulders in a who knows gesture, but the question hadn't felt casual. Before they could get into more depth, Herschel appeared in the kitchen.

"Ah, Sydney, thanks for coming by." He looked pointedly at Amanda, who nodded slightly. "Let's go into my office and talk."

Sydney followed him with some trepidation in light of what Tanner had told her about his suspicions. *He's suspicious of everyone, it's not just me*, she repeated to herself as she followed him to his office.

The office was the same as she remembered it from her brief inspection the night of the party. Gellar invited her to have a seat in one of the padded chairs across from his desk, and he walked over to a small bar in the corner of the room. "Something to chase that water down?"

Syd looked down at the still full glass of water in her hand that she'd taken from Amanda out of sheer politeness and decided to do the same again here. "I'll have whatever you're having." She watched as Gellar poured two whiskeys, neat, and tried not to grimace. "This is a beautiful office. I meant to tell you that the night of the party." She pointed at the long row of bookshelves on the far side of the room housing what looked to be a large volume of antique books. "I particularly admire your collection."

Gellar's well-stroked ego surfaced and he wore a big grin. "I've been collecting for years. First edition books dissecting the War of Northern Aggression." He whispered the moniker for the Civil War in an ironic nod to his own political incorrectness. He pulled a volume from the shelf and handed it to her. Syd feigned interest with a few murmured oohs and aahs before handing it back to him. "They're in such good condition," was the only praise she could manage.

"Thank you."

Syd watched as he lovingly replaced the book in its designated space. Hoping she'd done enough socializing, she got to the point. "Would you like an update on my work so far?"

"I imagine you're just barely getting started. The task force has been working for a while, and they've compiled a ton of material even if they've utterly failed at cutting off the Zetas' operation in North Texas. Arturo Vargas may be in prison, but his brother Sergio is free, and there's no sign that they are any closer to catching him."

"The Vargases are known for their ability to hide out, which makes the fact that you were able to capture Arturo a pretty big deal." Syd watched him puff up at her assessment, pleased to see that tagging him with Arturo's capture bought her some brownie points. "And the fact you managed to shut down Cyrus Gantry and their money laundering avenue means it's only a matter of time before their business fades out."

"Unless they find another way."

"They already approached their niece, Jade Vargas, and she rebuffed them. I take the fact they were willing to ask her as a sign of desperation." She raised her glass. "Desperate people make mistakes."

He met her air toast and drank from his glass, signaling her to join him. She took a small sip and managed not to grimace at the strong burn of bourbon coursing down her throat. The heat gave her the courage to ask, "Why did you want to see me? And why not at the office?"

Herschel set his glass down and steepled his hands on the desk. "Did Agent Cohen tell you what I said to her the other night? About being suspicious about whether there was some other reason you'd been assigned to this office, this case?"

Uh-oh. He knew something, but exactly what was a complete mystery. Syd knew she was walking a minefield. Either that or he was playing an elaborate mind game designed to pit her against the task force members, or at least Tanner. Her brain churned through a list of possible responses to his question, rejecting each one in turn for taking too much risk. The best way to win at poker was to bluff hard. "Tanner and I have spoken quite a bit since I was assigned here, but she hasn't mentioned any suspicions about case assignments. I confess most of our conversation has to do with memories from law school. We were both enrolled at Jefferson at the same time but haven't seen each other since, and we've been catching up."

Gellar nodded slightly. His hooded eyes kept her from detecting if he believed her. She watched him take another drink from his glass, set it on the desk, and lightly drum his fingers on the surface, clearly expecting her to say more. She clasped her hands in her lap and waited him out. She didn't have to wait long.

"I like Agent Cohen," he said. "She seems to be trustworthy, but I've learned it's wise not to place too much trust in any one person."

Syd cast about for some innocuous but responsive reply. "I don't know her very well, but I agree with your assessment." Two lies in one, but she didn't have much of a choice. Besides, it was true that she didn't know Tanner very well. Not anymore. The little glimpses here and there of the Tanner she used to know were only a piece of the bigger picture, and the person Tanner was now was a stranger to Syd. What she needed to do was point the conversation in the direction of some other topic and make Herschel forget Tanner and any suspicions he might have about either one of them. "Was there something else you wanted to talk to me about?"

"What's your plan? Long term, I mean. I will be presenting my case against the Vargases and Cyrus Gantry to the grand jury before their term expires at the end of the month. I've put it off long enough, but once we go forward, I need to know that you've reviewed everything and made sure that any issues have been resolved."

Syd took a drink and considered her options. This was the perfect time to point out that although he wanted her to clear his case to go forward, he wasn't sharing all the information he had. She could drop Agent Kelly's name and see how he reacted, but doing so would likely mess up whatever clandestine plan Tanner and the rest of the group were hatching. She settled instead on a vague reply. "Your team has been working on this for a couple of years, so it's a lot to review, but I should be finished by next week. I can have a summary for you then that should be a good outline for your grand jury presentation."

"Excellent," Gellar said, rising from his chair to signal the meeting was over. "Thanks for coming by and don't forget what I said. Trust no one."

Syd smiled and nodded, but all she could think was the only person she knew for sure she couldn't trust was him.

❖

Tanner slid into the booth at Snuffers and faced Dale and Mary. "What's the emergency?"

"Order a beer. Bianca and Peyton are joining us in a few," Dale said.

"Is this a new thing? We're no longer meeting at the ranch? And where's Syd?"

"Syd got called to Gellar's house for a secret meeting," Mary said. "And Lily had the wedding planner out at the ranch tonight."

Tanner barely heard the last part. "What do you mean a secret meeting at Gellar's? What's it about? You do remember he's suspicious of her, right?"

"He's suspicious of all of us, in case you haven't been paying attention." Dale delivered the words with a frown. "Do you think she can't handle a meeting alone with him?"

"No, it's not that." Tanner paused, not sure why she was worked up about Syd meeting with Gellar at his house. Of course Syd could handle whatever Gellar might throw her way, but why had he wanted the meeting at his house and not the office? Something was off, but until she could figure out exactly what it was, she just sounded like a worrywart, so she let it go for now. No sooner had she settled on her response than Bianca and Peyton appeared at the table.

"Sorry we're late," Peyton said. "Docket ran long." She motioned Bianca into the booth, slid in beside her, and set a file on the table. "Did you start without us?"

Dale shook her head. "Nope. I wanted to see what you found out before we got into it."

Tanner's head swiveled between them. "Start what? And what are we getting into?"

Their server reappeared before anyone could respond, and Tanner tapped her foot impatiently while Peyton and Bianca ordered drinks. When the waitress finally wandered off to the bar, Peyton opened the file and pushed a piece of paper toward her. She knew just enough Spanish to make out that it was a police report from Ciudad Juarez. "Tell me what I'm supposed to be seeing here?"

"Gellar's friend and party guest Carlos Aguilar is under investigation by the Juarez police," Peyton said. She pointed at the police report. "His right hand, Jorge Salazar, was arrested by the police in Juarez for the murder of one of Carlos's rivals."

"Okay." Tanner looked around the table, sensing there was more to this and everyone but her knew. "I assume by right hand you mean this Salazar guy was helping Aguilar with business interests besides the restaurant industry?"

"Drugs, human trafficking, smuggling. You name it, Aguilar has his hands in it. His entry into the underworld is fairly recent. Apparently, he was groomed by Fernando Lopez to take over his businesses a few years ago."

Tanner sat back in her chair and took a long drink from her beer. Fernando Lopez had been a dominant player in the Mexican criminal element until his death last year. With no sons to inherit his interests, rival factions had battled over his business interests, legitimate and illegal. "I don't get it. I thought his interests had been absorbed by the other cartels."

"That's what we thought too, but apparently, Carlos was lying in wait, letting them battle each other while he waited to make his move. That time has come, and the authorities in Mexico say he's taken significant steps to solidify his interests over the past year, and his next step is to put together a distribution network to funnel drugs and money to the US."

"By expanding his chain of restaurants," Tanner said.

"Exactly."

She remembered Gellar and Aguilar mucking it up at Gellar's party. "Do you really think Gellar's mixed up with this guy?"

"I don't know," Peyton said. "But I do think it's strange that Aguilar showed up at his party." She directed her questions to Dale and Mary. "Have you turned up anything to connect the two?"

"Nothing," Mary said. "We checked phone and travel records and found nothing to show Gellar talking to Aguilar or making any trips to either Mexico or El Paso, where his US operation is based. No record of money transfers either way. Of course, all the fishy bank transactions we have from Gellar have to do with cash deposits, so there's the possibility that if Aguilar is paying Gellar off, he's doing it in cash."

"Paying him off for what exactly?"

"I don't know, but it's at the top of the list of things we need to find out."

Tanner's mind was racing with possibilities, and when she noticed the shadow fall over the table, she figured it was the waitress returning to check on them. She looked up to tell her they were fine, but found she was staring into Syd's eyes.

"What have I missed?" she asked.

Tanner watched while Peyton filled Syd in. She hadn't seen Syd since the other night at her place, but she'd thought about little else since. She wished everyone else around the table would disappear so she could have a moment alone with her. Not to rekindle their old romance, but to recalibrate and start over because it was too hard to go from old lovers to nothing. Surely they could find a happy middle, find some way to enjoy the time they had together before they both resumed their separate lives.

"You know," Syd was saying, "Carlos was eerily interested in me at the Gellars' party. Maybe we could use that to our advantage."

"What?" Tanner yelped, a little too loud. "That's a stupid idea." She ignored the quizzical look on Peyton's face and pressed on. "You don't know anything about this guy. For all we know he was interested in you because he wanted to make sure you weren't investigating him. If he's a Mexican drug lord and he gets one whiff that you're trying to get information from him, he's going to..." She couldn't, wouldn't speak the horrible things that came to mind.

"I hear you, Cohen," Dale said, "but Syd's got a point. He did seem really interested in her. We can keep her safe, but we should definitely use that."

"He's probably not even in town anymore," Tanner said, holding out hope that was the case.

"But he is," Dale said. "He's staying at the Ritz Carlton. Rented out the penthouse indefinitely."

Tanner looked around the table for someone, anyone, to agree that this was a crazy idea, and she settled on Bianca. "What do you think?"

Bianca shook her head. "These people are all dangerous, but we have to do something. We've all had to play a part to try to take them down. I didn't hear you objecting when these clowns," she waved a hand at Peyton and Dale, "wanted to set me up with Jade to try to get information on her uncles. But look how well that turned out. If Syd wants to step up, then we should let her."

"This is different," Tanner said, struggling to tamp down the rising panic in her voice. It was different because although they'd all risked something in this investigation, and she would gladly risk her own safety, she was certain Syd had no real clue what she was signing up for. She employed her best litigation skills to make her case. "Syd, tell me the last time you went undercover as part of an investigation of any kind?"

"I haven't, but—"

"And isn't it true that if you do this thing and discover evidence, you can't simultaneously serve as a witness and as counsel?"

"Yes, but—"

Tanner nodded as her point was made and started to launch in again, but Peyton placed a hand on her arm. "I think we can all agree there's some amount of risk, but when it comes to technicalities, we can work around that. Let's start small. Syd will meet with Carlos, someplace casual. She'll talk to him and let us know if she gets a gut feeling for whether he's involved with Gellar, and then we can decide what to do from there. It'll be a daytime meeting and we'll keep a close eye on her." Peyton looked around the table. "Everyone in favor, raise their drink."

As a group, they toasted the decision. All except Tanner, who kept her glass on the table but gripped it with all her might, certain this idea was doomed to disaster.

CHAPTER FOURTEEN

I think it's sweet that you're worried about me."

"I'm not," Tanner barked as she paced Syd's hotel room.

Syd let the lie go unchecked, but she knew better. Tanner hadn't spoken to her since they'd left the bar with a plan of action day before yesterday, and now she would barely make eye contact. While it was comforting to know Tanner's method of dealing with stress hadn't changed from the time they'd been a couple, Syd wished she would take a breath and stop worrying about her imminent meeting with Carlos Aguilar.

Setting up the meeting had been easy. Syd had contacted Paladar's US headquarters and left a message. Carlos had called her back within the hour, leaving no doubt that his interest at the party had not been feigned. She asked if they could meet for lunch to discuss some business and asked him to be discreet. If he was working with Gellar he'd probably call him right away, and if he wasn't, he'd probably be extra curious about what she wanted to discuss. Either way, her goal was to keep him guessing.

As if she could read her mind, Tanner asked, "Has Gellar given you any indication that he knows about this meeting?"

"He hasn't said a word and he's acting the same as always, although that doesn't say much. How did this guy get appointed in the first place?"

"You know how it is. Cronyism. He was qualified on paper and probably did some favor for someone and the appointment to US attorney was payback. It's all politics."

"Do you ever wish you'd chosen some other profession?" Syd asked. "One where you didn't have to spend your life fighting for what is right?"

"Like what? Barista? Trash collector?"

"Yeah. I mean those are important jobs, right? We all need coffee, and life would be pretty gross if no one picked up the trash."

Tanner smiled. "You have a point there. Those jobs are important, but anyone can do them. Don't you think it's wrong to waste your skill and intellect?"

"I agree with you, mostly. But sometimes...sometimes I wish things were as easy as clocking in and out."

Tanner reached for her hand. "That's not you, Syd. You'd last about one day, maybe. Are you having second thoughts about meeting with Carlos? Because we can call this off."

Syd sighed. "That's not it. I promise." She started to say more but wasn't sure how to put into words the sudden bout of melancholy that had swept over her. It would pass. It had to. Life wasn't simple, and there were no easy solutions to the hard work that needed to be done. Tanner had always risen to the challenge and she would too. "Tell me what you and the others have planned."

"You'll take an Uber to the restaurant since it will be harder for any of his people to track you that way. We're not going to risk any listening devices. Mary is going to be sitting at the bar. She won't make contact with you, but if you run into trouble, put your hand on your throat and act like you're choking. She'll rush over and say she's a doctor, make a fuss, and get you the hell out of there."

Syd tried to imagine what kind of trouble could happen in broad daylight in a public restaurant that would necessitate a fake choking fit to invoke a rescue mission, but she came up with nothing. Tanner was overreacting. The question was why. She pushed it aside for now. "Sounds good. I'll tell him

I'm considering a change of pace. Law isn't what it used to be. Business is where it's at and I'm interested in learning more about his success as a source of inspiration. Allude to the idea that law and order is a little too confining for my tastes."

"This is Peyton's idea?"

"We came up with it together. It's not completely out of the realm of possibility, and he might believe me. Worst-case scenario, if what I say gets back to Gellar, then we know they're talking."

"No. The worst-case scenario is that he believes you want to cross over to the dark side and he asks you to prove yourself."

Syd heard the frustration in Tanner's voice and tried to add some levity. "Cross over to the dark side? A little melodramatic, don't you think?"

"Syd, you haven't had firsthand interaction with people like Carlos. He's charming and suave, but if he thinks you're trying to cross him, he will do unspeakable things, things that I won't even say out loud for fear they might come true."

Torn between being touched that Tanner was worried about her and annoyed that Tanner didn't think she could handle a simple meeting, Syd fought to keep her tone even. "I appreciate your concern, but I promise you I can handle this. Rest assured, if I run into trouble, I'll put on a choking performance worthy of the Academy."

"Whatever." She rolled her shoulders. "When the meeting's over, come straight back here. Don't stop anywhere or talk to anyone. Understood?"

Syd wanted to buck against the restraints, but decided this wasn't a battle worth fighting. "Understood." She stood in front of the mirror and applied a coat of lipstick and dropped the tube in her purse. "Are you waiting here or downstairs?"

Tanner stood and looked around awkwardly. "I guess it's best if I wait at the bar."

"Why don't you wait here in the room? It shouldn't be too

long." Syd wasn't sure what prompted the invitation, but she decided it was probably better that Tanner cool off here in the room than by pacing around impatiently in the lobby.

"Yeah, okay. Good idea."

Syd grabbed her purse and strode across the room, placing her free hand on Tanner's shoulder. "It's a late lunch in a public place. You have nothing to worry about." On impulse, she reached up and lightly kissed Tanner's cheek. Airy, friendly—the kind of kiss you give to a close friend or a sister. Why then did she suddenly feel things that friends shouldn't feel?

The bellman convinced her one of the waiting cabs would be faster than an Uber, and she couldn't think of a valid reason to turn him down. Strike one, she thought, as she settled into the back seat. Tanner had been planning to keep track of her movements by signing into her Uber app, and she was probably pissed. Syd considered calling her, but phone calls weren't part of the plan and Aguilar's hotel was literally five minutes away. Mary would text Tanner the moment she saw her. Tanner would just have to wait.

The maître d' led her to the back corner of the restaurant. On the way, she spotted Mary but didn't make eye contact. When they arrived at the table, Carlos was already seated with a champagne bottle already on ice. So much for business. Carlos was out of his chair before she reached the table. He clasped both her hands in his and kissed them in a move that she supposed some women would view as chivalrous but she thought was pretty smarmy.

"How wonderful to see you again," Carlos said, holding out a chair for her. "And such a better venue, more suitable for actual conversation."

Syd made a show of looking around. "This is very nice, and they seem to know you here. Business must be good."

He laughed. "I'm a lucky man. Much good fortune has come my way." He pointed at the champagne bottle and raised an eyebrow. She nodded and watched as he poured. He wore a single plain wedding band and sported the most understated model of Rolex. Champagne aside, he wasn't a show-off.

"I was surprised to get your call," he said after they placed their orders.

"I must admit I hesitated to reach out to you."

"And why is that?"

She decided to lead with honesty. "Well, for one thing, I don't know you, and this is a very private matter."

"You can count on me to be discreet. What else caused your hesitation?"

Syd fiddled with her napkin. She didn't need more time to answer, but now she was venturing into the lying part of the program and she needed to sell it. "I've been saving my entire adult life. I never had a particular goal for my nest egg, but lately I'm itching for an opportunity to transition from the law to something else."

"The law doesn't hold your interest?"

"It did once, but for a while now it's felt a bit too restrictive. I could do so much more if I weren't bound by the structure of my position." She took a drink from the glass while the waiter set their plates. When he finally wandered off, she took up the thread again. "You can see why I'm hesitant to say anything. If my boss, or anyone else, like Mr. Gellar, for instance, knew I was exploring other options, they might take it the wrong way."

"And what way would that be?"

"Let's just say I think the world would be a much better place if there weren't so many rules." Syd relaxed into her role as the disaffected prosecutor. "I would like some means of earning a living that isn't so restrictive."

"And you are worried that if Herschel Gellar knew how you felt, he would find you lacking?"

Syd chose her next words carefully. "I do not know Mr. Gellar well enough to make that assumption. Am I off base?"

Carlos ignored her question and cut into his steak. He pointed at the meat with his knife. "This is a perfect steak. It's so easy to accomplish, but so rare to find." He smiled. "No pun intended." He took a bite and chewed slowly. "Do you know why I am so successful?"

"Is that a trick question?"

He laughed. "No, but it is a rhetorical one. I am successful because I settle for nothing less than perfection. Rules have a way of stifling perfection. Do you agree?"

"I do."

He pointed at her plate. "Eat your meal. I believe that food is meant to be enjoyed. We will discuss pleasurable things now and business after." He didn't wait for her to respond and tucked into his steak. While they ate, he talked about his family in Mexico, particularly his grandmother. "My *abuela* taught me to cook when I was only five years old. Every recipe direct from her head to mine. We wrote nothing down. Important things are easy to memorize. Secret recipes remain so when they live only in the mind."

Syd chewed her food slowly, certain there was some undercurrent of meaning in his words. The food was good, but she hoped she wasn't in over her head. When the waiter came back to clear their plates and ask about dessert, she deferred to Carlos.

"We'll have my usual, but upstairs." As the waiter wandered off, Carlos stood. "I have something to show you."

Syd looked around, a bit disconcerted. "Here?"

"Close by."

Uh-oh, she thought. Leaving the restaurant with Carlos wasn't part of the plan, but since she hadn't managed to get any information from him so far about whether he was working with Gellar, she wasn't ready to rule out going off script for a bit. "I should get back to the office," she said half-heartedly.

"Where is the woman who was talking about breaking rules?" he challenged. "I promise it won't take long, and if you are truly interested in changing your life for the better, you will want to see what I have to show you."

Tanner would come unglued if she left here with Carlos and no one knew where they were headed, but Syd knew if she didn't go with him now, there probably wouldn't be another chance. She said a silent prayer that wherever they were going, Mary could keep tabs on them, and she feigned an excitement she didn't feel. "Then by all means, lead the way."

❖

"What do you mean she left with him?" Tanner gripped the phone as if she could squeeze a different answer from the speaker.

"They ate lunch and then left together. I followed as close as I could, but I lost them when they got on the elevator." Mary cleared her throat. "She didn't look like she was under duress."

Tanner held back a sarcastic retort about how Mary barely knew Syd, so how would she know if she were under duress or not? The simple fact was she should have been the one at the restaurant, keeping an eye on Syd, but instead she'd spent the last hour and change sitting in Syd's hotel room trying not to think about the fact the bed where Syd slept every night was only a few feet away. Having Syd meet with Aguilar had been a stupid idea from the start, and now the team that had come up with it had lost control. "How long ago did they leave? Do you even know if they're still in the hotel?"

"They left about twenty minutes ago. Dale is checking with the valet to see if Aguilar's car has been checked out, but we're trying to be subtle. I don't think they've left the hotel, though."

Tanner heard a slight inflection in Mary's voice. "Why do you say that?"

"I saw a couple of guys seated not far from Aguilar at the restaurant. They didn't order any food, and when he left with Syd, the guys followed. I'm betting they're Aguilar's body men. They're in the lobby right now."

"Shit." Tanner stared at the wall in Syd's room, trying desperately to formulate a plan, but all she could come up with was for the entire team to bust down Aguilar's hotel room door and go in guns drawn. She needed to get a grip and figure out something workable, but the column of fear twisting around her spine was paralyzing. "What's your plan, and please say something other than wait for Syd to make contact?"

"Where are you?"

"What?"

"I'm heading your way so we can talk this out. Where are you?"

"No. I'm coming to you."

"Tanner, you know Syd better than any of us. Do you really think she'd take a big risk if she didn't feel like she could handle it?"

I used to know her. Tanner forced her breath to slow and rolled Mary's words over in her head. Syd was a planner. Meticulous and orderly. She charted a path and stuck with it. That's the Syd she used to know. But the Syd who'd walked back into her life a few weeks ago was different. This Syd risked her career by becoming a whistle-blower. She'd abandoned her dream job to work for the government. She'd volunteered to meet one-on-one with a guy who might very well be a cutthroat cartel boss. This Syd wasn't the one she knew. Not at all.

"I'm at Syd's hotel. Don't come here. If anyone happened to make you and they followed you here..." Tanner ran a hand through her hair. "Besides, I'd rather you stick close in case you spot her. I'll be there in a few minutes."

"Bad idea. I've got Dale watching outside the building and I'm inside. What are you going to do, charge into the penthouse?" Mary dropped her voice to a whisper. "I get that you're worried, but there's nothing you can do right now. Wait there, and I'll keep you posted."

Tanner paced the length of the room, doing her best to tamp down her frustration. Several times, she started to send Syd a text and ask what the hell she was doing, but if Syd was in trouble, a bunch of concerned texts from an FBI agent would only exacerbate the situation. The wait was aggravating, but even more so was the lack of information. Tanner could handle anything if she knew what she was up against, but Syd's reappearance in her life and the uncertainty of what it meant for her future had thrown her completely off balance, and the unknown was going to do her in.

❖

In her time at the law firm, Syd had seen plenty of posh places from client offices to private suites at expensive hotels, but Carlos's suite at the Ritz was next level. They entered via a private entrance that opened into a massive living area. He excused himself to make a call, and she spent a moment taking in her surroundings, partly out of curiosity, but mostly in case she needed to make a sudden getaway. Silly really, since Carlos had been the consummate gentleman. If Peyton hadn't told her he was suspected to be behind a dangerous cartel, she wouldn't have guessed he was anything but what he purported to be—an entrepreneurial restaurateur bringing the food of his heritage to the public.

She walked the length of the living room and spotted a hallway that led to four closed doors. Was Carlos's food empire big enough to support what must have been a lavish expense, or was this luxury funded by illicit income? Was evidence of either behind one of those doors?

Carlos's voice intruded on her musings. "It's an extravagance, I know, but I have meetings with potential investors here, and it's important that they believe in my success."

"Believe or know?" Syd asked.

"You are very insightful, Ms. Braswell." He walked over to the window that offered an irresistible view of the Dallas skyline. "I do not lack for anything, but that doesn't mean I am satisfied. Nothing is more dangerous than for a man to think he is satisfied."

"Or a woman." Sydney could do this word dance as long as he could, but she wanted to push things along. "I appreciate your desire to be subtle, and maybe it's the crass American in me, but I don't see anything wrong with admitting that you are wildly successful and able to afford whatever luxuries you want."

She waited for him to recoil, but he only smiled and changed the subject. "Have a seat. Dessert will be here in a few minutes, but in the meantime, I'd like to hear all about what brought you to Dallas and your work with our mutual friend."

Syd thought quickly. Her first instinct was to deflect, but she'd done that at the party the first time he asked about why she was in town. If she put him off again, he'd likely shut down, and she wanted just the opposite. Decision made, she opened her mouth and offered a fictionalized version of the truth. "This is not public knowledge." She stopped and waited for him to nod a promise of silence. "The task force that Herschel has been running has gone a bit rogue, and he wanted someone to bring them into check. He's much too busy to watch their every move, so that's why I'm here. While they should be doing everything in their power to put together the strongest possible case against the Vargases and Cyrus Gantry, who was laundering money for them, they have lost focus."

"And how are you getting them back on track?"

"It's not easy, but I have insisted on overseeing their work, reviewing all of the evidence and having them account for all their time. They don't like the oversight, but it's not up to them."

"And this evidence, does it support the case?"

His body tensed slightly as he waited for her answer, sending the signal that his interest was way more than casual. Syd nodded vigorously. "There's absolutely no doubt that Cyrus Gantry had been laundering money for the Vargases, who are not only behind one of the biggest drug operations in this part of the country, but they were responsible for kidnapping that reporter, Lindsey Ryan, and," she lowered her voice to a conspiratorial whisper, "we have reports that they were also behind the death of a federal prosecutor, Maria Escobar."

As she said Maria's name, she scrutinized his face, hoping he'd have some reaction that she could read, but she got nothing. His eyes were focused on hers and they were piercingly interested, but he didn't flinch or smile or shrug at her declarations. She didn't know what she'd expected. She didn't have any reason to believe he knew anything about the crimes she'd described, so why would he have any kind of reaction? Coming here was a dumb idea.

The doorbell to the suite rang, and Carlos excused himself again. A moment later, he returned with a tray of cookies in his hand and a maid behind him with a coffee service. He directed her to pour them each a cup and then he set the tray on the table and resumed his seat on the couch. "Eat, please. These are biscochitos. The pastry chef makes them especially for me when I visit. I shared a version of my *abuela*'s recipe with him." He handed her a small plate with several cookies. "You see, these are the kind of luxuries you can indulge when you are, how did you put it, 'wildly successful.'"

Okay, maybe I don't suck at this after all. Syd vowed to be patient since it was becoming clear that Carlos would only reveal information at his own pace. She ate one of the cookies and moaned her response. "These are amazing. I can only imagine what the authentic recipe must be like."

"You can try them sometime. We serve them at Paladar."

"The source of all your success."

"A smart man does not rely on any one source for his success unless that source is his own ingenuity."

"The same is true for a smart woman."

He nodded. "This is true. I suspect you are a very smart woman, Ms. Braswell."

"Please call me Sydney."

"Sydney it is. Would you like to see some plans I have for expanding into the north Texas market?"

"Absolutely." She didn't have a lick of interest in looking

at a restaurant business plan, but the longer she was here, the more likely she'd stumble onto something that might show a connection to Gellar.

Carlos walked over to the desk against the wall and opened a drawer, but before he could get any farther, a piercing ring filled the room, and someone started beating on the door. Sydney placed her hands over her ears and Carlos lunged toward the door. Syd heard shouting, and Carlos reached into his jacket, the door flew open, and two large men charged into the suite. She should've listened to Tanner.

CHAPTER FIFTEEN

Tanner cursed the four people in the elevator who'd each stopped on a different floor. When the car finally reached the main floor, she stormed through the lobby of the Adolphus, desperate to get outside. Her phone conversation with Mary had been abruptly cut short when a loud noise broke through the line and she hadn't had any luck getting her back on the line. Phone calls to Dale had gone unanswered, and no fucking way was she going to sit here and wait to find out what the hell was going on.

When she pushed through the doors, she paused for only a second to consider her options. Her car was parked almost half the distance between here and the Ritz. She could wait on an Uber, take one of the cabs idling nearby, or run through downtown. She had her hand on the door of a cab when she heard a voice shouting her name. She looked up and Dale was jogging toward her. Tanner waved the cab on and stepped back. "What the hell are you doing here?" she shouted at Dale.

Dale didn't respond until she was standing right next to her. "Get a grip, Cohen. She's fine."

Tanner stared at Dale, not quite willing to believe what she couldn't see for herself and too disconcerted to act nonchalant. "Where is she? Aren't you supposed to be the second set of eyes? Why in the hell did you and Mary let her leave that restaurant? This was the dumbest idea ever."

"Can't say I disagree with you. When Syd didn't show up after a while, I pulled the fire alarm at the hotel to smoke them out. Mary spotted her in the lobby and sent her a text that she was needed at the office."

"Why didn't you do that in the first place?"

"Because as much as you can't see it right now, some risk was worth letting her try to get some information. She's fine and she's probably on her way back here."

"Tanner?"

Tanner froze at the sound of the familiar voice, cutting through her aggravation at what Dale had just told her. All these years, all the tension between them, and Syd's voice still filled her with hope and promise. But despite her relief, she wasn't ready to set aside what had just happened. She turned slowly to face Syd. "Why did you do it?"

Syd's eyes narrowed slightly like she was trying to puzzle out the words, and then her expression softened into a gentle smile. She held out a hand. "Let's go inside and talk."

Syd jerked her chin at Dale and Dale looked between them, nodded, and walked away. Tanner watched her go, part of her wanting to follow to avoid whatever fallout was about to occur, but her legs betrayed her and stayed rooted in place. When Dale was out of sight, Syd moved closer, slipping an arm around her waist. "Tanner, come with me. Please?"

She let Syd lead her through the lobby, into the elevator, down the hall, and into Syd's room. She'd left this space mere moments before, but the waiting had been like a haze that enveloped her with its shadows. Syd walked over to the desk and poured whiskey from a bottle into a short, fat glass. Tanner opened her mouth to say, "You don't like whiskey," but the words stuck in her throat. What Syd liked and didn't wasn't her business anymore. Neither was whether Syd chose to take foolish risks that might jeopardize her life. Syd had made the choice to walk away from their relationship, and no amount of time or distance could repair the break between them.

"Drink this." Syd pushed the glass into her hand. "Then let's talk."

Tanner stubbornly refused to accept the drink. "I don't want to talk."

"Then you drink and I'll talk."

"There's nothing left to say." Tanner paused to try to slip the paralysis that was taking hold. "I asked you not to do this thing, and you did it anyway. I asked you not to take unnecessary risks, and you ignored me." She wagged a finger between them. "Nothing has changed."

Syd looked down at the glass in her hand, then raised it to her own lips, taking a deep drink. Tanner watched her eyes water from the burn of the whiskey and then darken with steely resolve. Syd set the glass down hard. "You're right. Nothing has changed, but this time it's me doing something that doesn't fit your plan. When it comes to our past, maybe I should have reacted differently when you went behind my back and signed on for a career that was exactly the opposite of everything we'd ever planned, but that's easy to say now. At the time, you didn't care how I felt or how your selfish decision swept away all of our dreams."

"Our dreams? Big law, big house, big bank accounts? Those were never my dreams, only yours. You never gave me a chance to explain I didn't want those things. Besides, look how well they turned out for you." Tanner spat the harsh words, and the lack of a filter felt liberating. Until she saw sadness drape Syd's face as she backed away. Torn between doubling down and backing off, she simply said, "Syd, wait."

Syd held up a hand. "Don't." Hurt cracked through Syd's voice and Tanner stepped closer.

"I'm sorry."

"Don't say you're sorry. You're not sorry." Syd gathered steam. "You made a choice and you've never regretted it. You haven't had to live your entire life wondering what might have been. You walked away and never looked back." Syd shook her head. "You always were the smarter one."

The hollow echo of her sadness pierced Tanner's heart and

she gathered Syd into her arms. She wasn't the smarter one. She'd never been the smarter one. She'd given up the one great love she'd ever had for what? A life dedicated to protecting strangers and slumming with criminals. She tilted Syd's face toward hers. The pain in her eyes reflected years of missed memories they would never be able to recapture, but in this moment she could share the fire that burned through her regret. Before she could think the feeling away, she leaned down and took Syd's lips between her own, and everything else—the case, the conflict, the past—fell away.

❖

Syd groaned at the familiar feel of Tanner's mouth on hers, immediately reconnecting with every sense memory she'd held tightly in reserve for the last ten years. Soft lips, firm touch, hooded, soulful eyes drinking in her reactions. Seconds into the searing kiss, her own eyes fluttered shut to let her absorb the onslaught of emotion. Was Tanner still watching?

And then the sensations stopped. "I'm so sorry," Tanner murmured. "Are you okay?"

Syd opened her eyes and looked deeply into Tanner's. She wanted to ask if she was really sorry, but she didn't want to know. All she wanted was the press of Tanner's lips on hers again and to forget about everything else. "Kiss me again," she said. "Just like that. And this time, don't stop."

Tanner answered by running her hands up Syd's side. Syd craned her neck, arching into Tanner's touch, craving it with increasing urgency, but Tanner made her wait, leaving whisper soft kisses on her neck as if they had all the time in the world. Syd reached her hands around Tanner's waist and tugged her shirt loose. She skimmed her hands over Tanner's tightly muscled abdomen with light, leisurely touches that mirrored the excruciatingly slow strokes Tanner was teasing her with. Tanner moaned. "You're making me crazy."

Syd smiled but didn't stop. "Welcome to my world." She slid her fingers inside the rim of Tanner's pants and traced her skin. "There's a bed right behind us. I vote we take off these clothes." There. She'd said what she wanted, and the moment she did she knew she'd wanted Tanner this way since the first moment she'd seen her again. Hell, she'd never stopped wanting Tanner. Wanting wasn't the issue. Before practical thoughts could intrude, she helped the situation along by pulling Tanner's shirt over her head and tossing it onto the floor. She sucked in a breath at the sight of her naked torso, as beautiful as she remembered, and Syd licked her lips with desire.

Tanner moved closer, her hands on either side of her head pulling her into a deep, pulsing kiss that left her swooning. When they broke for air, Tanner whispered in her ear, "Are you sure?"

She wasn't and she was. The swirl of her warring emotions was a force of its own, and she surrendered to the only certainty she knew. No one before or after Tanner had made her feel like this. The world fell away and everything that was important was in this room, making her heart race and her body thrum with anticipation. She'd spent her life trying to control every little detail, and she'd failed miserably. But here in this moment, she had complete control, and she was going to do the thing that would make her happy, even if it wouldn't last. "I've never been more sure."

The words were barely out of her mouth before Tanner swept her into her arms and carried her to the bed. She'd set the stage and now she relaxed and let Tanner take the lead. Tanner slowly undressed her, taking time as she removed each garment to check in with gentle kisses that stoked the growing heat between them. By the time they were both naked, Syd's entire body was on fire. "I'm so ready for you."

Tanner lazily drew a finger through her very wet center and traced it along her thigh. "Really? I can't tell."

Syd reached up and rubbed her flattened palm over Tanner's breast, smiling as Tanner shuddered in response. "Two can tease."

"Who's teasing?" Tanner leaned down and captured Syd's nipple between her teeth, slowly circling it with her tongue. Syd fisted the bedsheets and arched into the intimate embrace, riding the thrilling combination of pain and pleasure to the edge. When Tanner moved to her other breast, Syd thrashed on the bed, desperate for release but determined to prolong the pleasure.

"I'm so close," she managed to whisper between whimpers of pleasure.

Tanner cradled her close, her hand drifting lower. "I want whatever you want. Tell me."

Words she'd longed to hear. In a different context, a different time, the message would have been life-altering, but for now she was happy just to be here with Tanner even if this paradise was limited to the confines of these four walls for only as long as they could stave off the rest of the world. "I want you."

Tanner nodded, her eyes reflecting a familiarity Syd had never felt with anyone else. Tanner settled between her legs and stroked softly with her tongue, her fingers easing inside, building pressure in a slow and steady pace. Syd surrendered to the sensations that transported her to another place, a place where there was no past or future, only the here and now, and she came in fantastic, rushing waves of ecstasy.

Tanner heard footfalls in the hall and she tiptoed to the door, shoved a twenty-dollar tip at the room service waiter, and waved him away. She slowly rolled the cart into the room, trying her best not to wake the woman she'd made love with for the past three hours.

"I smell cheeseburgers. Please, God, let there be cheeseburgers." Syd sat up and rubbed her eyes.

"I'm sorry," Tanner said as she leaned down to kiss Syd. "I was trying not to wake you."

"You didn't wake me. Cheeseburgers woke me." She

tugged Tanner to her and kissed her soundly on the lips. "You are perfectly innocent. Except, wait. How did the cheeseburgers know where I was? Did you tell them?"

"Guilty."

"Seventeen orgasms *and* cheeseburgers. What more could a girl ask for?"

"There may not have been exactly seventeen orgasms, but there were a lot."

"Who's counting?"

"Apparently, you." Tanner reached for a French fry. "I'm starving."

"You always are after..." Syd's face reddened. "I mean, you always were, you know, after we..." She sat up straight and assumed what Tanner knew to be her "I'm in control" face. "Is this weird? And by this, I mean—"

"I think I know what you mean," Tanner said, not entirely sure she wanted to have this conversation.

"I mean is it weird, having sex again with someone you used to have sex with a very long time ago?" She looked down the covers where her fingers were nervously fiddling with the sheets. "Having sex with me?"

Was it? Tanner had been rolling the same question over in her head for the past hour while she'd lain awake and Syd snored like a freight train. She'd never imagined she'd have another shot with Syd, especially not after all these years, and she wasn't sure what it meant that they'd fallen into each other's arms. It hadn't been weird. It had been spectacular. They'd made love with the same energy and passion they'd had when they were young twenty-somethings, fresh in the throes of newness. She'd had an hour to piece together what to say when Syd woke up, and all she'd been able to come up with was some version of *let's try this again*, but she hadn't quite concluded whether the "this" was the romp in bed or something more.

Which led her to examine Syd's choice of words. Was this just sex to Syd? For Tanner, the intimacy they'd just shared had closed the distance between them, but maybe the markers of distance were too entrenched for Syd to see what just happened as anything more than a physical connection. She wanted to know, but she was scared to ask and ruin the moment, so instead she simply said, "Nothing weird about it. Other than your obsession with cheeseburgers."

"They're the perfect food." Syd pointed at the barely two bites left on her plate. "All the food groups are represented and you can eat it with your hands." She cast a longing glance at Tanner's plate. "Are you going to eat the rest of yours?"

"Did Aguilar not feed you any lunch?"

"Holy shit!" Syd swung her legs out of bed and walked across the room to her purse. "I totally forgot."

Tanner cursed her timing. She hadn't meant to bring up anything that might allude to their earlier argument, but Syd looked to be on a mission. "Come back to bed."

"Wait." Syd held up one hand while she dug in her purse with the other. "This may not be important, but it was the only thing I could grab while the alarms were going off." She pulled her hand from the bag in a voilà gesture, waving what looked like a business card in the air. She tossed it to Tanner like a paper football. "I don't know if this is important, but there are numbers on the back, so I figured it might be worth looking into."

Tanner picked up the card and examined both sides. On the front was the name of a restaurant supply company, Bastrop's, with a phone number but no address. On the back was a series of handwritten numbers. She read them several times but didn't see any obvious pattern to indicate the numbers were related. "What is this?"

"I don't know. I don't even know if it belongs to Carlos, but it was in between the seats of the couch in his super-expensive suite at the Ritz. Five rooms, not including the living room, dining room, and kitchen. Do you really think a guy selling homemade Mexican food makes that kind of money?"

"No, Syd, I don't, which is why I was so freaking worried when you went off the grid with him."

"I was fine. I promise."

Tanner sighed. Syd was as stubborn as ever, but it was hard to be mad at her when she was sitting naked in bed, picking over the last of the French fries. She tapped the card against her thigh. "You realize that if this turns out to be important, it might not be usable because of how you procured it?"

"Let me worry about that. If those numbers on the back are bank accounts, then it doesn't really matter how I came by them since we don't need a subpoena to get the records."

"We have to call Peyton."

"What?"

"Yes, dear. Your little adventure with evidence has to take precedence over this." Tanner pointed at the bed. "If these are bank account numbers, which is a stretch, and your pal Carlos discovers them missing, the accounts might suddenly disappear."

"Damn. I was hoping now that I have my energy back, we could go again."

Tanner wished the same thing. Whatever this was between her and Syd, even if it didn't mean anything beyond the pleasure it provided, she wasn't ready to let it go. "Two hours max. We meet with the team and then come back here. Okay?"

Syd sighed dramatically. "Okay."

Tanner placed the call to Peyton, struggling to keep her focus on the conversation and not Sydney, who took her sweet time deciding what to wear. When they were both dressed and ready to go, Syd looped her arm through Tanner's and led the way like the whole thing had been her idea. Tanner had no choice but to follow.

CHAPTER SIXTEEN

Syd walked through the door at Peyton's ranch, acutely conscious Tanner had established a distinct physical distance from her the moment they arrived. She got it, or thought she did. Tanner didn't want the team to know how she and Tanner had spent the afternoon. The problem was she didn't know if Tanner's distance was about respect or regret. She couldn't help but notice Tanner had stepped around the issue when she'd asked how she felt, but since she didn't know how she felt about it either, why should she expect Tanner to be able to articulate her feelings?

Bianca greeted them the moment they walked in. "Hey, you two. I was beginning to think Syd had flown back to DC, but I see she was in good hands." She winked at Tanner and then focused on Syd. "Did Tanner take good care of you?"

Syd struggled for a response, but shock at Bianca's implication robbed her of words. Could she possibly know that Tanner had spent the last few hours taking exceedingly good care of her? She shot a stinging look at Tanner, who jumped into the conversation.

"Syd's fine. You think a little adventure with a cartel boss is going to throw her off her game?"

"Cool," Bianca said to Tanner and then leaned close to Syd to whisper, "These federal agents think they do all the dangerous work. *Please.*"

Bianca led the way to the kitchen and Tanner started to

follow, but Syd jerked her back. "What did you tell everyone about where we've been this afternoon?"

Tanner frowned. "Nothing." She held her hands up. "I swear. They didn't ask and I didn't tell. All I said when I called was that you had something to show them and we should meet soon."

"Okay." Syd's heart rate started to slow. "Sorry. I didn't mean to jump down your throat."

Tanner squeezed her shoulder. "No worries. What happened is just between us. I'm not about to tell these guys about it."

Syd supposed she should thank Tanner for the discretion, but her words stung. *Get a grip, Braswell.* Syd didn't want her personal life laid bare, especially not when she'd scolded most of the group about boundaries. Tanner was right. Whatever had happened between them needed to stay between them, which made sense since it wasn't going anywhere. It wasn't like they were going to be picking out wedding venues and inviting all their friends along to witness public professions of love. Love wasn't even on the table.

Suddenly very uncomfortable with the thought train in her head, Sydney rushed past Tanner into the kitchen where the rest of the team had already assembled. She needed conversation neither with nor about Tanner. Peyton looked up as she walked in and grinned. "Hey, Syd, I hear you set the hotel on fire this afternoon."

"What? What are you talking about?" she sputtered.

"Just kidding. Don't worry. I've already given Dale a hard time about pulling the alarm, but we need to figure out a better plan if you plan to go rogue in the future."

"Rogue. Very funny," Syd said, her pulse settling into a normal rhythm. "The guy said he wanted to show me something and I was supposed to say no thanks? Ask one of these fine federal agents sitting around the table what they would've done in my place."

Dale jumped in. "She's got a point, but Peyton's right too. We do need a better system."

"No, we don't," Tanner said. When everyone looked at her, she kept going. "There's not going to be a next time. If someone's going to get close to Aguilar, it's not going to be Syd."

Syd started to say that was none of Tanner's business, but Peyton interjected. "Let's table this subject for now and talk about what happened today. Syd?"

"Lunch was pretty vanilla. He talked about his grandmother and her recipes and how she inspired his vision for the restaurant chain. I threw out a few hooks about how I was looking for new challenges, ones that were way more lucrative, and he was very Yoda in his responses. Veiled comments suggesting that if I wanted to learn from the master, I had to earn the master's trust and all that."

"Strange," Peyton said. "But not unexpected. It's not like he can afford to trust anyone in his line of business. What did he want to show you?"

"I don't know." Syd fake frowned at Dale. "Someone set off the fire alarm in the building. But I think he was going to show me expansion plans for his business. He made some comments about how it wasn't enough to own the restaurants—to control the output, he needed to control all the systems."

"Sounds to me like he was talking about more than just the restaurant biz," Mary said. "The most successful cartels control everything from growing to packaging to distribution."

"Show them what you found," Tanner said.

Syd pulled the card out of her purse and passed it to Bianca, who was sitting next to her. "I found this in the couch cushions and grabbed it as we were leaving the room. No one saw me take it, and I probably shouldn't have, but it seemed harmless and I wanted to have something to show for my little foray into undercover work." She pointed at the card. "Check out the numbers on the back."

Bianca flipped the card over and held it up for everyone to see. "Any clue what these are?"

"Too long to be phone numbers or bank routing numbers. Account numbers maybe?"

"Account numbers were my first thought," Tanner said. "If that's correct and Aguilar figures out someone has them, you can bet he's going to shut down these accounts."

"It's a little like looking for a needle in a haystack, don't you think?" Syd said. "It's not like we have time to call every bank there is and ask if they have accounts matching these numbers."

"Hey, Tanner," Peyton said. "Don't your people have fancy computers designed to sort data? Can you get one of them to run these numbers through their list of databases and see what they come up with?"

"Not without raising some flags. We're still working the Gellar angle, right?"

"Yeah, bad idea."

"Wait a minute," Syd said. "I might know someone who can help. She used to be assigned to the Behavioral Analysis Unit but transferred here a couple of years ago and works in white-collar. If she still has contacts at the BAU, they have crazy good access to information, and no way would it get back to Gellar."

"Excellent," Peyton said. "Check that out. Now, let's talk about this Agent Kelly that Gellar has working on the case. We need to figure out how best to use her."

Syd listened to them discuss a way to test Kelly's loyalty, but after a few minutes, she tuned out. Tanner's thigh was nestled close to hers under the table, and she couldn't quite tell if she was the only one pressing into the touch or if Tanner was too. Her head swam with memories of how they spent the afternoon, and all she could think about was getting Tanner back in bed. Ironic that naked and vulnerable, it felt much easier to cover the problems in their past that had caused them to break up. There was a message there, but taking the time to dissect it would only pull her out of the very good, very comfortable feeling of enjoying whatever she and Tanner had right now. There would be plenty of time, when this case was over and when she had to head back to her real life, to sort out what this all meant, but right now, she only wanted to feel, and making love with Tanner felt perfect.

❖

Tanner didn't start to feel strange until they walked into the lobby of Syd's hotel, but when they crossed through the doors, she was struck with a sudden sense of nerves. She motioned to the bar. "Do you want to grab a drink?"

Syd looked at her like she was a space alien. "Uh, we have alcohol in the room."

"I know, but I also know you'd much rather have some sugary concoction than straight whiskey."

"Why do I think you're speaking in code?" Syd ran her hand down Tanner's arm. "Are you the sugary concoction or the whiskey neat?"

Tanner grinned. Syd had always been able to cut through bullshit and get to what mattered, and all that mattered in this moment was pleasure, not any worries about what the future might hold or what all of this meant. Right?

Tanner wasn't completely convinced. Syd's words and actions both conveyed that the few hours they'd spent naked in her bed were about nothing more than sex. Good sex. Great sex. The kind of perfect sex that only two people who knew each other's bodies extremely well could have. Once, that intimate knowledge meant more than sex, but Tanner had no idea what it meant now. She had a nagging feeling they should sort that out before they got naked again, and if they were going to talk, it would be easier to do so if they weren't a few feet from Syd's bed.

Syd tugged on her arm, but she held her ground. "Should we talk?"

"Do you want to talk?"

"I don't know."

"Me either." Syd cast a glance at the elevators. "It's been a long day. We could talk later and perhaps do something a little more relaxing now."

Syd was as convincing as ever, and Tanner gave in. "But this time, we get pizza."

They were standing at Syd's door when Tanner's phone rang. She pulled it out of her pocket to turn off the ringer, when she saw Agent Kelly's number on the screen. Damn. "I need to take this."

Syd opened the door. "Go ahead. I'll be in the bathroom when you're done." She sashayed off with a sexy grin.

Tanner swiped the screen. "Talk to me."

"You didn't hear this from me. A couple of marshals just picked up Cyrus Gantry as he was leaving dinner at Al Biernat's."

"Marshals? What's going on?"

"I don't know. I got wind something was going down from our mutual friend about five minutes before it happened. I don't have the whole story, but it appears that his bond is being revoked. I have to go. I'll let you know if I find out more."

Kelly disconnected the call, and Tanner immediately called Peyton.

"I heard," Peyton said in place of hello. "Lily just got a call from the family lawyer. He was having dinner with Cyrus not ten minutes before the arrest."

"Gellar has to be behind this."

"Someone had to file a motion from our office. Obviously, there's nothing I can do without raising a ruckus, but Lily's pretty upset and she's headed to meet with the lawyer. I know it's been a long day, but is there any chance you could find out what's going on and where they're taking him?"

Tanner looked over at the closed bathroom door. She could hear the shower running and let her eyes flutter shut and imagined Syd standing naked under the cascading water, steam rising from her body. Hot, sexy, and waiting for her. When she opened her eyes again, Peyton was still on the phone, waiting on an answer. She wanted to ask Peyton to call Dale or Mary, but she didn't want to reveal why she couldn't do this very personal favor herself. She sighed. "I'm on it. I'll call you as soon as I know something."

The longer she waited, the harder it would be to leave, so she didn't waste any time. The bathroom door wasn't locked and Syd was in the shower, exactly as she imagined. Syd reached for her hand, but Tanner shook her head. "Duty calls. I have to go."

"Are you okay? What is it?"

Tanner handed her a towel. "Babe, you're either going to have to cover up or I'm going to wait outside."

"Seriously?" Syd wrapped the towel around her body and stepped out of the shower. "What's going on?"

"All I know is Cyrus was arrested by a couple of marshals for a bond violation, but I don't know what the violation is or who filed the motion to revoke the bond. Could have been Pretrial Services or it could have been—"

"Gellar." Syd interrupted. "I'd bet money it was him. Something's up and he's trying to hustle things along."

"You really think so?"

"Based on what everyone has said, this is exactly the kind of headline-grabbing diversion Gellar would pull if he was trying to distract from something else. Think about it. If Carlos really is in town to do some kind of deal with Gellar, what better way to distract from that than to put his case against Cyrus Gantry back on the front page? I bet all the news outlets will be leading with this story in the morning."

"You may be right. Maybe you should do all your theorizing while naked." She reached out and ran her finger along the edge of Syd's towel, savoring the feel of her warm skin. She sucked in a breath. "I promised Peyton I would find out where they're taking Cyrus and get Lily in to see him."

"Then you should go."

"I'd rather stay."

"That makes two of us." Syd pulled a robe from the back of the door and slipped it on. "You go and help Lily, and I'll talk to Bianca and see if we can sort out who filed the motion. If we can't be in bed, at least we can both be working on the same thing, right?"

"Sure. Right." Tanner took one last look at Syd, damp and steamy from the shower, and cursed the job. "I'll call you as soon as I know something."

CHAPTER SEVENTEEN

An hour later, Tanner was within minutes of the Seagoville Federal Detention Facility when Dale called. "Cohen."

"Did you find him? Peyton left me a message, but I just got it."

"Hello to you too," Tanner shot back. "Where have you been?"

"Lindsey's leaving tomorrow and won't be back for a week. Need I say more?"

Tanner started to tell Dale she wasn't the only one who would rather be spending quality time with her girlfriend, but the words skidded to a halt before she could say them out loud. Girlfriend? Where had that come from? Syd wasn't her girlfriend. She hadn't been for years, and she wasn't ever going to be again.

Then what was Syd to her now? The question had been tickling her subconscious all day, but she hadn't wanted to examine it too closely. Syd obviously enjoyed the sex and had made it pretty clear sex was all it was, so who was she to ruin a good thing? But she couldn't fault Dale for not calling in since sex with an ex didn't trump two women in love sharing an intimate evening before being separated. "No, you definitely do not need to say more. I talked to a buddy of mine at the marshals office. He said they're checking Cyrus in at Seagoville tonight, and I'm headed there now. He didn't know anything about the reason for the revocation. He said the paperwork was sealed."

"Sealed? That's strange."

"You're right about that." Tanner hesitated for a moment. "Syd had a crazy theory about this."

"Oh, she does, does she?"

Tanner tried to ignore the "I know more than you think I know" tone in Dale's voice, but it rubbed her the wrong way. "You want to hear it or not?"

"Shoot."

Tanner told Dale what Syd had said about Gellar having Cyrus arrested to distract from something else.

"So, what's the something else?"

"It's a theory, not a roadmap. She doesn't know, but she suspects it has something to do with Aguilar. She's convinced that he's got some plan with Gellar, and arresting Cyrus right now is a diversion."

"Maybe she's on to something. Your ex is pretty smart."

"Don't call her that." Tanner slapped her hand on the steering wheel. The word "ex" rubbed her the wrong way, but she didn't feel like figuring out why.

"Something going on between you two? Are you back at odds?"

"No. Not even. It's all good. Can we focus on the case?"

"Sure. Just trying to keep up. You want some company out there? I can be there in twenty."

Tanner considered her options. She was about to show up at a federal detention center where a high-profile defendant had been arrested on a bond revocation, and the defendant's daughter was on the way to see him. There was no way the prison guards would let Lily in to see Cyrus unless Tanner came up with some plausible reason it was necessary for the case. Her arguments might be more convincing if she had another agent along as a show of force. "Sure, I'll wait for you outside the building."

When Tanner pulled up to the detention center, there were only a couple of cars in the parking lot. She spotted Lily's SUV right away, parked next to a Bentley that she tagged as the lawyer's. She got out of her car and strode over to Lily's vehicle. The window lowered as she approached, and she spotted Lily in the driver's seat and a ruddy, well-fed, well-dressed sixtyish man seated next to her.

"Hey, Lily," Tanner said. "You want to introduce me to your friend?"

Lily grimaced. "Agent Tanner Cohen, this is my father's lawyer, Nester Rawlins."

Tanner stuck her head in the window and addressed the lawyer directly. "Mr. Rawlins, if you don't mind, I'd like a word with Ms. Gantry alone."

"I do mind," he sputtered. "I have represented Cyrus Gantry and the entire Gantry family's business and personal interests for over thirty years. If a federal agent wants to question Mr. Gantry's only daughter, you can damn well bet I'm going to be right there next to her."

Tanner rolled her eyes at Lily, who turned to Rawlins and said, "Nester, walk around the parking lot for five minutes. I'll wave when we're done."

When Rawlins was out of earshot, Lily apologized. "I know he thinks he's taking care of Daddy's affairs, but Nester doesn't know jack about criminal law. His bluster is a cover. Do you know anything?"

"Not much. I think it would be helpful if we can talk to your dad, but he's not going to talk to us with Mr. Super Lawyer over there telling him what to do. Dale's on her way. Do you think you could get your dad to speak to us?"

"He owes me after the whole 'hiding who my mother really was and that I had a sister all these years' thing. If you can get me in to see him, I'll get him to talk to you."

Tanner had no idea how she was going to fulfill her end of the bargain, but she was going to do her best. Lily pointed at a pickup pulling into the lot. "Looks like Dale's here."

"I'll talk to her while you get Nester to back off."

As Tanner started to walk away, Lily grabbed her arm.

"Look, I know my dad isn't the best guy, but he's always looked out for me." She pointed at the prison. "Jade's uncle is in there, and there's no telling what he thinks about Cyrus after everything that's happened. It's possible he may believe Cyrus has betrayed them. I don't want to see Cyrus get hurt."

Tanner nodded as Lily's words inspired a plan. She walked over to where Dale had parked and filled her in, and then the four of them walked into the lobby. Tanner told Rawlins and Lily to have a seat while she and Dale approached the desk. They both flashed their badges, and Tanner asked to speak to the night warden. A few minutes later, a tall, slender guy entered through the door behind the desk and asked what they needed.

Tanner glanced back at Rawlins and Lily, and kept her voice low. "You have a prisoner that was dropped off about thirty minutes ago by the Marshals Service, Cyrus Gantry. I need to speak with him in one of your attorney rooms, and I need to bring a witness in with me."

The warden cocked his head like he wasn't quite sure what he'd just heard. "Say again?"

"Cyrus Gantry is about to go on trial for helping two leaders of the Zetas Cartel launder their drug money. You have one of those leaders in your facility right now. I'm a special agent working directly with US Attorney Herschel Gellar, and I need to speak to Gantry about an urgent matter that may require some motivation." She motioned over her shoulder. "I brought the person who can provide the motivation, but we need a private place to speak. No records, no one listening in. Mr. Gantry's safety is crucial to the government's case. If you want to see my bar card so you can justify letting me talk to him in one of the rooms, I'd be happy to show it to you."

The commander rocked back on his heels. Tanner looked at Dale, who drummed her fingers on the desk while they waited for him to respond. Finally, the guy made up his mind. "Okay, but just the girl and you. Fifteen minutes and that's it." He pointed at the conveyor belt to the side of the desk. "Let's go."

Tanner waved Lily over while Dale moved quickly to intercept Rawlins, who was barreling over to find out why his client's daughter could get in but he couldn't. She whispered a quick set of instructions to Lily. "Everything goes through the machine. Don't talk to anyone. Follow my lead."

This wasn't Tanner's first trip to the detention center, but it was her first time to escort a defendant's family member in to see one of the detainees. The first time she'd met Lily Gantry, Lily had been sitting in her father's office when Tanner and a fleet of other FBI agents descended on Gantry Oil's headquarters armed with a search warrant. Cyrus had ducked out of the building immediately before they arrived, leaving his daughter to answer Tanner's questions about whether she knew what her father had been up to. Initially, she didn't buy that Lily was an innocent bystander in her father's money laundering for the Vargases, but as the investigation progressed, she found out Lily had no direct involvement in the family business and was as surprised as anyone to learn that her father was in business with Sergio and Arturo Vargas.

Cyrus was still in a suit when the guards brought him into one of the attorney conference rooms. His eyes widened when he spotted Lily, and Tanner subtly placed a finger over her lips, hoping he would get the message to keep quiet until the guards left the room. When the door shut, she motioned for Cyrus to have a seat. The guards were not supposed to tape the conversations that took place in these rooms because attorney-client communications were privileged. She might be an attorney, but Cyrus wasn't her client, so she couldn't be absolutely sure the guards would follow the rules and she proceeded with caution.

"Mr. Gantry, my name is Tanner Cohen and I'm a special agent with the FBI assigned to the task force that has been investigating Sergio and Arturo Vargas. I need to speak with you about an urgent matter, and as a show of good faith, I brought your daughter here to see you."

Lily started to speak, but Cyrus raised a hand, signaling for her to be quiet. "You have some nerve showing up here like this without my attorney present."

"Mr. Rawlins is in the lobby. Even he can't get in to see you right now. Not until you are processed. I'm an attorney and I know the rules. I'm not here to question you about your case. In fact, what I'm here to talk to you about could potentially help you." She paused for a moment, and he rolled his hand, urging her to continue. "Here's what I propose. I'll tell you some things that I know, and when I'm done, you can decide if you want to talk to me. If you don't, I'll give you a few moments with your daughter and then we'll leave. If you do, then I'll arrange to have you moved to another location. You are aware that Arturo is at this facility pending trial?"

Cyrus nodded, and she caught a glimpse of fear in his expression. "Before we get started, let me ask you one question. Do you have any idea why you were arrested tonight?"

"No."

"The marshals didn't give you any paperwork or say anything?"

"They said my bond was being revoked and that my attorney would receive a copy of the motion to revoke. That's it." He settled back in his chair and crossed his arms. "That was more than one question, Agent Cohen."

"True." Tanner looked over at Lily. She'd prefer Lily not hear everything she was about to say, but for all she knew Peyton had shared some of the details with her already. Best just to dive right in. "We know you laundered money for the Vargases and that you did it to protect Lily, but we think someone has been trying to put you completely out of business so they can take over. We have reason to believe a person in a position of authority has been helping that someone achieve their goal."

Cyrus nodded at first, but it looked more like a reflex than agreement until she got to the part about a powerful position of authority. At those words, he slapped his palm on the table and jabbed his finger at her.

"Take it easy or the guards will come in. Keep your reactions calm. Okay?"

"Okay," he replied. "Tell me more."

"Within the week, I expect you will be indicted for conspiring to kill a federal prosecutor. Her name was Maria Escobar, and she led this task force until the time of her death." Tanner heard Lily's gasp, but she kept her eyes trained on Cyrus, gauging every tic, every eye movement. To her well-trained eye, his reaction signaled nothing to implicate him. "I'm sure you know what the penalty will be if you are convicted of such a crime."

He shook his head slowly but didn't say anything.

"Mr. Gantry?" Tanner prompted him.

"What do you want me to say? I can't admit to something I didn't do, but I don't expect you to believe me."

"Actually," Tanner said. "I've been trying to figure out what motive you would have had. Things were rocking along pretty well for you until Ms. Escobar was killed, but it wasn't too long after that when someone tipped the FBI off that you might be involved with the Vargases."

"You might think I handled financial transactions for those devils, but you can't possibly think I would commit murder. That prosecutor and those people in that truck…" He shuddered and hung his head. "Those were despicable acts committed by cowards."

"You might not have pulled the trigger or left those people to die," Tanner said, "but if you withhold information that could help us find who was responsible, then you are just as guilty as they are. If you are willing to work with us, I will do everything within my power to help you."

Cyrus crossed his arms and shook his head, but Lily grabbed his hands. "Look at me." When he raised his head, she said, "You have a chance to make things right." She pulled back, and her stare was kind but unwavering. "If you drag our family through a trial, you will ruin everything about your legacy. No matter what the verdict, we will all be tainted, and you will never regain what you have lost."

"You want me to stand in front of a judge and tell him that I laundered money for drug dealers?"

"I want you to be the man I always thought you were—honorable and honest. I know your hand was forced, but no one is forcing you now. Will you do the right thing?"

Tanner watched the exchange feeling a bit like a voyeur, but Lily's impassioned plea to her father was riveting. She'd barely spent any time with Lily, and she hated to admit that she'd always assumed Lily was more fluffy socialite than steel magnolia. She should have known Peyton would not be with a woman who didn't have a strong sense of justice and the fortitude to back it up.

Tanner's mind flashed to Syd, another woman she'd underestimated. When their relationship ended, she'd been convinced Syd was the weaker one, chasing money and success over the things that really mattered, but she, not Syd, was the one who'd walked away from love. And for what? She'd had a decorated career but no one to share it with. The time she'd spent in bed with Syd this afternoon was the closest thing to true intimacy she'd experienced since they'd parted ways ten years ago. Was she going to spend the rest of her life waiting for another great love to stumble into her life?

"I'll do it," Cyrus said.

Tanner snapped out of her reverie. Lily was smiling, and Cyrus wore a resigned expression but appeared at peace. "You'll help us?"

"Yes, if you'll help me." Cyrus squeezed Lily's hand. "I've made a lot of mistakes in my life, but I hope it's not too late to make it up to the ones I love."

Tanner couldn't agree more.

CHAPTER EIGHTEEN

Syd pulled up at Peyton's house hoping someone was home since she hadn't bothered calling first. Sitting in the hotel room where she and Tanner had spent the afternoon making love had been too much to bear alone, and she needed a distraction. She'd called Bianca, who'd promised to look into the bond issue, but she was with her daughter and couldn't get away. Syd parked the rental and walked up the steps to Peyton's house where she found Peyton sprawled in the front porch swing. "Hey, mind if I join you?"

Peyton scooted over, and Syd settled in, enjoying the gentle sway of the swing. "I thought you might appreciate some company. Have you heard anything?"

"Not yet," Peyton said.

"I bet it was hard not to go with her."

"Nearly impossible. As much of an ass as Cyrus has been, I don't want Lily to have to see him behind bars."

Syd rubbed Peyton's shoulder. "Tanner will take good care of her."

"She seems like good people."

"She is." Syd wanted to say more. She wanted to tell Peyton that Tanner was a rock and she'd never felt more loved and protected than when she and Tanner had been together, but it struck her as odd to say those things to Peyton when she hadn't been able or willing to tell Tanner how she felt.

"You're still in love with her."

Peyton's words were like a bucket of ice. "That's crazy."

"It might be crazy, but it's also true," Peyton said. "You look for her every time you enter a room. She does the same thing. And the thin layer of discord you both have going barely covers some pretty palpable surges of electricity."

Syd's jaw dropped at Peyton's astute observations. She did look for Tanner every time she walked into a room, and only felt truly settled when Tanner was within reach. In all the years they'd spent apart, no one had ever made her feel the level of passion Tanner did, whether the source was aggravation or arousal. She'd almost forgotten how to feel anything, but now she knew the life she'd been living was no life at all. She'd been going through the motions, waiting for something, someone to wake her soul, and Tanner had done exactly that. She could deny it or she could own her feelings, and now was as good a time as any. "I never stopped loving her."

"You should tell her. Life has a way of trying to rob us of the ones we love."

Syd nodded, but before she could process the suggestion, her cell phone rang. She dug frantically in her purse, certain it was Tanner calling and not caring if Peyton thought she was a mess for jumping on the call. A glance at the screen told her it wasn't Tanner, but someone she'd been hoping to hear from. "Hey, Flores, tell me you have some good news." Syd had worked on a couple of cases with Special Agent Sarah Flores when Sarah had been assigned to the BAU, back in DC. Sarah had transferred to the Dallas field office a few years ago to work in their white-collar crime division, but she and Syd had kept in touch with the occasional email. When she'd reached out to Sarah about using the BAU database, Sarah had been eager to help.

"I'm still running those numbers you sent," Sarah said. "I do think they're account numbers, but without a routing number it may take a while to make anything of them, but I did find some info on that other stuff you sent."

"Sarah, do you mind if I put you on speaker? I've got AUSA

Peyton Davis here with me. She's one of the good ones." Syd punched the speaker button and propped the phone up between her and Peyton. "Okay, go."

"I ran searches on all the cases involving known Barrio Azteca members and narrowed the parameters to only those handled in the Northern District in the past three years. There were over a hundred defendants, some of them indicted together in the same case."

"Anything stand out?" Peyton asked.

"Funny you should ask. This can't be right, but it appears that US Attorney Herschel Gellar handled the plea in most of these."

Syd and Peyton exchanged surprised looks. "It probably just looks that way on paper," Syd said. "Because the pleadings would have his name stamped on them. Trust me, this guy wouldn't handle anything that wasn't high profile."

"Then the majority of these cases were high profile because his name is all over them, and not just on the pleadings. He's showing up at hearings, on the record, in court." The sound of paper rustling came through the phone. "Looks like the last case was about two months ago."

"Right before I started at the office," Peyton said. "Sarah, I don't suppose you have a list of outcomes, do you?"

"Matter of fact, I do. You want the details or just a summary?"

"Summary is good."

More rustling. "I'd say roughly ninety percent of these cases pled out on the low end of the range, and more than half of those below the statutory minimum."

Syd practically bounced in her seat. "Any idea how many of those cases had 5K1 motions filed?" she asked, referring to requests prosecutors filed with the court to ask for special consideration for cooperating defendants.

"I don't have exact numbers, but it's a lot."

Syd picked up the phone. "Can you hang on for a second?" She barely waited for an answer before putting the phone on mute and turning to Peyton. "Sounds like certain gang members are getting special treatment from the big boss. This might be the hook we need."

"Maybe," Peyton said. "But no one's going to issue a search warrant for Gellar's house based on just this. Besides, we don't know if there was special treatment. All we have is proof a sitting US attorney took a special interest in the drug cases that affected his community. That's how he'll spin it anyway. For all we know, he showed up in court in cases involving defendants from all the other gangs in the drug trade, and they got good deals too."

"Let's find out." Syd switched the sound back on. "Hey, Sarah, how long would it take you to run a comparison of the outcomes in these cases versus similar cases where the defendants are members of other gangs, like the Zetas, for instance."

"I had a feeling you might want that, so I already searched the data."

"And?" Syd clutched the phone in anticipation.

"Outcomes aren't even close. The district's convictions have most drug offenders going away for mid-range to maximum time, unless they are Barrio Azteca. And the big guy doesn't seem to take a special interest in those other cases."

After Sarah promised to send Syd an encrypted file with the data to her personal email address, Syd clicked off the line and stared at Peyton. "This is big."

"It's huge," Peyton agreed. "But I'm not sure what to do with it yet."

"Time for a meeting?"

"Absolutely. As soon as we hear from Tanner and you get that email from Flores, let's set something up."

Syd rocked back and forth with Peyton in the swing waiting for her email notifications to ping and wishing Tanner were sitting next to her. She couldn't wait to tell Tanner what they'd found out, but mostly she couldn't wait to see her.

❖

Tanner sped down the highway with Lily in the seat beside her. She'd offered to drive Lily back to the ranch to save her from having to spend time listening to Nester Rawlins pontificate on how the charges against Cyrus were trumped up and he was going to prove it in a court of law. Cyrus had made the right decision. A jury would hate Rawlins the minute he opened his mouth, and Cyrus by association.

She took the turnoff to Peyton's ranch and looked over at Lily who was slumped against the passenger side window as she'd been since they got in the car. "Are you okay?"

"Okay is about all I can manage," Lily said with a half-smile. "This is supposed to be the happiest time of my life. I found out my mother is alive, I have a sister, and I'm about to get married to an amazing woman."

"I hear a 'but.' Let me guess. You always imagined your father being at your wedding, dancing with him, maybe even having him walk you down the aisle, but never in your wildest dreams did you think he'd be in custody, having to make a choice between his personal safety and spending the rest of his life in prison."

"That about sums it up." Lily straightened in her seat. "Sorry. My problems are minor in comparison to the people who've suffered at the hands of these horrible monsters."

"For the record, I don't count your father among the monsters," Tanner said. "What he did was wrong, but he acted out of fear for your safety, and it's not for me to judge whether he had a better choice."

Lily reached over and squeezed her shoulder. "Thank you."

Tanner pulled into the drive in front of the ranch house and immediately spotted Syd's rental. She froze for a second as a litany of things that could have possibly gone wrong to bring Syd out to the ranch this late ran through her mind.

"Tanner?" Lily was looking at her with her brow furrowed. "Guess it's my turn to ask if everything's okay."

"Sorry." She parked the car and took a deep, calming breath.

There had to be a reasonable explanation for Syd's late-night visit. She pointed at the rental. "Wasn't expecting Syd to be here."

Lily smiled. "It's hard to tell from your tone if that's a good thing or a bad thing." She unbuckled her seat belt. "Would you like to come in?"

"It's late."

"Come in. I think you really want to."

She did and not just out of concern about Syd. She'd had to use incredible powers of concentration to focus on everything that happened at Seagoville tonight because every cell in her body wanted to be back at the hotel room with Syd, watching her in the shower, joining her in the shower, spending the entire night making love with her. She was only steps away from seeing her now, but she was full of trepidation. Why? Could she only handle being with Syd when there was no need for conversation, when sex was the only thing on their minds?

There was only one way to find out. Tanner followed Lily into the house, where they found Peyton and Syd in the kitchen raiding the refrigerator. Syd looked up from the open door with a sheepish grin on her face, and Tanner started to say something about her insatiable hunger, but she bit back the words as too revealing, too private. Instead she strode over to the fridge and stood beside her to peer inside. "Can I be invited to this smorgasbord?"

Syd stuffed a piece of ham in her mouth. "Maybe. There might be a little left after I'm done making all the sandwiches I can eat out of this incredible ham. Who has ham like this sitting in their refrigerator on a regular weekend?"

Tanner hitched her shoulders. "It's not even close to Easter."

"I know, right?" Syd mumbled with her mouth full and then pointed behind Tanner. Peyton and Lily stared at them like they were freaks of nature. "What?"

"You two should take this routine on the road," Peyton said. "And don't eat all the ham. Everyone else is on the way."

Tanner raised her eyebrows. "Define everyone."

"Mary, Dale, Lindsey, Bianca, Jade."

"I'm guessing you've been working tonight."

"Yep. Well, Syd has, and she found some information that might blow this case wide open."

"I did." Syd nodded. "Or my pal from BAU did. I'll tell you everything as soon as the rest of the gang gets here."

"Fine, then I guess I'll wait to share what we have to say until then too," Tanner said. "Unless Lily wants to share. It was all her doing."

"Thanks, Tanner," Lily said, "But it was truly a team effort. Cyrus is going to cooperate. Tanner arranged to have him moved out of Seagoville tonight before he's fully booked in. Doesn't make him perfectly safe, but it should buy you some time. She's going to talk to Judge Casey personally first thing in the morning to see if she can get him in protective custody."

"That's fantastic news," Peyton said. "I knew you were the right person to call."

Tanner accepted the praise, feeling a twinge of guilt that she'd almost blown Peyton off in favor of sex with Syd. When she saw the proud look on Syd's face, she knew she'd done the right thing. They worked together to pile a platter high with ham sandwiches, and then set out chips and pickles, plates and napkins. No sooner was the table set than the rest of the group poured into the house ready to work.

Between large bites of her sandwich, Syd relayed the information she'd obtained from Sarah Flores. Everyone shook their heads in disbelief, but they universally agreed Gellar's special treatment of the Barrio Azteca cases showed a clear bias. "It's not enough to get a warrant, but let's see if we can figure out a way to leverage this information to find out more."

"No luck on the numbers you found in Carlos's hotel room?" Dale asked.

"Not yet. Sarah's still working on that."

Peyton pulled out a large poster board and a marker. "Let's do this the old-fashioned way, by listing all the people of interest and loose ends, and then we can figure out how to tie them up. Start calling things out."

"Sergio," Jade said. "He's still on the loose." Peyton wrote his name and drew a box around it. Across the page she did the same with Carlos Aguilar. "What else?"

A few minutes later, they had a flow chart of sorts with various names in boxes and solid or dotted lines between the boxes to indicate relationships. In the center of the board was Herschel Gellar. She stabbed at the name with her marker. "Our job is to smoke out how all of the rest of these folks relate to him and why."

"And catch Sergio," Dale chimed in. "And get the goods on Carlos Aguilar while we're at it."

Tanner sat back in her chair and stared at the board. What had at first seemed like a random jumble of loosely related concepts started to form a pattern, and her brain rearranged the boxes into a perfectly logical sequence. She was deep in thought when Syd leaned over and playfully punched her in the side. "You falling asleep?"

"Not hardly." Tanner raised her voice. "Bear with me, y'all. This is going to sound crazy, but promise you'll hear me out to the end. I have a plan."

CHAPTER NINETEEN

Syd rolled onto her side, slipped her arm around Tanner's waist, and snuggled close into big spoon position. "Are you awake?"

"Hmm, almost."

Syd shifted slightly to check the clock. Six a.m. She should let Tanner sleep, but she'd barely slept the entire night even after another incredible bout of sex. Her thoughts and fears were starting to get the best of her. After leaving Peyton's house, they'd spent the night at Tanner's, where Syd had made Tanner detail her entire plan again without the rest of the team shouting out their ideas. No matter how many times she heard it, it sounded like folly, but she'd been the lone holdout of the group.

She'd give Tanner thirty more minutes of sleep before she started bugging her, and she'd count Tanner's heartbeats to pass the time.

"Are you listening to me breathe?" Tanner turned in her arms and smiled at her with groggy eyes.

"Close. I was measuring your pulse. You're in pretty good shape for your age."

"For my age?" Tanner leaned up on her shoulder and started tickling her ribs. "Take it back."

"Don't!" Syd arched away, laughing. "I hate being tickled."

"Is that so?" Tanner stopped suddenly and assumed a solemn expression. "I'm sorry." She acted like she was sitting back against the bed, but like lightning, she reached for Syd and started tickling her again. "Not sorry!"

For the next few moments, they rolled around on the bed like kids without a care in the world, laughing hysterically. When the laughter finally subsided and they both lay panting in the sheets, Syd wondered if they'd ever felt like this before. When they were in school, she'd been worried all the time—about grades, class rank, and job prospects. She'd had fun with Tanner, but there had always been an undercurrent of seriousness. She'd been a woman on a mission, and love had never been the primary objective.

"What're you thinking?" Tanner asked.

Too many things at once. Syd reached over and grabbed Tanner's hand. "I'm sorry."

Tanner turned her head and smiled. "I'm pretty sure I tickled you first."

"You did, but that's not what I was talking about." Syd paused to gather courage. "I'm sorry I spent our entire relationship trying to lay a foundation for the future at the expense of building something lasting between us. Maybe if I'd been honest, we could've gotten past our differences and found some common ground."

"It wasn't just you. I wasn't clear about what I really wanted and I let you believe we wanted the same things."

Syd pulled Tanner into a hug and held her tight. It was a relief to finally have some closure. But if this was closure, then why was she so reluctant to let go? Tanner's what-if echoed in her mind, but it didn't matter. They hadn't gotten past their differences then, and now years had passed, widening the distance between them.

Or had it? She looked down at their naked bodies, loosely covered with a thin sheet. Maybe what they were sharing now wasn't closure, but a chance at a new beginning.

"Besides, that's all in the past." Tanner patted her leg. "If this plan works out, you'll be going back to DC soon, but I'd like to stay in touch, if that's okay with you." Tanner's brow scrunched up like she wasn't quite sure what she wanted to say next. "We can be friends, right?"

Friends. That didn't bode well for a new beginning, but if that's all Tanner had to offer, Syd wasn't about to say no. Friends who had occasional, incredible sex was better than nothing. She stuck out her hand. "Friends for sure." Suddenly feeling vulnerable, she pulled the sheet up over her breasts. "Okay, friend, explain this plan of yours in full detail one more time."

Tanner's eyes brightened and she sat up in bed with her legs crossed. "The goal is to create a perfect storm with Gellar as the eye."

"That sounds way more poetic than it should. Details, please. Everyone was talking over each other last night."

"Our aim is to take down Aguilar, Gellar, and as a special bonus, flush out Sergio Vargas. The plan rests on the assumption that somehow Aguilar has bribed, cajoled, or blackmailed Gellar into helping him and his Barrio Azteca pals take over the drug trade in this area."

"Big assumption, but let's go with it."

"We will put three things into motion. First, we start a rumor that Jade is stepping in to take over her uncle's business."

"You kind of lost me on that one. Isn't that what her uncles wanted?"

"Not exactly. They wanted her to do their bidding, but we're going to make them and everyone else think that she's going to run the empire and push them out. After all, Arturo is in custody and Sergio is on the run. Jade has decided they are ineffectual and it's the perfect opportunity for her to jump in and take over the reins."

"And this is supposed to flush Sergio out of hiding?"

"Oh, it will. He won't be able to contain his anger at the idea of being betrayed, and he'll want to put her in her place."

"And how is he going to find out about her takeover bid if he's on the run?"

"We know for a fact that Arturo has been communicating with him through channels. Lindsey is going to pay him a visit under the guise of producing a report for her show, and ask him to comment about Jade taking over the family business, but we also need Gellar to find out about this, and that's where you come in to help with the second part of the plan."

"I told you last night I'm not sure I want to do this."

"It's one lie for the greater good."

Syd groaned. "You want me to tell Gellar that I've suspended Bianca from any involvement in the case because her girlfriend is taking over her family's drug business, and I'm supposed to say that with a straight face?"

"You won't have to try very hard. He already thinks most of the task force is up to no good."

"Fine. But I'm not clear on how this all culminates into a bonanza of arrests."

"If Aguilar is focused on moving in on the Vargases' territory, he's probably pretty confident right now because his buddy Gellar has got Arturo and Sergio and their money laundering man on the ropes. The third thing is to secure Cyrus's release. He was moved last night. Before you fake suspend Bianca, she and I are going to see Judge Casey this morning to talk to him about the motion to revoke and get him to let Cyrus back out on bond pending trial."

"Assuming you're able to get him released, how does that help?"

"When Aguilar finds out Cyrus is back out on bond, he's going to question Gellar's loyalty. Couple that with the information that one of Gellar's subordinates is in bed with the new local head of the Zetas Cartel, and he's going to have to act, and that's when we get Jade to request a meeting with him to discuss their mutual interests. He'll know Jade is way more like him than her uncles are. Both of them went to fancy business schools and know the value of having a legitimate cover for their more nefarious enterprises. Jade will send him a message inviting him to the ranch for a meeting. Lindsey will make sure Arturo knows about the meeting. She'll tell Arturo she heard about it from a source, and I bet he doesn't waste any time getting word to Sergio. If Sergio shows up at the ranch, then we'll have them all in one place."

"And then what? Do you really think they're all going to sit down and confess? And what's Jade supposed to do while all this is going on?"

Tanner shifted on the bed. "It's not a perfect plan, but that's kind of hard to come by. Even if we only manage to arrest Sergio as a result, it will be a success, but if Aguilar and/or Gellar show up, that very act implicates them. How else are they going to explain their presence except they were invited to talk business with a self-proclaimed drug lord? Or is it drug lady?"

"Don't joke. Jade could get hurt. For all you know this storm you're creating could devolve into a shoot-out."

"It's not the O.K. Corral. None of these people have any interest in leaving a trail of bodies over what is simply a conversation. Besides…"

Syd's ears perked at the wary tone. "What?"

"Last night when we were leaving and you were talking to Lily about her wedding plans, Dale and Peyton and I decided that I should pose as Jade for the meeting at the ranch. We're about the same height, and our hair color is close. If someone is keeping an eye on the place, from a distance, they won't be able to tell I'm not Jade."

Syd's heart pounded. "Until they actually see you face-to-face. Fuck, Tanner, it's a meeting. They're going to know you're not Jade the minute you come out with your hand outstretched, and then what? And if Sergio shows up, he's going to be expecting to see his niece. You think these people are going to handle being double-crossed?"

"We've got a plan. Dale and Mary will be at the ranch and they're getting some other agents, people Gellar doesn't know, to pose as Jade's inner circle. They'll handle the preliminaries, and I'll only have to show my face if necessary."

"Don't do this." Syd shook her head. "You haven't thought this through. We need a plan. A real plan takes time to get the pieces in place. This is too thrown together. It's never going to work." She reached for her phone on the nightstand. "I'm going to talk to Peyton and call this off. We'll meet again and work out something better."

Tanner gently put her hand on the phone. "Syd, listen to me. This is my specialty, and I've been doing this a while. There are times when all the pieces are in play and you have to strike right away or lose the opportunity. Any minute now, Aguilar could discover that card you found is missing. Gellar could find out Cyrus has been transferred, suspect something's up, and press the grand jury for an indictment. Sergio Vargas could disappear. We have to act now or risk everything we've worked for being undone."

"But why do you have to be at risk?"

"It's my job. This is what I do. You have to trust that I know how to do it well."

Syd knew she was right, but that knowledge didn't change her overwhelming sense of dread at the prospect of Tanner in the eye of this so-called perfect storm—way more concern than a friend would feel, but she shoved that thought aside. She had to put some serious distance between her feelings for Tanner and her focus on the case if she was going to get through this.

❖

Just after noon the next day, Tanner held the door from Judge Casey's chambers open for Bianca and followed her into the hall. "That went well," she whispered.

"Easy for you to say," Bianca whispered back. "You're not the one about to be suspended."

Tanner held back a grin. She and Bianca had just put the first piece of their plan in place. Judge Casey had listened to their spiel about how yes, the US attorney's office had filed the motion to revoke Cyrus's bond, but they'd had a change of heart and Cyrus was going to be a key witness and they needed him out of jail to fully utilize his contacts. Tanner had known Judge Casey for a long time and considered him a man of unimpeachable integrity that she could trust to be discreet. He wouldn't tell anyone about their conversation, not even Gellar, mostly because he would assume Gellar knew and he didn't much care for the sitting US attorney.

They had to move fast now because once Gellar found out Cyrus's attorney hadn't requested a hearing on the bond, he would suspect something was up. "You better get back to the office. Syd's with Gellar now, and she's going to be looking for you after."

"When's Lindsey going to Seagoville?"

"She's probably on her way there now."

"And you've got the meeting set up for tonight?"

Tanner nodded. "Dale and Mary are already at the ranch. Later this afternoon, I'll be at your mom's. You and Jade will come by, and I'll take Jade's car and drive out to the ranch."

"You know, we don't usually drive to my mom's. She's literally a block away."

"Be creative. Load some boxes, a piece of furniture. Anything that would make it look like you had to drive instead of walk."

"Got it. Anything else?"

"Yes, a couple of hours before we meet, text me a picture of what Jade's wearing. Tell her to stick to something simple—ranch-type clothes would be best and solid colors to make it easier for me to duplicate the look. Pretty sure I won't look as good as she does, but I'll do my best."

Bianca punched her in the shoulder. "You sell yourself short, pal. You're a catch, and I'm pretty sure I'm not the only one who thinks so."

"What's that supposed to mean?"

"I've seen the way Syd looks at you, and Dale and Mary

filled me in on your past. Such a romantic story. Two lovers reunited as they join forces to take down a criminal empire."

"Anyone ever tell you that you have a flair for the dramatic?"

"Anyone ever tell you that you're good at trying to change the subject? Key word trying. I'm a woman in love, and when you're in love, everything is rosy and full of possibility. You should try it sometime."

Tanner sighed. When Bianca got in one of her "fully focused on one thing" moods, it was easiest just to play along. Besides, she didn't want to be the one to tell Bianca that love wasn't all it was cracked up to be once you got past the initial fluff. Bianca and Jade were in for a lot of sacrifice and pain, if they even survived past the initial blush of new love.

"Hey," Bianca said, waving her hand in front of Tanner's eyes. "You zoning out on me?"

Tanner's mind snapped back into focus. "Just running through the details in my head. Are you ready for your meeting with Syd?"

"As ready as I'll ever be. I've never been part of a super-secret sting before. Should I be scared?"

Syd's voice played in Tanner's head, reminding her how many moving pieces there were to this plan and how it could all go wrong. "It's all good. Don't try and win an Academy Award or anything."

"Roger that." Bianca started to walk away but paused and turned back. "Hey, be careful, okay?"

"Always." Tanner watched her go and wondered how she was going to kill the next few hours before it was time for her role in the sting to begin. She was a quick elevator ride from the US attorney's office where Syd was right now, but dropping by to see her would probably mess with Syd's head, not to mention her own. Despite what she'd told Syd this morning, there were risks, and all the training in the world couldn't prepare her for what might happen if things got out of hand.

She wasn't normally skittish before a big operation, but she hadn't been able to shake a nervous edge today. She was probably just internalizing Syd's concern. Better to spend the next few hours alone so she could tune out any distractions. She walked to the elevator and rode down to the lobby, away from Syd and whatever was brewing between them.

CHAPTER TWENTY

Gellar sat forward in his chair. "You want to suspend Bianca Cruz?"

"Yes," Syd said, noting his barely perceptible surprise. "Effective immediately. I've uncovered information that her girlfriend, Jade Vargas, has plans to take over her uncles' drug business. I don't know yet if Bianca is involved, but this puts her in direct conflict with the work of your office."

He slapped his hand on the desk and his smile was gloating. "I knew it. The task force is tainted, and I've been saying it for some time now."

Syd feigned nonchalance, not wanting to feed into his response with a reaction of her own. "I'm still looking into the rest of the team members. I should have a full report to you soon."

"Excellent," Gellar said. "I have no doubt you'll find plenty of issues." He shifted slightly in his seat. "How do you think Jade Vargas will react at the news her girlfriend no longer has the inside track?"

"I have no idea," Syd replied, trying to gauge if nerves drove him to ask the question.

"I guess it doesn't matter." He placed his hand on the desk phone. "Was there anything else?"

"No, that's it for now." Syd stood, choosing not to react to the blatant dismissal, and left the room. Frankly, she'd expected him to be a bit more worried than he appeared to be about the news that the Vargas empire would have a new leader. Was it possible Tanner's theory was completely off base? Or maybe he was a better actor than they'd given him credit for, and he was calling Aguilar now to give him the news. Either way, Syd hoped Tanner's plan didn't backfire.

Later that evening, Syd stood at the back door of Bianca's mother's house and knocked a second time, hoping she was at the right place since it was hard to tell from the alley. She'd about decided to give up when the blinds popped open and a woman the spitting image of Bianca, or how Bianca would look twenty years from now, was staring back at her. As quickly as they opened, the blinds shut again and Syd heard an exaggerated whisper before the blinds opened again and Bianca grinned at her and the door swung open.

"Come in quick," Bianca said. She peered out the door. "This is a nice surprise. Did anyone see you?"

Syd ignored the surprise comment. "I was careful. I did exactly what Tanner had planned. I took an Uber and had them drop me off on the street behind and came in through the alley."

"She left already."

Syd forced a smile but decided not to feign ignorance. "I figured she'd be gone."

"But you kinda hoped she'd be here."

Did she? If something happened to Tanner tonight, would she rather have the memory of being naked in bed with her or would she prefer saying her good-byes in front of other people, knowing her words weren't enough to keep Tanner from going off and doing something crazy? The echoes of the past were impossible to deny. She didn't have any sway over Tanner's thoughts and desires, and as much as she understood the call to duty, she hated that Tanner would choose it over her every single time.

Overcome with embarrassment that she'd shown up here chasing a fantasy, Syd mumbled that she was only checking in and should go now. She turned to leave, but Bianca reached out and gently tugged on her arm.

"Stay. You should be with friends. We'll keep each other sane."

Syd wasn't sure that was possible, but if she went back to the hotel to wait, she'd be bombarded with memories of Tanner, and sanity would be hard fought.

"We're having homemade tamales for dinner."

"You probably should've led with that. I love tamales." Syd didn't think she'd be able to eat anything, but pushing food around a plate with these people, her people, was better than worrying alone.

She followed Bianca into the kitchen where Jade was on the phone and the Bianca look-alike was pulling plates from the cabinet. Bianca introduced her to her mother, Lourdes Cruz, who examined Syd from head to toe and quickly pronounced her in need of a good meal. Syd offered to help and was put to work putting ice in glasses and pouring tea. While she handled the simple task, she eavesdropped on Jade's conversation and determined she was talking to Lily.

"Do you know where he is now?" Jade asked. Long pause. "I'm sure he's safe. Do you want me to ask Syd? She just showed up." Jade placed a hand over the phone and turned to Syd. "It's Lily. She's worried about Cyrus. Do you have any information about where he's been moved?"

"No, but it's best that way. The marshals are trained to keep him safe, and if none of us knows where he is, nothing can make us divulge the information. We'll see what goes down tonight and then make a decision about whether it's safe for him to come out of hiding."

What she didn't say was that Tanner told her this morning the marshals had offered her the information, but she had declined. Tanner didn't say why, but Syd figured it was because whatever did go down tonight, Tanner didn't want to be in the position of having to choose between her own safety and Peyton's soon-to-be father-in-law if it came down to a choice. She shuddered to think about any situation that would leave Tanner in desperate straits. "I don't know about you, but I could use a distraction. Mrs. Cruz, those tamales smell amazing. I hear they are a ton of trouble to prepare. Do you make them often?"

"It's an intense process, but everything good is worth doing, yes?" Lourdes rubbed her hands on her apron. "When you girls are not in the middle of a big case, you can come back and I'll teach you how it's done."

"Mama, we're not girls," Bianca said. "We're women."

Lourdes raised her hands in the air. "Women who talk back to their mamas. That's a fine thing." She patted Syd on the arm. "She usually has much better manners. Now, go set the table for four. It's just us girls tonight."

"That's too bad, I was hoping to meet Bianca's daughter."

"Papa took Emma to her favorite pizza place and then they are going to the library for a reading. I didn't want her to be here in case, you know."

Syd did know, but instead of being upset about being reminded of the trouble Tanner was walking into, she was coming around to the idea that being around other people was the best way to handle her discomfort. She stole a look at her watch. Tanner would probably be at the ranch by now, setting up to wait for Aguilar to arrive. Would Sergio show up? Would Gellar? Too many what-ifs when all she wanted was a solid answer. It had almost been easier when Tanner left her to join the FBI. She'd had a fuzzy notion then that Tanner might face danger, but there was nothing tangible to worry about. But now, after having worked for the Justice Department, she was acutely conscious of the specific dangers that could be inflicted by the criminal element. *Please don't let this morning be the last time I see her.*

They were almost finished with their tamale dinner when Bianca announced, "She's there."

"What?"

Bianca shoved her phone at Syd. "Text from Dale."

Syd read the brief line: *She's here.* "Dale's not big on sharing a lot of detail, is she?"

"She's definitely not the touchy-feely type, but aside from Tanner, there's no one I'd rather have watching my back than Dale or Mary."

"I wish we could have set up a way to listen in."

"Dale said there wasn't enough time to set something up. She said if she could work out an open phone line, she'd make it happen, but it's not worth the risk if it would compromise the operation."

Bianca's mother stood up and started clearing plates, stopping to hug her daughter from behind and kiss the top of her head. "Would you listen to *mija*, talking about such things? She does such important work."

Syd smiled at the sweet display of affection, and then a thought occurred to her. "Jade, where is your mother tonight?"

"She's staying at Peyton's with Lily. It's a good cover since she's been over there a lot helping plan the wedding."

Syd started to ask about the wedding plans as a way to distract them all from what was happening at Jade's ranch, but a loud ringing pierced the air, causing her to nearly jump out of her seat. She looked around the table, but everyone was staring back at her, and she quickly realized it was her phone. "Sorry," she said. The display said only Unknown Caller. She pressed the answer button and braced for whatever was on the other end. "Hello?"

"Syd, is that you? It's Sarah."

Syd smiled at the sound of the familiar voice. "Hey you. Did you find something?"

"Yes, but you're not going to believe me when I tell you."

"Spill."

"I did some cross-checking on those numbers and finally got a hit on a bank in St. Kitts. The numbers correspond to a set of accounts opened approximately two years ago. I've got a contact down there, and he's sending me the full details, but these accounts are flush with cash and have been extremely active. They're all registered to the same person."

Syd gripped the phone. "It's Aguilar, isn't it? Can you trace any of the transactions back to Herschel Gellar?"

"I've traced quite a few and I'm working on others, but, Syd, I'm not seeing Herschel Gellar's name or any of his accounts from that list you gave me on any of this."

Syd sank into her chair, dismayed to learn her theory about the Aguilar-Gellar connection wasn't panning out and wondering what that meant for the meeting at the ranch tonight. She needed to get word to Tanner so she could determine how she wanted to play this new piece of information. "Thanks for checking into this for us. I've got to make a call to someone. Maybe we can catch up before I head back to DC?"

"Hang on a minute. Don't you want to know who Aguilar was wiring money to?"

An urgent undertone in Sarah's voice set Syd on high alert. She'd assumed that because whatever Sarah found didn't support her theory, it didn't affect the work of this particular task force, but maybe she was wrong. "Who?"

Sarah spoke a name, and a rush of white noise flooded Syd's ears, blocking out the rest of what Sarah had to say. Syd grabbed the edge of the table and held on while her mind whirred through every piece of evidence she'd reviewed, every conversation she'd had since she arrived in Dallas, but she kept cycling back to the same conclusion. Sarah's revelation came out of nowhere.

Tanner found Dale and Mary waiting for her in Jade's ranch house. Tanner had been here several times before and she liked the place. If she ever had a spread, she'd want it to be like this—a unique combination of rustic ambience and modern conveniences.

"How many other agents are here?" Tanner asked.

"Two more in the house, two at the stables, and a few others spread around the property. They're all dressed like ranch hands, and Jade's regular employees are gone for the day. If anyone is watching the place, they're going to expect that Jade beefed up staff to help her with her takeover of her uncle's business."

"Aguilar's going to know it's me the minute he walks in that door."

"Sure he will, but he doesn't know us. A good captain lets her lieutenants vet the visitors. Besides, you're just the bait to get them here. We'll talk to him first and see if we can get him to make some admissions in the interest of developing a business relationship with you."

"What's the matter, you think an FBI agent can't handle a sting?"

Dale grinned. "Well, we know you kids can handle simple jobs, but you should leave the big cases to the drug and gun folks."

"As if. Okay, where do you want me?"

"Jade's room is upstairs and it's got a great view of the road in. Go up there, and whoever sees Aguilar approaching first will text the other. We'll talk to him and see what we can get before he pushes to meet with Jade personally."

"And if he won't talk to you at all?"

"We're going to have to improvise."

Tanner nodded. She'd expected as much and was ready. Worst-case, she'd have to tell Aguilar she was the reason Gellar was suspicious of the task force, that she was working for Jade, and while he'd come here to meet the boss, he'd have to settle for second in charge. She couldn't imagine he would believe her, but it might be enough to get him to say something incriminating about Gellar. Or it could get her killed.

"Hey, if things go sideways tonight—"

"Shut up," Dale said, holding her palm up. "Don't even go there."

"Yeah, okay." Tanner nodded at Mary, who gave her a sympathetic look, and then she climbed the stairs to Jade's room.

The room was clean and simple, with hardly any personal items in view except a single framed photo on the nightstand of

Jade, Bianca, and Emma standing in front of the stables. Emma was grinning wide between the women, who were looking at each other instead of the camera. Tanner wondered if Jade and Lily's mother, Sophia, had taken the picture and how she'd managed to capture such happiness, love, and joy in one click. Tanner ran a finger around the frame, tracing the captured moment. Once upon a time, she'd wished for a wife and a life full of love and family. Spending time with Sydney had stirred those longings, and she wondered if the feelings would subside when this case was over and Syd returned to her home. They had to.

She heard the SUV before she saw it, its tires crunching on the gravel drive as it slowly approached the ranch house. It was dusk out and the headlights shimmered in the haze of the setting sun. Her phone buzzed and she looked down to see a text from Dale. *Ready?*

She stared at the display for a moment, hesitating— something she'd never done before when it came to the job. Risks were part of the package, and she'd never shied away from them for any reason. More so, she'd always embraced risk as a way to show her allegiance to duty, but the images of Syd in her arms flashed in front of everything else she'd ever considered important. For the first time in her life, she realized there were some things, some people, that a person shouldn't risk losing for any reason.

Her thumbs hovered over the keyboard on her phone. She was ready. Ready for this operation to be over so she could find Syd and tell her she loved her, that she'd never stopped loving her. That she'd been wrong to walk away and she wanted to spend the rest of her life making it up to her. Tanner typed the single word, and turned the vibration off on her phone. She stepped back to the window and took one last look, squaring her shoulders for whatever was about to happen, certain she could handle whatever risk this night might bring. But when the door to the SUV opened and Amanda Gellar stepped out, Tanner knew none of them were ready for this.

CHAPTER TWENTY-ONE

Tanner stood at the top of the stairs and listened as Amanda Gellar calmly explained to Dale and Mary that she was here to see Jade and had no interest in explaining her business to a couple of Jade's lackeys. Tanner's relief that Amanda appeared not to know who Dale and Mary really were turned to dread. Amanda for sure knew who she was, and there was little to no chance she could sell Gellar's wife on the story she'd planned for Aguilar.

The bigger question was why in the hell had Amanda Gellar shown up for a meeting with the new head of the Zetas Cartel?

Two large men escorted Amanda from the SUV to the house. Tanner stepped back to the window, but from this vantage point, she couldn't see if they were waiting outside or if there was anyone still in the SUV. Tanner pulled out her phone to text the team covering the stables. Maybe they could see if Amanda had more personnel waiting in the car, but a text from Syd popped up and stole her attention. *Bank accounts are in St. Kitts. They belong to Amanda Gellar. She was getting money from Aguilar through back channels. Be careful.*

What the fuck? Tanner sent a quick text to the team outside and shoved her phone into her pocket. If Syd already had proof Amanda Gellar had sketchy dealings with Aguilar, Tanner didn't see any point in putting off the inevitable. She descended the stairs, prepared to leverage this information into the full story.

Amanda almost hid her reaction when she walked into the

room, but Tanner caught a hint of surprise in her eyes. "Special Agent Cohen, how nice to see you."

Tanner's eyes swept the room. One very large and frighteningly ugly man stood hulking behind Amanda, who was seated at the kitchen table. Dale sat across from her with Mary standing behind. Judging by the bulge near this guy's heart, he was armed with some serious firepower. Amanda was dressed in a sleek black cocktail dress, like she was headed to a gala instead of a business meeting. After assessing the room, Tanner turned her attention back to Amanda. "Call me Tanner. I mean, what's the point of being formal when I already know so much about you?"

"Tanner it is," Amanda said without missing a beat. "Please join us."

Tanner didn't want to sit down, but she needed to make Amanda feel completely at ease if she was going to get her to talk. She thought back to the conversation she'd had with Amanda during the holiday party when Amanda had spoken so disparagingly about her husband, and it gave her an idea. She motioned to Dale who, like a pro, didn't ask questions, but merely gave up her seat. Once she was sitting across from Amanda, Tanner said, "I'm glad you could make it."

"Confess, Tanner, that you are surprised to see me."

Tanner smiled and steepled her fingers. "I've been doing this for a while. Nothing surprises me."

Amanda arched her eyebrows. "Nothing?"

"Would you like an example?" Tanner waited a beat, and when Amanda didn't respond, she pressed on. "There was a time when I thought everyone involved in law enforcement, from prosecutors to police, was above reproach. Granted, I was young and fresh out of the academy."

"While it would be a treat, I'm sure, to hear the tales of your youth," Amanda said, "I can think of other, more pressing matters."

"I have no doubt. Bear with me, I'm getting to the point."

Tanner cleared her throat and wished there was some way she could alert Dale and Mary about what Syd had told her. "Back in the day, the idea that a sitting US attorney would frame an innocent man for the death of a federal prosecutor to appease his business partner, a drug lord, well, that would have blown my mind. But now…" Tanner didn't bother finishing. Amanda's contorted features told her she'd guessed exactly the right pressure points. "Is something the matter?"

Amanda's tone had a slight edge. "You overestimate my husband."

"I don't think so. He's actually pretty brilliant. It was only by chance we found him out. He probably should've chosen a more experienced agent to do his dirty work, one who was already jaded by years of seeing criminals succeed where law enforcement failed. One who'd grown tired of subsisting on paltry raises when men like Aguilar live like kings. An agent like that wouldn't have rolled on him because she would've understood what she was risking, and your husband's perfect plan to put the Vargases out of business in exchange for the generous support of Carlos Aguilar would never have been detected."

Tanner studied Amanda, detecting micro signals of discomfort from the slight shift in her posture to the way her eyes seemed to focus on nothing in particular. Tanner was trying to figure out what exactly she could do to push her over the edge, when Amanda turned to the thug behind her. "I would like to speak to Agent Cohen alone."

The big guy stepped back, and Amanda pointed at Dale and Mary. Tanner nodded and Dale and Mary led Hulk out of the room. Amanda waited until they were completely out of sight before she spoke.

"You're smart enough to know my husband is not a criminal mastermind."

Tanner shrugged. "It doesn't really matter what I think, only what the evidence can prove."

"You don't give yourself enough credit. Evidence can be

massaged. I've been married to Herschel long enough to know that." She leaned back in the chair, assuming an air of confidence. "I can tell you don't care for my husband. You're not alone. But there's no reason the breadth of your investigation has to extend to Carlos Aguilar. What if you could be rid of Herschel and live like a king yourself? I can make sure you have sufficient resources to fund your wildest dreams along with enough evidence to put Herschel away for his crimes. It's a win for everyone. The Vargases will still be out of business and you can close the case on Maria Escobar's death."

Tanner struggled not to act surprised at Amanda's callous suggestion, not to mention her command of the specifics. Tanner never would've expected her to know Maria Escobar's name. And what was Amanda's relationship with Aguilar that she was willing to pitch her husband to the wolves? Were they lovers? She decided to call Amanda's hand. "How long have you and Carlos been lovers?"

A look of confusion crossed Amanda's face, but before she could reply, a loud shout and sounds of a scuffle from the front of the house interrupted their conversation. Another shout and Tanner could swear she was hearing "Jade." Tanner shot out of her seat and drew her gun, and carefully eased into the living room in time to see a man and a woman she didn't know burst in through the front door holding a struggling Hispanic male between them, followed closely by Dale and Mary.

"They're with us," Mary called out.

Tanner looked at the man the strangers were holding and narrowed her eyes. "Sergio Vargas?"

He spat on the floor by way of response, but Dale said, "Yep." She jerked her chin. "These two found him out by the stables. Agents Mars and Ruben, meet Agent Cohen." Dale pulled Tanner aside and in a low voice said, "Sorry to interrupt your little charade, but while they were taking Sergio down, Mrs. Gellar's bodyguard rushed outside and a couple of other guys jumped out of her car. Pretty sure they planned to whack Sergio, but with the other agents stationed outside, we managed to get everyone separated and detained. We searched Mrs. Gellar's car and there's some pretty serious firepower inside."

Tanner clasped Dale on the shoulder. "You did the right thing. Taking Sergio down is a huge win. Besides, Syd sent me a text earlier—they've traced the money from Aguilar to none other than Amanda Gellar. She's in there, throwing her husband under the bus." Tanner pointed toward the kitchen where she could see the table she'd been sitting at with Amanda, but Amanda was no longer in her seat. Tanner jogged back across the room, her pulse quickening with dread. When she reached the doorway, the room was empty and curtains fluttered in the breeze of the open window.

"Shit!" Tanner backed up into Dale. "She went out the window." Without another word, the two of them raced toward the front door of the ranch house. They ran toward Amanda's SUV, but there was no sign of her. "We should split up," Tanner said. "You check the stables, and I'll head that way." She pointed to the wooded area on the other side of the field next to the house. She had a hard time imagining Amanda Gellar in her fancy dress dashing through a field, but desperation made people do crazy things. Tanner had just started to run toward the woods when two men emerged with Amanda between them. Unlike Sergio, she didn't struggle, but she wore the signs of her attempted escape in straws of hay adorning her dress.

Dale jogged up to Tanner's side as the men holding Amanda approached. "Our guys," she said.

One of the men handed Dale a cell phone and said, "She was on the phone when we found her, but she hung up."

Tanner took the phone and checked the number Amanda had called. It looked familiar. She pulled out her own phone and scrolled through her pictures until she found the one she'd taken of the card Syd had found in Aguilar's suite at the Ritz. The number Amanda had just called matched the number to the restaurant supply company listed on the front of the card.

"She called Aguilar." She handed Amanda's phone back to Dale. "Probably not directly, but he'll get the message and be on the run in no time."

Dale told the other agents to take Amanda in for questioning and turned to Tanner. "Let's go get Mary and track this bastard down."

Tanner barely registered Dale's words. She was staring at her own phone and a succession of texts that must have come in while she was talking to Amanda Gellar.

Did you get the message about Amanda?

Y or N, it would go a long way toward alleviating what is probably unnecessary panic on my part.

Come back safe. Please.

Nothing too personal. Each message could be interpreted as one colleague checking on another, but Tanner knew it was more. Syd was concerned not just about the operation, but about her. Where once she'd pushed back from Syd's pressing concern about every little thing, now she was ready to embrace it. Syd was waiting for her and there was nothing she wanted to do more than to get back to her.

She looked up from her phone to see Dale and Mary walking toward her. Dale pointed at her truck and motioned for Tanner to join them. Duty called. Bad guys were still on the loose and good guys had to track them down. Tanner had spent the last ten years being one of the good guys. Could she walk away from her calling even if it was for love?

❖

"Something's happened. Something bad." Syd paced the living room at Bianca's mother's house not caring that Lourdes looked at her like she was losing her mind. It had been two hours since she'd sent the text to Tanner about Amanda Gellar and she hadn't heard jack. She totally got that they were in the middle of a sting and Tanner wouldn't be watching her phone, but the lack of information was killing her. Now she knew how hard it had been for Tanner to wait without word when she met with Carlos Aguilar. Her last text, asking Tanner to at least reply with a Y or N to acknowledge she was still alive, had been pure desperation.

On her third loop around the room, Jade and Bianca intercepted her path. "I get it," Bianca said. "You're freaking out, but you're wearing a hole in my mother's carpet. Tanner, Dale, and Mary know what they're doing. If you haven't heard from them it's because they're busy being badasses." Bianca shot a look at her mother, who was shaking her head. "Sorry, Mama, but I'm right." She looked back at Syd. "Maybe your text about Amanda was perfectly timed. I bet Aguilar and Gellar showed up at the ranch together and Tanner and the others are luring them into confessing everything. Right? And while Aguilar and Gellar are spilling their guts, Sergio appears out of nowhere and—"

"It wasn't quite like that, but close," a low voice said from the other side of the room.

Syd whirled at the sound of Tanner's voice and watched the woman she loved step out of the shadow of the foyer. Syd launched across the room but pulled up short when an older man and a young girl entered the room with Tanner.

"*Mija!*" Bianca cried out, stretching her arms toward the girl.

Syd saw Emma run to her mother in her peripheral vision, but her gaze was trained on Tanner, who still stood framed in the entry, like she wasn't quite sure if she should come or go. Syd paused, waiting for Tanner to take the first step, but then she realized she'd spent the last ten years waiting for something to bring her back to Tanner when what she should have been doing instead was closing the distance all on her own. Not caring what anyone else in the room thought, Syd ran across the room and gathered Tanner tightly into her arms, silently vowing never to let her go.

"Hey," Tanner whispered. "It's okay. I'm okay. I'm sorry I didn't call. I just wanted to see you and a voice over the phone wasn't going to be enough." She leaned down and gently tipped Syd's head back so they were face-to-face. "Are you okay?"

"Are you?" Syd ran her hands down Tanner's arms, squeezing tightly every few inches to be sure it was really Tanner, that she was really okay, standing right here in her arms. "I have to tell you something."

"I know. Me too."

"I love you," Syd blurted out before she could think about the consequences or the fact Bianca's entire family was watching her intimate moment with Tanner go down.

"I love you too," Tanner said, pulling Syd closer into her arms. "I never stopped."

"Kiss!" the girl called out, and Syd heard Bianca say, "Emma, hush," but before she could assure Bianca it was okay, Tanner's mouth was on hers and she melted into the firm command of her hungry lips, forgetting everyone else was in the room. When Tanner released her, Syd struggled to keep her balance and then blushed while Emma, Lourdes, and Bianca applauded. In a gambit to add some levity to what she was certain had been an R-rated kiss, she took a bow and thanked the audience.

"Now that the kissing portion of the evening has concluded, do we get to find out what happened at the ranch?" Bianca asked.

"Time for bed, right, Emma?" Lourdes grabbed her husband's arm, and together they led Emma down a hallway toward the other end of the house.

When they were out of earshot, the rest of the group settled onto the sectional in the living room. Syd sat close to Tanner and launched into her first round of questions. "You got my text, didn't you? Were you able to use the information against Aguilar? Did Gellar show up?" At Tanner's grin, she took a deep breath. "Sorry, it was kind of hard sitting here not having a clue what was going on."

Tanner's smile was tender. "I get it. Actually, Bianca was partly right. Aguilar didn't show up at the ranch, but Gellar did. Amanda Gellar, not Herschel."

"You're kidding."

"Not even close. Herschel's no innocent, but Amanda is the brains behind everything he's done, and there's no love lost between the two. She essentially offered me whatever I wanted if I would make Herschel disappear."

"So she's in custody?"

"Yes, despite the fact she climbed out a window and ran into the woods in a fancy cocktail dress. We've got agents keeping an eye on Herschel to make sure he doesn't take off when he gets the news his wife has been arrested."

Syd nodded, already thinking ahead to the report she'd need to file with Main Justice if they were going to get permission to bring charges against Herschel.

"In related news," Tanner said, "Sergio showed up and was arrested with very little fuss. Jade, he was very disappointed to find out you weren't following in his footsteps after all."

Jade grimaced. "He and Arturo will be running a prison gang in no time, but I'll only rest easy if they're never released."

"What about Aguilar?" Bianca asked.

Tanner shook her head. "I guess he sent Amanda as his proxy, but we have a lead, and Dale and Mary are following up."

Syd watched Tanner's face, certain she detected a hint of unease. "Why aren't you with them?"

"What?"

"Can't they use all the help they can get? If Aguilar gets word that you've arrested Amanda and have Gellar under surveillance, he's going to make a break for it." Syd watched a parade of emotions march across Tanner's face and reached for her hand, threading their fingers together. All these years she'd thought Tanner had chosen the job over her, but now Syd knew it hadn't been a choice. Tanner was meant to do this work and so was she. They were both drawn to righting wrongs, but the pursuit of justice didn't have to be at the exclusion of each other. "I'm glad you came back so I could see you're alive, but you've got work to do." She stood up and pulled Tanner with her. "So, kiss me again and then get your butt out there and do your job. I'll do mine, and I'll see you when we're done."

CHAPTER TWENTY-TWO

Two weeks later

Syd rolled over in bed to find Tanner propped up on one arm, staring at her with a goofy grin. She poked Tanner in the chest. "Are you sleep stalking me?"

"Kind of." Tanner's eyes twinkled with mischief. "Mostly I was wondering how someone so pretty and feminine can make such loud noises while sleeping."

"Shut up!" Syd sat up in bed. "You snore too, you know."

"Sure. Right."

"You do." Syd play smacked her with a pillow to emphasize her point, and for the next few minutes, they wound up wrestling in the sheets. When they were both out of breath, Syd snuggled in close and draped an arm over Tanner's chest. "This has been the best two weeks of my life."

"Mine too," Tanner said. "I've never worked so hard, but it's never been easier." She kissed the top of Syd's head. "I like working with you, but I like this most of all." She wagged a finger back and forth between them and sighed. "Being naked with you is the best employee benefit ever. How long do you think we can make this case last?"

Syd heard the undercurrent of melancholy in Tanner's voice. She felt it too. They'd worked twenty-hour days since the night Sergio and Amanda had been arrested at Jade's ranch, but her energy was boundless since she and Tanner had rekindled their feelings. Syd was a woman in love, and knowing Tanner loved her too made it easy to live in the moment. At some point they'd both need to talk about the future and where they would go from here.

The case was wrapping up faster than they'd anticipated. Tanner had been with Dale and Mary when they arrested Aguilar at a private airstrip near Denton the night Amanda Gellar had been arrested at Jade's ranch. Both Aguilar and Amanda had steadfastly refused to talk, but Herschel was another story. He was only too happy to share that his wife and her cousin, Carlos Aguilar, had used him to expand Aguilar's criminal enterprises to North Texas. They'd opened bank accounts in Herschel's name and stocked them with cash that could be traced to dubious offshore accounts for which Amanda had records that she held over Gellar's head to get him to do Aguilar's bidding. The bidding consisted of putting the Vargases out of business, including their main money laundering source, Cyrus Gantry, and going easy in court on Barrio Azteca gang members who worked for Aguilar.

No one on the task force believed Herschel was the innocent victim he proclaimed to be, but as long as he was willing to cooperate, they were willing to postpone an indictment and consider working out a deal. He had loaded them up with specifics about how Aguilar's business worked, including storing money in the pretend wine cellar at Gellar's house. Herschel's biggest bombshell had been about Maria Escobar. While he claimed to have had nothing to do with her death, he did say Maria had confronted him about the way he was handling the Barrio Azteca cases. He made up some on-the-fly excuse about prison-based gangs like BA being more dangerous because they felt like they had nothing to lose, and if he wanted to handle some cases personally to keep his litigation chops sharp, it was his prerogative as the head of the office to do so. Maria seemed to accept his explanation, and he'd decided not to worry about it, but he'd mentioned the conversation to Amanda in passing. Within days, Maria had been gunned down on her front lawn, and for the first time, Herschel had realized he was no longer in charge.

There was still a lot of work to do, but Syd knew at any moment she might get the call to return to DC and let the locals handle the rest of the case on their own. Whether she would go back and whether Tanner wanted her to were topics they'd avoided in favor of spending the free moments they had making up for lost time. She'd spent every night at Tanner's, basking in their reclaimed love, but neither one of them had broached the subject of what the future held, and right now, it was easier to talk about safer subjects.

"Do you think Cyrus will be at the wedding?" Syd asked.

"I think so, but not in the traditional, walk his daughter down the aisle kind of way. Peyton said he didn't want to divert any attention from the ceremony, so he'll stay in the background." Tanner sat up and pointed at the clock on the nightstand. "We should probably start getting ready."

"You're right." Syd kissed Tanner and crawled out of bed. She went to the window and peered through the blinds. It was a beautiful, sunny autumn day—perfect for an outdoor wedding. She started to turn away from the window but felt the press of Tanner's naked body against her back.

"Whatcha thinking?" Tanner asked.

Syd's mind whirred through the dozens of things pulling at her attention, most of which had nothing to do with Carlos Aguilar, the Gellars, and the Vargases but everything to do with what the future held for her and Tanner. But today was a day to celebrate, and she didn't want to mar it with a serious discussion, so she said the first true thing that came to her mind.

"It's a beautiful day for a wedding."

❖

Tanner tried not to squirm in her seat, but she was feeling claustrophobic in the new suit and tie she'd purchased for the wedding. Peyton was waiting at the front of the rows of chairs, standing underneath an arbor laced with dozens of poinsettias, and Tanner thought she looked way too relaxed considering what was about to happen. Tanner envied Peyton's calm, and she crossed and recrossed her legs, finally settling both feet firmly on the floor with her elbows resting on her knees, when the music started and she, along with the dozens of other guests, scrambled to their feet and turned to look at the bride.

"Are you okay?" Syd whispered.

Tanner kept her eyes focused on the aisle. "Sure. Of course. Why?"

"Because you look like you want to make a break for it, and you're not the one in the penguin suit."

Tanner fumbled, trying to formulate a response. She didn't know why she was so restless, but she was positive it wasn't just the suit. She'd been jumpy since they'd arrived at the Circle Six, barely able to concentrate on any of the conversations around her, and there were plenty, since the entire community was still buzzing with news of the indictment of Amanda Gellar.

"Tanner?"

She squeezed Syd's hand. "Sorry. I'm good."

At that moment, the crowd gasped as Lily appeared at the back of the crowd in a gorgeous white dress, her eyes firmly focused on Peyton. Tanner looked down at Syd and smiled. Excitement shined in her eyes, and it was infectious. When Syd met her eyes, Tanner grinned to signal everything was okay, or if it wasn't now, it would be. They had so much yet to work out, but if they both wanted to, surely they could find a way through it.

With each vow that was spoken, a cylinder clicked into place, and by the time Judge Casey pronounced Peyton and Lily married for all eternity, a soothing sense of calm settled over Tanner's mind, and her heart told her exactly what to do.

The reception featured a popular local cover band that

happily took requests from the guests, and they played Tanner's selection immediately after Peyton and Lily's first dance.

"I love this song," Syd said, swaying in place to Whitney Houston's "I Look to You."

"I remember," Tanner said, holding out her hand. They danced close, and the song was halfway over before Tanner finally made up her mind that this was indeed the perfect moment. She stopped in place on the dance floor. When Syd looked up to see what was up, Tanner spoke quickly. "I asked them to play this song, our song. I look to you, Syd. I always have, even when I was too hardheaded to admit it. You are the one true, great love of my life and I never want to be without you again. Will you marry me?"

Syd's eyes brimmed with tears, but the huge smile on her face told Tanner they were tears of happiness. "Yes," Syd said. "Absolutely yes." Tanner pulled her close, and they sealed the promise with a searing kiss.

They danced the next few songs, neither willing to let go of the moment, but when the band took a break, Peyton waved them over to where she and Lily were standing with Dale, Lindsey, Bianca, Jade, and Mary. She handed them each a glass of champagne. "Since we're all here, I thought we might steal a moment and toast our work on the task force. It's not over yet, but we're well on our way to closing some of the biggest cases this area has ever seen. To all of you and to Maria, who I never had the pleasure of meeting, but who has inspired all of us to keep doing this good work." Peyton nodded at Dale and then raised her glass, and everyone else joined in the toast.

While everyone drank, Tanner, fueled by the mood and maybe a little bit by the champagne, raised her glass next. "I'd like to propose a toast to friendships, old and new. May we treasure all of our relationships and never let go of the people that are important to us."

Bianca was the first to raise her glass in response. "I'll drink to that if you'll tell us what you two have been up to. You and

Syd are acting like kids who found the hidden stash of Halloween candy."

Tanner glanced at Syd, who grinned back at her. "Just happy to be alive."

"Nope, I'm not buying it," Dale said. "They're up to something."

Syd raised a hand. "Seriously. This is Peyton and Lily's special day. Let's focus on them."

"No way!" Bianca squealed. "You got engaged, didn't you?"

"What?" Tanner said, looking to Syd to help her out. "Engaged? No way."

Syd smiled back at her. "Honey, I don't know how you've made it this long in law enforcement. You can't lie worth a damn." Syd grabbed her hand and held it tight while she announced, "Yes, we're engaged. No, we haven't worked out the details, but we're super grateful to Peyton and Lily for providing the perfect romantic setting for Tanner to pop the question."

"You know," Peyton said, "this setting is perfect for more than proposals." She turned to Lily. "What do you think?"

Lily grinned and nodded her response, and Peyton looked over the crowd and waved to Judge Casey, who started toward them. As Tanner watched him approach, she realized what Peyton had in mind. "Wait. No." She felt Syd squeeze her hand.

"I'm ready if you are."

Tanner's heart stopped and she took a moment to catch her breath. This was really happening, and the knowledge that it wasn't a champagne-infused dream sent any last nerves she had skittering away to make room for calm assurance that she'd never be separated from Syd again. Only one last lingering doubt remained. "I'm ready. I've never been more ready. But," she held up a hand to stave off Syd's protest, "Peyton and Lily's generous offer aside, don't you want a big wedding of your own?"

Syd's eyes glimmered with affection. "I used to. I used to want a lot of things, but none of those things ever made me happy. The only thing I want for the rest of my life is to be married to you, and I don't want to waste another minute waiting for that to happen."

Judge Casey happily obliged the request to perform a second set of nuptials, waving off any concerns about license and waiting periods with assurances that nothing should get in the way of true love and he would take care of those silly formalities. An hour later, there were two new happily married couples cutting the cake as their friends cheered them on, celebrating the twists of circumstance that had brought them all together.

About the Author

Carsen Taite's goal as an author is to spin tales with plot lines as interesting as the cases she encountered in her career as a criminal defense lawyer. She is the award-winning author of numerous novels of romance and romantic intrigue, including the Luca Bennett Bounty Hunter series and the Lone Star Law series.

Books Available From Bold Strokes Books

Breakthrough by Kris Bryant. Falling for a sexy ranger is one thing, but is the possibility of love worth giving up the career Kennedy Wells has always dreamed of? (978-1-63555-179-2)

Certain Requirements by Elinor Zimmerman. Phoenix has always kept her love of kinky submission strictly behind the bedroom door and inside the bounds of romantic relationships, until she meets Kris Andersen. (978-1-63555-195-2)

Dark Euphoria by Ronica Black. When a high-profile case drops in Detective Maria Diaz's lap, she forges ahead only to discover this case, and her main suspect, aren't like any other. (978-1-63555-141-9)

Fore Play by Julie Cannon. Executive Leigh Marshall falls hard for Peyton Broader, her golf pro...and an ex-con. Will she risk sabotaging her career for love? (978-1-63555-102-0)

Love Came Calling by C. A. Popovich. Can a romantic looking for a long-term, committed relationship and a jaded cynic too busy for love conquer life's struggles and find their way to what matters most? (978-1-63555-205-8)

Outside the Law by Carsen Taite. Former sweethearts Tanner Cohen and Sydney Braswell must work together on a federal task force to see justice served, but will they choose to embrace their second chance at love? (978-1-63555-039-9)

The Princess Deception by Nell Stark. When journalist Missy Duke realizes Prince Sebastian is really his twin sister Viola in disguise, she plays along, but when sparks flare between them, will the double deception doom their fairy-tale romance? (978-1-62639-979-2)

The Smell of Rain by Cameron MacElvee. Reyha Arslan, a wise and elegant woman with a tragic past, shows Chrys that there's still beauty to embrace and reason to hope despite the world's cruelty. (978-1-63555-166-2)

The Talebearer by Sheri Lewis Wohl. Liz's visions show her the faces of the lost and the killers who took their lives. As one by one, the murdered are found, a stranger works to stop Liz before the serial killer is brought to justice. (978-1-635550-126-6)

White Wings Weeping by Lesley Davis. The world is full of discord and hatred, but how much of it is just human nature when an evil with sinister intent is invading people's hearts? (978-1-63555-191-4)

A Call Away by KC Richardson. Can a businesswoman from a big city find the answers she's looking for, and possibly love, on a small-town farm? (978-1-63555-025-2)

Berlin Hungers by Justine Saracen. Can the love between an RAF woman and the wife of a Luftwaffe pilot, former enemies, survive in besieged Berlin during the aftermath of World War II? (978-1-63555-116-7)

Blend by Georgia Beers. Lindsay and Piper are like night and day. Working together won't be easy, but not falling in love might prove the hardest job of all. (978-1-63555-189-1)

Hunger for You by Jenny Frame. Principe of an ancient vampire clan Byron Debrek must save her one true love from falling into the hands of her enemies and into the middle of a vampire war. (978-1-63555-168-6)

Mercy by Michelle Larkin. FBI Special Agent Mercy Parker and psychic ex-profiler Piper Vasey learn to love again as they race to stop a man with supernatural gifts who's bent on annihilating humankind. (978-1-63555-202-7)

Pride and Porters by Charlotte Greene. Will pride and prejudice prevent these modern-day lovers from living happily ever after? (978-1-63555-158-7)

Rocks and Stars by Sam Ledel. Kyle's struggle to own who she is and what she really wants may end up landing her on the bench and without the woman of her dreams. (978-1-63555-156-3)

The Boss of Her: Office Romance Novellas by Julie Cannon, Aurora Rey, and M. Ullrich. Going to work never felt so good. Three office romance novellas from talented writers Julie Cannon, Aurora Rey, and M. Ullrich. (978-1-63555-145-7)

The Deep End by Ellie Hart. When family ties become entangled in murder and deception, it's time to find a way out... (978-1-63555-288-1)

A Country Girl's Heart by Dena Blake. When Kat Jackson gets a second chance at love, following her heart will prove the hardest decision of all. (978-1-63555-134-1)

Dangerous Waters by Radclyffe. Life, death, and war on the home front. Two women join forces against a powerful opponent, nature itself. (978-1-63555-233-1)

Fury's Death by Brey Willows. When all we hold sacred fails, who will be there to save us? (978-1-63555-063-4)

It's Not a Date by Heather Blackmore. Kade's desire to keep things with Jen on a professional level is in Jen's best interest. Yet what's in Kade's best interest...is Jen. (978-1-63555-149-5)

Killer Winter by Kay Bigelow. Just when she thought things could get no worse, homicide Lieutenant Leah Samuels learns the woman she loves has betrayed her in devastating ways. (978-1-63555-177-8)

Score by MJ Williamz. Will an addiction to pain pills destroy Ronda's chance with the woman she loves, or will she come out on top and score a happily ever after? (978-1-62639-807-8)

Spring's Wake by Aurora Rey. When wanderer Willa Lange falls for Provincetown B&B owner Nora Calhoun, will past hurts and a fifteen-year age gap keep them from finding love? (978-1-63555-035-1)

The Northwoods by Jane Hoppen. When Evelyn Bauer, disguised as her dead husband, George, travels to a Northwoods logging camp to work, she and the camp cook Sarah Bell forge a friendship fraught with both tenderness and turmoil. (978-1-63555-143-3)

Truth or Dare by C. Spencer. For a group of six lesbian friends, life changes course after one long snow-filled weekend. (978-1-63555-148-8)